# Also by the Author

# Brain Damage

The Erin O'Reilly Mysteries
Book Twenty-Four

Steven Henry

Clickworks Press • Baltimore, MD

First publication: Clickworks Press, 2024
Release: CWP-EOR24-INT-P.IS-1.0

Sign up for updates, deals, and exclusive sneak peeks at clickworkspress.com/join.

Ebook ISBN: 979-8-88900-020-4
Paperback ISBN: 979-8-88900-021-1
Hardcover ISBN: 979-8-88900-022-8

For those struggling with injuries of the brain,
and those who care for them.

# Brain Damage,
## aka "Hemorrhage Shot"

*Mix 2 oz. peach schnapps and 1 oz. Irish cream in a shot glass. Do not stir. Gently tilt glass to help mixture curdle. Add a dash of grenadine and swirl the glass slightly.*

# Chapter 1

"We really don't understand the human brain as well as we'd like."

"Thanks, Doc," Erin O'Reilly said. "That's just what I like to hear. It gives me confidence."

Doctor Mifflin didn't smile. His face wasn't built for it. He had a permanent frown line between his eyebrows and the sort of mouth that drooped at the corners, reminding Erin of a basset hound. Come to think of it, he had long ears, too. Maybe he really was part hound, part neurologist.

"You've suffered at least two severe concussions," Mifflin went on. "We have to consider the cumulative effects."

"It's rough out there on the street," she said. "Sometimes you have to take some hard knocks."

"This is serious," Mifflin insisted. "You may already be looking at permanent damage. Do you experience persistent, recurring headaches?"

"Sometimes." She had a headache that very minute, and talking to the neurologist was making it worse.

"Anxiety?"

"I'm a cop."

"Fatigue and sleep disturbance?"

"I'd have to get sleep in order for it to be disturbed."

Once again, her feeble joke failed to crack Mifflin's façade. "Irritability or mood swings?" he went on relentlessly.

"Did you hear the part where I said I'm a cop? That stuff happens to us all the time."

Mifflin sighed. "I'm only trying to do my job, Miss O'Reilly."

"And I want to get back out there and do mine," she shot back. "What do all those fancy machines say?"

"We haven't found any evidence of serious long-term damage," Mifflin admitted. "But, as I was saying, we're nowhere close to fully understanding the human brain. If you suffer another, similar injury, your prognosis will be much more serious."

"Doc, I got *shot* in the *head*," she reminded him. "I'm still walking around and breathing. You don't need to tell me how much worse it's likely to be if it happens again."

As she said it, she thought of Lieutenant Philip Stachowski. Phil had been shot shortly before Erin had taken her own bullet, and while he was still breathing too, she'd been lucky and he hadn't. He was in the same hospital where she was wrapping up her checkup, but he wouldn't be leaving any time soon. The damage to his brain had been much more extensive. He had blackouts and lack of motor control. He couldn't walk, had only limited use of his hands and arms, and his speech centers had been affected. Ironically, Erin had learned a new word to describe one of his problems: aphasia. Her brother the trauma surgeon had told her it meant a disconnect between thought and speech, resulting in poor Phil being unable to turn his thoughts into coherent words some of the time.

"You're cleared to return to duty," Mifflin said slowly.

"Full duty?" Erin asked, a little too eagerly. She slid off the examining table and bounced on the balls of her feet. "Not limited assignment? No desk duty?"

"There's no point," Mifflin said. "Whatever damage you've sustained, it's already happened. Your skull is intact and there's no swelling of cerebral tissue. You'll be in just as much danger in a week as you are right this minute. In fact, you're better off limiting your time in front of computer screens, so being on the move might, oddly enough, be the best thing for you."

"Good enough for me," Erin said. "Thanks, Doc."

She started for the exit and hesitated. The long-term Neurology rooms were just down the hall. It wouldn't take her more than a few minutes to drop in on Phil Stachowski.

She owed him the visit. Hell, she probably owed him her life. He'd taken a bullet for her and his reward had been a serious brain injury. He couldn't walk and could only haltingly talk. She'd already been in to see him more than once. But this time she wasn't sure.

Maybe it was guilt. Both of them had been shot by the same man. She'd recovered, he hadn't. She knew Phil wouldn't resent her. He'd be glad she was healthy. But in a way, that only made it worse. He didn't deserve what had happened to him. She wasn't sure she could look him in the face at that moment and see what the world did to good men.

A uniformed officer was posted outside Phil's door. Erin could see him, a pudgy middle-aged officer reading the *Times* from the dubious comfort of a hospital chair. She took a step toward the room, then another smaller step.

There'd be time to visit Phil later, she told herself. She had work to do. He'd understand. And he wasn't going anywhere.

The rationalizations were weak and Erin knew it. Even as she turned her back, she felt like she was running away. She didn't even know exactly what she was scared of. It was an unfamiliar feeling and she didn't like it.

She got out of the hospital as fast as she could. She'd already spent more time there than she wanted. It was the holiday season, just before Christmas, and she'd wasted the past five days twiddling her thumbs and waiting on the doctors to sign off on her file. It was a toss-up whether she or Rolf was going crazier, stuck around the apartment with nothing to do. The K-9 had gone through three new chew-toys and she didn't like the way he'd started eyeing her boyfriend's good dress shoes.

Erin went home first, swinging by the Barley Corner and hurrying through the pub to get to the upstairs apartment she shared with Morton Carlyle. He was fast asleep, which wasn't unusual. Pub owners and gangsters lived by night, and Carlyle was both. At ten o'clock in the morning, he'd been in bed less than eight hours.

But Rolf was very much awake. The German Shepherd met her at the top of the stairs, ears perked, tail wagging, leash held in his jaws. He hated being left behind, but was prepared to forgive her if she'd take him with her this time.

"Back to work, kiddo," she said quietly.

Rolf made a half-leap into the air, his front paws nearly smacking Erin in the face. Then he remembered his training and subsided, though his toes continued doing a happy tap-dance on the floorboards. He panted excitedly and stuck as close to her as he could, his snout almost in contact with her hip.

Erin slipped into the bedroom, easing the door carefully open like a burglar entering a booby-trapped vault. The room was almost pitch black, but she knew her way around. She found the nightstand on her side of the bed and opened the drawer, feeling around inside it for the familiar shapes of her sidearm and shield. The gold detective's shield with the numbers 4640 went just to the left of her belt buckle. The Glock automatic pistol rested on her right hip. Her little snub-nosed .38 revolver was already nestled in its concealed ankle holster.

Erin bent down and very lightly kissed Carlyle's cheek.

Then she tiptoed out of the room, Rolf still pacing her, and made her way out of the building, into the cold December air.

The week before, New York had suffered one of the worst blizzards in its history. Huge heaps of snow were still piled along the curbs, hampering driver visibility and pedestrian mobility. Erin drove cautiously, watching for careless motorists. It wouldn't pay to get in a car crash on the way back to work. She could just imagine the look on Doctor Mifflin's sad-eyed face if the EMTs wheeled her right back into the neuro ward.

\* \* \*

A present was waiting on Erin's desk in the Precinct 8 Major Crimes office. Vic Neshenko, Zofia Piekarski, and Lieutenant Webb were all at their computers, either working or pretending to work. Nobody so much as said a word to her and Rolf as they entered. But Vic and Piekarski were watching her out of the corners of their eyes, which made Erin immediately suspicious.

The package on her desk was about the right size to hold a basketball. It was gift-wrapped in the bright pink and purple paper a six-year-old girl might want on a birthday present. A pink bow decorated the top.

There was no getting away from it, so Erin tore open the paper. She stared at the gift for a moment.

"Har, har," she said dryly, hefting a brand-new bicycle helmet. It was pastel pink, with a threaded hole in the upper forehead. This hole, the package informed her, was for a rainbow-striped unicorn horn, included in the package. The helmet sported big cartoon eyes with long eyelashes.

Vic was snorting with suppressed laughter. Piekarski was giggling. Even Webb had a smile on his face.

"Welcome back, O'Reilly," Webb said. "Detective Neshenko

and Officer Piekarski thought you ought to have a little something to commemorate your recent adventures, and to greet you when you came back on duty. I assume your visit to the neurologist went as planned?"

"Clean bill of health, sir," Erin said. "So I guess I won't be needing this." She set the helmet on the corner of her desk, where it stared at Vic with its enormous eyes.

"You sure?" Vic asked. "You can use the horn when you head-butt the bad guys. Hell, you won't even need to pull your gun. Just the look of that thing will scare the hell out of them."

"How is this scary?" she asked.

"You'd have to be crazy to wear something like that on the street," Vic replied. "And criminals are scared of crazy people."

"*I'm* scared of crazy people," she said. "Anything happen this morning?"

"The Homicide boys down in Queens want to know if we're willing to take a look at something," Webb said.

"Who's dead?" Erin asked.

"Pizza delivery guy," Vic said. "Somebody beat his head in. Patrol unit found him in his truck, still behind the wheel."

Erin deflated. "That sounds like a pretty normal homicide," she said. "Mugging gone wrong. What makes this a Major Crimes case?"

"Something else you'd rather be doing, O'Reilly?" Webb asked.

"No, sir. It just seems a little weird they'd bring it to us. Are they shorthanded?"

"No, they're just idiots," Vic said.

"Oh, God," Erin said. "You don't mean..."

"Yeah," Vic said with relish. "It's Lyons and Spinelli, your old pals from the 116. You sure you don't want to wear that helmet?"

Erin rolled her eyes. "That's just what I need. Those two

bozos seeing me dressed up like a little girl? No thanks. I can't believe they'd call me."

"You're not the only member of this squad," Webb said. "You're not even the commanding officer, in case you've forgotten. Anyway, it was Lieutenant Murphy, your old CO, who called us. He thinks something's a little weird about this one."

"Weird how?"

"A man gets beaten to death in his company vehicle, but the windows aren't broken and his seatbelt's still fastened," Webb said. "Plus, he's got a record."

"I was just checking his priors," Piekarski said. "Floyd Shelton, age thirty-two, took two falls for burglary. He served two nickels upstate, only got paroled four months ago."

"A felon killed under suspicious circumstances?" Erin said. "That's more like it."

"I'm glad it meets with your approval," Webb said. "We've been waiting on you. CSU is processing the scene as we speak. I've had the others running background. I'll ride with you and let the lovebirds carpool."

"Tweet tweet, sir," Piekarski said.

"Cold pizza for lunch," Vic said. "This is gonna be a good day, I can feel it."

"Don't eat the evidence, Vic," Erin said.

# Chapter 2

"We ought to talk about your future," Webb said.

Erin braced herself. She kept looking out the windshield, avoiding her commanding officer's eye.

"You've been a detective less than two years," Webb went on. "But you've had what you might call an eventful career."

"You could call it that," Erin agreed.

"You've also been in more critical incidents than I can count," he said. "Gunfights, serious injuries, hostage situations, you name it."

"What's your point, sir?"

"You've been running on all cylinders," Webb said. "Don't you think it may be time to take a breather?"

She shot him an incredulous look. "I can't do that!" she snapped. "Not now!"

"I know, you've got something important in the works," he said. "But that'll be wrapped up within the next few weeks. It might actually be over by New Year's. Once you've taken care of that, you might seriously consider doing something else."

"Like what?" she asked. "I'm a cop, sir. This is all I know how to do."

"You'll be a cop with a great deal of pull," Webb said. "This is a career-making move. If you play your cards right, you can write your own ticket."

Erin didn't say anything. She turned her attention back to the road.

"What?" Webb demanded. "I was watching you right there. It was like someone flicked a switch behind your eyes and you shut down. I'm trying to give you some good advice. What did I say that was so awful?"

"Nothing," she sighed. "It just sounded like the sort of thing Lieutenant Keane would say."

"You say that like it's a bad thing."

"Do *you* like him?"

"Whether I like him isn't the point. He's smart, he's ambitious, he's the youngest—"

"The youngest Lieutenant in the NYPD," Erin interrupted. "Yeah, I know. He's also a ruthless, sneaky son of a bitch who'd pimp out his own mom to get ahead. I don't want to be him."

"Obviously," Webb said. "And you don't have to be. But you want to think what you'll be doing a year from now, or five years. I'll be retired before long, if I haven't kicked off from a heart attack. You're young. Relatively young, I mean."

"Thanks," she said wryly.

"You've got eight more years with the Department if you want to put in your twenty," he said. "You can't go on that whole time like you have been. There'll be nothing left of you to collect your pension. It adds up, O'Reilly. All of it. The injuries, the stress, the trauma. You keep writing checks on your future, sooner or later they're going to bounce."

"Are you *worried* about me, sir?" she asked.

"It's my job," he said.

"And now you sound like my dad."

"Your dad wore a shield for a quarter century," he reminded

her. "If he's got advice about being a cop, you might consider listening to it."

"So which is it? You think I should be advancing my career, or taking medical retirement?"

"I think you can't be a street detective forever. Do you want my job?"

Erin laughed. She couldn't help it. A vision of herself popped into her mind, fifteen years older and fifty pounds heavier, smoking like a chimney and counting the days to retirement.

"I'm serious," Webb said. "You could make Lieutenant one of these days. Maybe sooner than you think. That's assuming you don't get yourself crippled or killed."

"Thanks for the career counseling," she said, trying not to sound too sarcastic.

"Just keep it in mind," he said. "Opportunities are slippery things. If you don't grab on hard, they slide right past you."

"Do I detect a note of regret, sir?"

"A note?" Webb said. "My life's a whole symphony of it."

*     *     *

The pizza truck was in a parking garage just off Union Turnpike. The garage served Dasilva Memorial Field at St. John's University. Erin wasn't thrilled about that. The last time she'd been involved in a case at a college, she'd stepped on a few administrative toes and the head of campus security had demanded her resignation. But several NYPD vehicles were already on scene, together with a car bearing a security label, so maybe the red tape had already been cut away.

Among the official vehicles were the Crime Scene Unit forensics van, the coroner's van, a pair of NYPD blue-and-whites, and an unmarked sedan. Erin knew the last one was a police vehicle from the spotlight over the left rearview mirror, but also because it was familiar. The last time she'd seen it, her old enemy Detective Spinelli had been driving it.

Someone had already strung yellow tape around the victim's pickup. Two cold-looking Patrol officers stood guard while the evidence techs and the coroner did their thing. A pair of plainclothes guys watched, hands in their pockets. Erin recognized them, even from the rear. The big, broad-shouldered one was Detective Lyons. The little one that looked and moved like a weasel was Detective Spinelli. She hoped he'd at least gotten rid of his sleazy little mustache.

Vic and Piekarski arrived right behind Erin, Webb, and Rolf. They approached the scene together, already looking around for possible clues as to what had happened.

"These Homicide dicks are assholes," Vic said to Piekarski in a stage whisper. "But don't worry. If they get out of line, I'll give them a boot-leather enema."

"Are you offering to protect me because I'm female, or because I'm pregnant?" Piekarski hissed. "Because neither one is a compliment."

"I'm protecting you because I love you," Vic said indignantly. "And besides—"

"Can it, Neshenko," Webb interrupted. "You can fight with your girlfriend when you're off the clock. On duty, your ass is mine. And so is hers."

"Respectfully, sir, leave my ass out of this," Piekarski said. "It doesn't belong to anyone else, including Vic."

Spinelli heard them coming. He turned around, giving Erin a view of a sharp-featured face that still sported its ridiculous excuse for facial hair. He gave her a sour look.

"Your troubles are over," Vic announced. "Major Crimes is in the building."

"Good thing we're in a nice, spacious garage," Spinelli replied. "It's almost big enough for your ego."

"You think we asked to be here?" Vic shot back. "You guys called us, remember?"

"I apologize for my subordinate," Webb said blandly. "Believe it or not, he's on his best behavior. So, I trust, are you. We're here to help and we're all on the same team. What've we got?"

"Single victim," Lyons said, giving Erin a contemptuous glare. "Black, mid-thirties. Doc says cause of death is blunt force to the skull, probably a hammer. We're thinking robbery, smash-and-grab."

"Pizza delivery guys still get paid in cash a lot of the time," Spinelli said. "Plus tips."

"Yeah," Vic said. "A couple hundred bucks sounds like a fantastic motive for murder."

"I saw a guy get killed for seven-fifty in pocket change once," Spinelli retorted. "These guys aren't geniuses and they come cheap."

"Plenty of idiots in all kinds of professions," Vic said with a straight face. "Cheap losers, too."

"We were told the victim was found in the driver's seat, still wearing his belt," Webb said.

"That's right," Spinelli said. "Car was parked right where it is now. A school custodian found it about ninety minutes ago. Doors closed, engine off. Nobody around. He thought it was weird, so he came up and knocked on the window. He figured the driver was asleep, but then he saw the blood in the guy's hair and called campus security. They called us."

"Were the car doors locked?" Erin asked.

"Yeah," Spinelli said.

"Both of them?" she pressed.

Spinelli shifted uncomfortably.

"You did check the passenger door too, didn't you?" Vic asked.

"CSU is still processing the scene," Spinelli muttered.

"I think we'd better take a look for ourselves," Webb said.

The delivery car was a battered Toyota pickup from the late Nineties, wheel wells rusted out, a logo for Ninja Pizza ("Slice and Dice!") painted on the doors. A cartoon image of a black-masked ninja held a slice of pizza in one hand and was flinging a pair of dice with the other. Sarah Levine, the Medical Examiner, was in the process of examining the body behind the wheel.

"Morning, Doctor," Webb said.

Levine checked her watch. "Correct," she said. "But time of death was during the night. Judging from body temperature, the victim's heart stopped between one-thirty and two."

"How did we get an ID on him?" Erin asked.

"We called Ninja Pizza," Spinelli said. "They had a driver who didn't clock out at the end of his shift, and one of their trucks was missing. They gave us the name, so we e-mailed his boss his mugshot. He gave us a positive ID. CSU just printed him, and the prints are a match. It's Floyd Shelton, all right. Or it was."

"Good quick work," Webb said. "Have you been to Ninja Pizza yet?"

Spinelli shook his head. "We haven't had time. We've been canvassing the scene. Unfortunately, with the field closed and the snow piled up so high, nobody else seems to have been around."

"Nobody saw nothin'," Vic said with a sardonic smile.

Erin was looking at the dead man, watching Levine making her observations. "You said he got hit with a hammer?" she prompted.

"The trauma to the cranium is consistent with a blow from a hammer," Levine said. "He was struck three times, resulting in a depressed-skull fracture and massive intracranial hemorrhage. Unconsciousness would have likely been instantaneous, with death following within five to ten minutes. If you observe the impact points, you can see the strikes were made by an octagonal metallic object. This is consistent with some styles of hammer."

"Octagonal? Like a stop sign?"

"Correct. There is surprising variance in striking surfaces of hammers across different brands. Some are circular, some octagonal, some square. This narrows the possible number of murder weapons considerably."

"Hey guys," Erin said, directing her words to the nearest CSU tech. "Did you find a hammer anywhere? With or without blood on it?"

"Not yet," the technician replied. "But we're still looking."

"Looks like he got hit on the right side of his head," Erin said, trying to examine the injury with the same clinical detachment Levine always brought to bear.

"Correct," Levine said again. "All three blows struck his right temple."

Erin looked across the front seat of the car. The passenger door, like the driver's door, stood open. Another CSU guy was dusting the handle for fingerprints, which seemed optimistic to Erin. It had been a chilly night and the killer had almost certainly worn gloves.

"Was that door unlocked when you got here?" she asked.

"Yeah," the CSU guy said. "But the driver's door wasn't. The Patrol boys told us they used a Slim Jim to get it open so they could check his vitals."

"The killer was in the truck," Erin said.

"Obviously," Levine said. "It would not have been possible to strike him with a short-handled hammer from any other location, especially since he was secured by his seatbelt, even without taking into account the closed environment. A long-handled hammer, such as a sledge, would have left a different pattern of impact and would have damaged the windshield."

"The killer was sitting next to him," Erin said. "And our guy wasn't expecting to get whacked. He was looking the wrong way. Otherwise he would've been hit at least once in the face. If he'd been looking at the passenger, the headrest would've gotten in the way of these wounds."

"The ballistic arc of the hammer would have been interrupted," Levine said. "It would have resulted in a glancing blow at best. Your hypothesis is sound."

"No pizza," Vic announced. He'd been examining the cargo box behind the pickup's cab.

"Are you saying the bad guys stole the pizza along with our victim's pocket change?" Webb asked.

"Maybe," Vic said. "Or maybe he'd already made his delivery."

"Pizza delivery guys don't carry passengers," Erin said. "I've never seen them operate in pairs. So who was the passenger?"

"Someone he was meeting here?" Vic suggested.

"Maybe it was a hooker," Lyons said. "And he was getting a blowjob, so he didn't see it coming."

"His pants are zipped up, genius," Vic said, rolling his eyes.

"We still might be looking for a girl," Lyons insisted.

"It's possible," Webb said. "But male or female, I think they're more likely to be an accomplice than a romantic partner."

"Who said anything about romance?" Lyons asked. "I was talking about blowjobs."

"Stay classy, Lyons," Erin said under her breath.

"From what I see, we've got a convicted felon who's been murdered," Webb said. "The most obvious explanation is that he was involved in some sort of crime, and one of his associates killed him. That suggests either a conflict of personality or an argument over the loot."

"Let's find out who got robbed last night," Piekarski said.

"Good idea," Webb said. "See how many burglaries or robberies were reported last night. CSU has this scene in hand. Lyons and Spinelli, would you mind staying here and making sure the evidence is properly collected?"

"Glad to," Spinelli said through clenched teeth. He didn't like taking orders from an outsider, even when they were phrased as polite requests.

"The rest of us are taking a trip to Ninja Pizza," Webb said.

"I wonder if they have sushi as one of their toppings," Vic said. "I'm hungry and I've never had sushi pizza. That's some Italian-Japanese fusion cuisine I think the world's ready for."

# Chapter 3

Ninja Pizza was a hole-in-the-wall restaurant that reminded Erin of places she'd gone as a teenager. The brickwork was crumbling, the furnishings battered, but everything was clean and tidy. It looked, and smelled, like a small pizzeria that did most of its business via takeout and delivery. Three sedans and a pickup with the Ninja logo were parked in the little lot next to the strip mall.

Erin, Webb, Vic, and Rolf went into the restaurant. Piekarski followed them, eager to put off the less interesting work of robbery research as long as possible.

"Welcome to Ninja," the guy behind the counter said, flashing a cheerful smile that literally glittered. "Pickup or dine-in?" He had diamond-stud grilles on his teeth, five earrings in total, and tattoos covering every inch of exposed skin below the chin, plus a couple of ink spots on his face.

"Neither," Webb said, holding up his shield.

The man's smile faltered. "Oh," he said. "You're here about Floyd, aren't you."

"What do you know about that?" Vic demanded.

"Chill, man," the pizza guy said. "Your people called us just a little bit ago. Sucks, don't it? I'll fetch Mr. Martinelli."

"And he is...?" Webb asked.

"He's the boss. I just work here."

"Hold on a sec," Erin said. "What's your name?"

The man hesitated. It was just for a moment, but every cop noticed it, just like they'd noticed the piercings and tattoos. "Cross," he said. "Bode Cross. Look, you really oughta talk to Mr. Martinelli. He's in back. It'll just be a minute."

He scooted through the swinging doors into the kitchen before anyone could say anything else. The detectives looked at one another.

"Jailbird," Vic said. "You see his ink?"

"Yeah," Erin said.

"Quiz time, Officer Piekarski," Webb said. "What do his tats tell you?"

"If you're gonna make detective, you gotta pay attention to detail," Vic said, winking.

"This isn't the first time I've seen jailhouse ink," Piekarski said. "I worked Street Narcotics three years, remember? The spider-web on his neck means he's done time. The cross on his bicep means he's either religious, or he's a thief, or maybe both. The teardrop on his cheek means he's seen someone get murdered, probably a friend or fellow gang-member, or else that he attempted a murder but the guy didn't die."

"Because it's a hollow teardrop," Webb said, nodding. "If it was filled in, what would it mean?"

"It'd mean he killed the guy himself," Piekarski said.

"Conclusion?" Webb asked.

"Probably a repeat offender, but I'd guess a non-violent one," Piekarski said. "He comes from a gang background and might still be a member, but he's not wearing the colors of any gang I know."

"Very good," Webb said, nodding. "Anyone notice anything she missed?"

"Cats," Erin said. "Right arm, three black cats."

"Of course you'd notice the critters," Vic said, grinning.

"That means he's a burglar," Erin said. "Three means he was part of a crew of three guys."

Cross returned, trailed by a big-bellied, balding Italian man. The big guy came around the counter and offered his hand, which Webb shook.

"Luco Martinelli," the Italian guy said.

"Lieutenant Harry Webb, NYPD Major Crimes," Webb said. "This is Detective O'Reilly, Detective Neshenko, and Officer Piekarski."

"And Rolf," Erin added, nodding to the K-9. Rolf pricked his ears at the sound of his name and continued inhaling the aroma of the pizzeria. His nostrils were twitching. This place might or might not be full of bad guys, but it smelled *amazing*.

"Let's go to my office and talk," Martinelli said. "Bode, nothing to worry about."

Cross nodded, but he watched them all the way to the back of the restaurant.

Martinelli led the way through a door so narrow his bulk barely fit through it. Vic hunched his shoulders and shifted slightly sideways as he stepped in. The office was cramped, dark, and smelled like twenty years of cigarettes had been smoked in it. If anyone wanted to get rid of the stink, they'd have to rip up the carpet and burn it.

"You'll be wanting to talk about Floyd," Martinelli said. He shook his head sadly. "Terrible, just terrible. I can't hardly believe it."

"You run background checks on your employees, I assume," Webb said. "You must have been aware of Mr. Shelton's criminal record."

"Of course," Martinelli said. "Just like you pegged Bode for a man with a rap sheet the moment you walked in."

"Do you employ any other criminals?" Webb asked.

"I don't employ any criminals," Martinelli snapped. His dark eyes flashed with sudden anger. "I employ guys who need a second chance, good people who got criminal convictions in their past. When they come work for me, I give it to them straight. You screwed up once upon a time, I tell them. But that's in the past. You got a clean slate from this day forward. But you put one mark on it, you step out of line one time, that's it. You're gone. I'll have your parole officer haul your ass back to prison before it finishes bouncing on the sidewalk."

"Doesn't it strike you as a little risky to use convicted burglars as deliverymen?" Webb asked. "Given their past history, they could use the job to case homes and businesses."

Martinelli shrugged. "Anybody can be a crook," he said. "Somebody's gotta give these poor kids a break. Most of them, they never had nobody to believe in them. Half of them don't even know who their dad was, the other half remember him leaving or getting killed. They got no education, and ninety percent of the places they go looking for a job, the bastards take one look at their record and don't even bother asking no interview questions. So what do they do? They go right back to crime, because that's the only job they know, and it's the only one that's gonna hire them. I give these kids another choice."

"You've been through the system yourself," Erin said.

"Yeah," Martinelli said. "I was young and stupid once, my old man ran with LCN back in the Seventies and got himself clipped when I was eight. I ended up on the street, just like these kids."

"LCN?" Piekarski whispered.

"*La Cosa Nostra*," Vic translated. "He's talking about the Mafia."

"Which family?" Erin asked.

"What's it matter?" Martinelli retorted. "They're all the same, it don't make no difference to the rest of us. Main thing is, I did my time and got out. I got religion when I was inside, got clean. But I couldn't get nobody to hire me. So I worked those crappy minimum-wage jobs your PO gets you, where the boss is as crooked as the Mob guys. He skims twenty, twenty-five percent of your take-home and you can't do nothing about it or he'll violate you right back to prison. But I lived cheap and I saved, and when this old place came up for sale, I bought it and fixed it up. I've been running this joint ever since, and I promised God I'd use it to help other kids in the same spot like I was. And up until last night, I never lost one of my boys. Not one."

"How long have you been running Ninja Pizza?" Webb asked.

"Twenty-six years," Martinelli said proudly. "The secret's in the sauce. It's an old family recipe. My grandma, she could do things with tomatoes you can't even imagine if you're not Italian."

Vic snorted, which earned him an elbow from Piekarski.

"Just to be clear," Webb said. "If you'd suspected Shelton of being involved in further criminal activities, you would have fired him and reported him?"

"That's the deal," Martinelli said. "You gotta trust your boys, but you gotta have the stick ready. These boys gotta know I care about them, and that I won't let them screw up. It works, believe me."

"How long had Shelton worked here?" Erin asked.

"Four months. Since he got outta prison."

"Did you have any problems with him?" she asked.

"No problems," Martinelli said. "He was a good kid."

"Kid?" Vic said. "The guy was thirty-two."

Martinelli waved a dismissive hand. "They're all kids," he said. "They got stunted by their upbringing. People say you grow up too fast, but that's BS. These guys didn't get to grow up at all. They got no positive role models, nothing to grow into. You know I've had sixteen guys get their high school diplomas while they was working here? The oldest, he was forty-three when he got it. You believe that? He did night school, worked real hard, and you shoulda seen the look on his face when he got it. First guy in his family to finish high school."

"That's real sweet," Vic said. "My heart is just bleeding over here."

Piekarski elbowed him again.

"I'd think you'd be happy," Martinelli said. "If I didn't give these guys a place to be, they'd be your problem again, and you guys got enough to do. I'm doing the same work you are, I'm just more... what's the word?"

"Proactive?" Webb guessed.

"Yeah, proactive," Martinelli said.

"Who's Shelton's emergency contact?" Erin asked. "He must've had one on file."

"He's got a sister," Martinelli said. "Sweet lady, but she's had some hard times too."

"Is she local?" Erin asked.

"Yeah, I'll give you the address. I was gonna call her myself. Poor Alicia, it's gonna break her heart. Floyd was her baby brother."

"Floyd was driving a company vehicle," Webb said. "I assume he was on the clock last night?"

"Yeah," Martinelli said. "We're open until two. The University crowd, they like their late-night pizza. We do a lotta business after midnight. Floyd's last delivery went out around twelve-thirty. He shoulda been back in forty, forty-five minutes.

At one-thirty I tried calling him, but his cell went straight to voicemail. I tried him three more times, no luck."

"And you didn't report him?" Vic asked.

"No way," Martinelli said. "He coulda been in a crash, he coulda had engine trouble and his phone died. How do I know? And then, what if I call the cops and you guys get involved? Next thing I know, Floyd's on his way back upstate and he didn't do nothing. I wanted to give it a little time."

"Where was the delivery?" Webb asked.

"On campus," Martinelli said. "One of the dorms. Sullivan Hall, I think. I got the call log right here."

"We'll need the room number," Webb said.

"You think some college kids killed him?" Martinelli asked.

"I think they may have been the last people to see him alive," Webb replied. "He didn't have the pizza with him, so either he'd already made the delivery, or somebody stole the food. Either way, the kid who ordered is someone we want to talk to."

"Look," Martinelli said. "Anything I can do to help, I'll do it. Floyd was one of my guys. I hope he wasn't into nothing shady. He coulda been an innocent victim, you know. I gotta look after my boys."

"Of course," Webb said.

"I've got a question," Vic said. "Why the name? Ninja Pizza?"

"Oh, that," Martinelli said. "It was the Eighties. Ninjas were a whole thing back then. Remember the Ninja Turtles? They liked pizza and they lived in New York. In the sewers, I guess, but same difference. Seemed like good marketing, without infringing on nobody's copyrights. I think it helped, those first years, getting me established."

"So you don't have sushi pizza?" Vic asked.

Martinelli made a face. "What's the matter with you?" he demanded. "I'm Italian! I got some pride! Pepperoni's not good enough for you, or what?"

*    *    *

Alicia Shelton had lived with Floyd, just a few minutes' drive from the pizzeria. This was convenient, since it gave the detectives a chance to look over the victim's house. He hadn't been killed there, so getting a search warrant might prove problematic.

When they got out of their cars outside the three-story brick apartment, Vic was still carrying the box he'd snagged on his way out of Ninja Pizza. As Erin watched, Vic took out a slice of pepperoni and shoved half of it into his mouth.

"Wow," she said. "If the Lincoln Tunnel ever closes down again, they can use his mouth as a substitute."

"You ought to see him eat a hamburger," Piekarski said.

"I have," Erin said.

Vic chewed a few times and swallowed. "Laugh if you want," he said. "But this is damn good pizza, whatever those Italian grannies do with their vegetables."

"We're doing victim notification, Neshenko," Webb said. "Put your snack back in the car."

"Early lunch, not a snack," Vic corrected, but he did as he was told.

"Do we know if this lady's home?" Piekarski asked.

"If she's not, we'll leave a note and a calling card," Erin said. "Hopefully she'll give us a ring."

That wasn't necessary. The buzzer was answered by a harried female voice, a squalling baby providing backup vocals.

"Who is it?" the woman asked.

"New York Police Department, ma'am," Webb said. "May we come in? It's about your brother."

There was a pause. Then, with no further conversation, the front door clicked open. The cops trooped in. The Sheltons lived on the ground floor, unit 118.

The woman who answered the door looked like she'd been through the wars, or maybe a medium-strength hurricane. Her hair was frizzed out in all directions, face smudged, eyes shadowed and bloodshot. She was in her mid-thirties but looked much older. A screaming baby was balanced on her hip.

"Alicia Shelton?" Webb guessed.

"Yeah," Alicia said. "There's a lotta you guys, ain't there."

"Lieutenant Webb," he introduced himself. "These are Detectives Neshenko and O'Reilly, and Officer Piekarski."

"And Rolf," Erin added once again.

"You ain't Floyd's PO," Alicia said. "He's a fat bastard called Rorke, can't keep his eyes off my ass. I think he's a perv. Are you?"

"Ma'am, I'm with Major Crimes," Webb said, unsure how else to answer.

"None of us are pervs," Vic put in, trying unsuccessfully to be helpful. "Not even the dog."

Rolf cocked his head at Vic.

"You might as well come in," Alicia said. "Long as you don't mind the screaming."

The apartment was small and sparsely furnished, but well-kept, though Erin noted unwashed dishes in the sink. The living room didn't have enough seats for all of them. Webb and Piekarski took the love seat while Alicia sat in the only other chair. Erin and Vic had to bring chairs from the dining room.

"You got one on the way, huh?" Alicia said, glancing at the obviously pregnant Piekarski.

"Yeah," Piekarski said.

"See what you got to look forward to?" Alicia said, bouncing the baby on her knee. The kid was not quieted by her efforts.

"Is he okay?" Erin asked.

"Ear infection," Alicia said. "Just got the meds for him today. I figure he better start feeling better soon, or I'm gonna go right outta my mind. Thank God my job's got insurance and I got a little time off."

"Ma'am, we're here about your brother," Webb said.

"That's what you said," Alicia said. "Dammit, I knew this was gonna happen. I never shoulda listened to him. Family's family, I know, but I shoulda slammed the door in his face. He told me he needed a place to stay, or his PO would drop him in some piece of shit halfway house, so I said fine, he could crash here. And this is the thanks I get? Like I don't have enough problems."

"What was your brother involved in?" Webb asked.

"Beats the hell outta me," Alicia replied. "But you wouldn't be here if he hadn't done *something*. Just do me a favor, okay? Kick his douchebag friends' asses for me, will you?"

"So you're unaware of any criminal activity Floyd may have been participating in?" Webb pressed.

"I don't know nothin' about that," Alicia said. "But I know that boy's always in trouble. He's real good at making you feel sorry for him, he got those sad puppy-dog eyes, and he's my kid brother, so I love him, dammit, but he just couldn't never say no to nobody. Ever since we was growing up, some other kid would come to him with some big idea, and Floyd would go along with it. Then when it went sideways, he'd always end up taking the fall, and he never learned a thing from it."

"When's the last time you saw him?" Erin asked.

"When he left for work, yesterday afternoon," Alicia said. "About four o'clock. He's at that pizza place, Ninja Pizza. At least, that's where he said he was going. He never came back. I know, 'cause I was up half the goddamn night with this poor little guy screaming his head off. You ever have an ear infection? Hurts like a bastard."

"Did you report him missing when he didn't come back?" Webb asked.

Alicia gave him a scornful look. "Course not," she said. "You think I *want* the cops looking for him? That boy finds enough trouble without me throwing more his way. I figured he went out partying. He's a good-looking guy, maybe some college girl liked the looks of him and he got lucky. But now I figure he got pinched. Okay, you might as well tell me. What'd he do now?"

"Ma'am, your brother was found at Dasilva Stadium this morning," Webb said. "I'm sorry to say, he's been killed."

Alicia closed the eye nearest her baby and put a hand over that ear. "What?" she said. "I didn't catch that."

"Your brother's been killed, ma'am," Webb repeated. "Murdered."

"Oh sweet Jesus," Alicia said. Her eyes had gone very wide. "No, there's gotta be some mistake. Not Floyd, he's not dead."

"I'm sorry, ma'am," Webb said. "You'll be contacted shortly to identify and claim his body, but we've got a match on his fingerprints. There's no doubt."

"No," Alicia said. "No." Tears filled her eyes.

"We're trying to figure out what happened to him," Erin said. "Do you know if he was having problems with anybody? Had he gotten in any fights recently, made any enemies?"

"Floyd's a sweet guy," Alicia said, shaking her head. "He'd never hurt nobody. He'd steal stuff, sure, or do stupid pranks, but he wouldn't do nothing mean. Everybody likes him. Even in prison, he didn't make no enemies. Oh my God, poor Floyd. How... how did he..."

"Someone hit him in the head," Webb said.

"The Medical Examiner said it would've knocked him unconscious," Erin said. "He wasn't in any pain."

"Can you think of anybody who would've wanted to hurt him?" Webb asked. "Maybe a business associate? A partner?"

"I know who you should ask," Alicia said with sudden, tearful spite. "That other fat guy, Martinelli!"

"What do you think he knows?" Webb asked.

"He does this whole song and dance about helping cons," Alicia said. "All kinds of crooks hang out there. It's against their parole, they ain't supposed to associate with each other, but he says he's helping them get along in the world."

"We'll look into his associates there," Webb promised.

"Oh, God," Alicia said again. "What do I do?"

"I thought you didn't want him in your life," Vic said.

If looks could kill, Alicia Shelton would've become a cop killer on the spot. "You think I wanted *this*?" she demanded, angry tears spilling out of her eyes. "I love him! I meant, what do I *do*? Who do I call? I gotta take care of stuff."

"Here," Erin said, handing over a card. "There's a number of a grief counselor, and there's another number for the NYPD's helpline for victims and family. Call that, and there's people who'll help with the nuts and bolts of what needs to get done."

"Thanks," Alicia said bitterly, taking the card. "Jesus, I told myself maybe he'd do better this time, once he got out. That Martinelli, he said he helped guys like Floyd, and Floyd believed him, and I wanted to. God, he'd have done better if he'd gone right back to his old gang."

"Who are they?" Erin asked. "His old gang, I mean."

"Guys he used to hang with," Alicia said. "When we was growing up. Kids from the neighborhood."

"Are any of them still around?"

"Some of them moved out, some of the others got sent up. Bobby McAvoy OD'd on some bad smack, little Danny Sutton died in a car crash. There was this black kid, Bode Cross, who was in jail for a while. I dunno what happened to him. And Robbie Black, but Floyd didn't want nothing to do with him."

"Bode Cross," Webb repeated, raising an eyebrow at the other detectives. "That's interesting."

"But none of them woulda hurt Floyd," Alicia insisted. "They was, like, blood brothers."

"I'm sure you're right," Erin lied.

# Chapter 4

"Skeezy dorm life and cheap pizza," Piekarski said, looking at the brick and glass of the dormitory. "It's like a flashback to when I was nineteen."

"It's good pizza!" Vic objected.

"And Sullivan Hall isn't skeezy!" the security guard protested. He was a gray-haired campus rent-a-cop who'd been assigned as their liaison while they were on the grounds of St. John's. His name was Frank Wycliffe and he had a pleasant, grandfatherly aspect that Erin figured helped him deal with rowdy college kids.

"Sorry," Piekarski said.

"Don't apologize," Vic said. "All dorms are skeezy."

"Even the ones at religious schools?" Erin asked.

"*Especially* religious schools," Vic replied. "All those Catholic girls in their short plaid skirts..."

"I think you're confusing real life with Internet videos again," Piekarski said. "Or maybe Billy Joel songs."

"According to our security cameras, the pizza delivery was made to this door," Wycliffe said, ignoring Vic. "Todd Overholtz paid for it."

"You recognized the student?" Webb asked, surprised.

"I try to get to know all the kids," Wycliffe said. "Particularly the freshmen. They're away from home for the first time in their lives. Most of them make good choices, by and large, but a few can't handle the freedom and get in trouble. I try to steer them the right way when I can. Todd's a good kid, even if you count the skinny-dipping incident."

"The what?" Vic, Erin, and Piekarski asked in unison.

Wycliffe shrugged. "Back in September, he and a few other frosh snuck into the swimming pool at midnight for a little unsupervised swim."

"Wasn't it locked?" Webb asked.

"One of them picked the lock," Wycliffe said. "But they didn't know we had motion-sensors. I was a couple minutes away, so they'd just had time to strip down and jump in the pool before I got there."

Vic snickered. "Caught them with their pants down, huh?"

"And everything else," Wycliffe said. "Todd's buddies gave up, but Todd made a break for it. I got between him and his clothes, but he figured he didn't need them and took off. Stark naked. I don't know what he was thinking."

"Maybe he figured his buddies wouldn't rat him out," Vic said.

"His student ID was in his pants pocket," Wycliffe said. "I didn't need to chase him."

"What happened to him?" Vic asked.

Wycliffe smiled. "We called him to the security office the next morning and gave him back his clothes and ID, in exchange for a fine and a stern talking-to about the importance of safety and lifeguards. It wasn't a big deal, but I remembered his face."

"And other parts of him, I guess," Piekarski said, grinning. "You ransomed a guy's clothes back to him. That's fantastic."

"I've checked his schedule," Wycliffe said. "His next class isn't until this afternoon, so if he's not here, I hope we can find someone who knows where to find him."

The campus cop scanned his ID card at the door and let them in. They attracted interested stares from several students. Webb might have passed for a worn-out tenured professor, but Vic looked like a thug, Piekarski was obviously pregnant, and Erin was walking a large German Shepherd who was wearing a K-9 Kevlar vest.

Wycliffe led the way to Overholtz's room. The door was shut, but music was audible through the wood. Wycliffe rapped on the door with his knuckles.

"Hey, Todd," he called. "You in there?"

"C'mon in," someone replied from inside.

Wycliffe opened the door to reveal a typical crowded, messy dorm room. It looked like a triple to Erin. Two young men were lounging around; one reading a textbook, the other at his computer. The kid with the book blinked in surprise. Then his eyes got wide and he quickly sat up.

"Frank!" he said. "I can explain everything. It wasn't my fault!"

Vic started to say something, but Erin caught his eye and shook her head, letting Wycliffe take the lead.

"I think you'd better, Todd," Wycliffe said. "Don't worry, I'm sure it's not as bad as it seems."

"I swear, I didn't know about the frogs ahead of time," Overholtz said. "Brian said he could get us into the faculty lounge. We just wanted to borrow some beers. But Petey had this box with him, and he had it open before we knew what he was doing. And then they jumped out, and they were going everywhere in the dark. There was just no way we were going to catch them again."

"Frogs in the faculty lounge?" Wycliffe said. "And this would be Brian King and Peter Van Dorn?"

"Yeah, but we didn't even find any beers," Overholtz said. "Please don't be too hard on them. Wait a second, you didn't know about the frogs?"

"I do now," Wycliffe said with a twinkle in his eye.

"Oh, shit," Overholtz said.

The NYPD officers exchanged knowing grins. Talkative perps were easy to break. Sometimes they confessed to things you didn't even know they'd done.

"But... if this isn't about that, what're you doing here?" Overholtz asked.

"These folks are from the NYPD," Wycliffe said. "They want to talk about the pizza you ordered last night."

"Pizza? What for?" Overholtz was completely lost.

"You were the pizza guy's last delivery," Webb said. "We just have a few questions."

"Does that mean we can forget about the frogs?" Overholtz asked hopefully.

"Oh, we're going to talk about the frogs," Wycliffe promised. "We're going to have a nice, long conversation about amphibians."

"But we'll put in a good word for you if you cooperate," Erin said.

"What do you need to know?" the kid asked.

"Let's start with the timing," Webb said. "When did the pizza arrive?"

"Quarter to one, maybe," Overholtz said.

They already knew this from the security footage outside the hall. Webb was testing to see if the kid was telling the truth, and if his memory was reliable.

"Who was it for?" Webb asked.

"Me, Brian, Petey, Jamie, and Nick."

"What'd you order?" Vic asked.

"Two extra-larges. One pepperoni, one cheese."

"That's a lot of pizza," Erin said.

"For five college guys," Wycliffe said. "Don't you remember how much you ate when you were their age?"

"How did you pay?" Webb asked.

"Cash," Overholtz said.

"How much was it?"

"I think it was thirty," Overholtz said. "The other guys chipped in, and with tip, I don't remember exactly. Is that a problem?"

"It's fine," Webb said. "Do you remember anything about the driver?"

"The pizza guy?" Overholtz was still confused. "He was just this guy, you know? I guess I thought he was kinda old to be working a job like that."

"Old?" Webb prompted.

"Yeah. Back home, it's usually high-school kids delivering pizza. This guy was *old*. I mean, he must've been at least thirty."

Erin winced. She was thirty-six.

"He had tattoos," the kid said. "I saw one over the top of his collar. I couldn't tell what it was."

"Did he act unusual?" Webb asked.

"Unusual how?" Overholtz asked.

"If I knew how he was acting, it wouldn't be unusual," Webb said patiently. "That's why I'm asking. Was he upset? Angry? Nervous?"

"Now that you mention it, he was a little edgy," Overholtz said. "He was in kind of a hurry. I figured it was the next delivery he had to make. He didn't even count the money, just shoved it in his pocket and took off."

"Did he say anything?" Erin asked.

"He said 'thanks' when I paid him," Overholtz said. "Look, is this guy into something? Is he, like, a drug dealer or something?"

"Why would you say that?" she asked.

"Well, you said I was his last delivery," Overholtz said. "What about the other one on campus?"

"How do you know he had another campus delivery?" Erin asked.

"Because of the other pizza box."

Everyone stared at him.

"What?" Overholtz asked, shifting uncomfortably.

"Explain, please," Webb said.

"We ordered two large pizzas," Overholtz said, holding up the first two fingers on his right hand. Then he raised his ring finger. "But he had three boxes in his hands. He only gave me two."

"Did you see where he went?" Erin demanded. "Afterward?"

"No," the kid said. "Sorry. I went back inside. I was hungry."

"Anything else?" Webb asked.

"No." He looked hopefully at Wycliffe. "Am I still in trouble?"

"Not from them," Wycliffe said, poker-faced. "But we'll discuss the other thing later."

Overholtz sagged. "Just don't call my mom, okay? She'll flip."

"I think we're done here," Webb said.

"Except for one thing," Erin said. "What happened to the pizza boxes when you guys were done eating?"

\*   \*   \*

"We have to find that other pizza box," Erin said. She was holding Rolf's leash in one hand and an empty box in the other.

"Why?" Wycliffe asked.

"Because we're detectives," Vic said. "We don't like it when things go missing. It makes us nervous."

"We need to know where our victim went and what he was doing when he died," Webb explained. "Our victim was delivering pizza to Sullivan Hall at quarter to one. By one-thirty, two at the latest, he was dead in the parking garage over there. Where was he in the meantime?"

"Do you have cameras covering the whole campus?" Erin asked Wycliffe.

"No," he said. "We have the dorm entrances, the entrances to the academic buildings, and hallway coverage of the science and computer buildings, on account of the valuable equipment in those. But it'll take a while to review all that."

"Not as long as you might think," Webb said. "We're only looking at a forty-five minute window. Take Neshenko with you to the security station."

"Why me?" Vic asked.

"Piekarski needs to be reviewing robbery reports," Webb said. "And if my guess is right as to why O'Reilly wanted an empty pizza box, she and her dog are going to try a more old-fashioned method of tracking our guy."

"That's right," Erin said.

"What about you?" Vic asked.

"I don't review security footage," Webb said. "Because I'm a Lieutenant and RHIP."

Wycliffe raised his eyebrows. "Beg pardon?"

"Rank Hath Its Privileges," Erin and Vic chorused.

"Quit bitching, Vic," Piekarski said. "You might find the clue that cracks the case."

"I doubt it," Vic muttered. "Those goddamn cameras have the worst resolution on Earth. I can't believe our rent-a-cop recognized somebody he knew. Are you some sort of psychic?"

"I've got a good head for faces," Wycliffe said mildly. "And I'm not rented, I'm salaried."

"If you don't carry a gun, you're not a real cop," Vic retorted.

"If you need a gun to prove you're a cop, you can't be much of a cop," Wycliffe said.

Piekarski held up a finger and made a sizzling sound, grinning at Vic. "He's got you there."

"I'll show you to the security center," Wycliffe told Vic. "I don't want a murderer running around campus any more than you do. For all I know, he'll take out a student next."

"You boys play nice," Piekarski said.

"Here's a security badge," Wycliffe said, handing it to Webb. "It'll get you into the campus buildings. Try not to disrupt any of the classes."

"I'll tag along with you," Webb told Erin, clipping the badge to the flap of his trench coat.

"Rolf may not get the right scent," she warned him. "Five college boys might've handled this box. Or he might track it the wrong way, back to where the victim parked."

"Understood," Webb said. "But I've got faith in both of you."

Erin smiled. Rolf cocked his head at her, waiting for something to happen. She held the box in front of his snout and gave him his "search" command.

"Rolf, *such!*"

The K-9's nostrils flared as he inhaled. Most dogs would have enjoyed the lingering odors of cheese, grease, and pepperoni that clung to the cardboard, and Rolf was no exception, but he'd been trained to focus on the smell of humans.

Forensic science was founded on the principle of transference. Whenever you touched something, you got bits of it on you and you left bits of you on it. A good CSU team could prove where a person had been and what they'd handled by examining either the person or the environment. If you didn't find evidence, you weren't looking hard enough.

Rolf's nose worked the same way. Humans left skin cells, sweat, and glandular secretions on everything they came in contact with. Every human's scent was as unique as their fingerprints. There might be billions of people on Earth, but Rolf could tell every one of them apart with a single sniff.

The Shepherd paused, sorting through the various smells. More than one human had touched this box. Which one was he supposed to follow? He made a tight circle, checking the lingering smells outside the dormitory, and made his best guess.

"Damn," Erin muttered. Rolf had led them back to the front door of Sullivan Hall. He scratched at the base of the door and looked up at her expectantly.

"No," she told him. "Not that one, kiddo. Try again. *Such!*"

She held out the box again. Rolf was a bright enough dog to puzzle it out. His partner didn't want him following that human. But all the other smells led back through the same door. All of them except one.

Rolf set off along the sidewalk, tail wagging hesitantly. He paused and glanced back at Erin, seeking reassurance.

"Go on, kiddo," she said. "*Such!*"

Rolf trotted happily off, glad to be doing the right thing. His rubber Kong toy awaited at the end of the trail. He was already salivating a little at the prospect.

The K-9 led Erin and Webb along a sidewalk across campus. The scent trail was crisscrossed by the smells left by dozens of other humans, but Rolf wasn't shaken. He went more confidently every moment, trotting faster and faster until Erin had to pull back on the leash so the two-legged ones could match his pace. They passed in front of St. Albert Hall, moving southeast, then took a sharp left and fetched up at the southern entrance to St. Augustine Hall.

"All these buildings are named after saints," Webb observed, looking at the name over the door. "You're a good Catholic girl. You ought to feel right at home."

"To tell you the truth, sir, saints make me a little edgy," Erin said, rubbing her eyes and squinting. The sun on the bright white snow was dazzling, making her head hurt. The bullet wound on the side of her skull was throbbing dully.

"Really? How come?"

"Cops never trust anyone who seems too good to be true," she said. "The better the PR, the worse the person hiding behind it."

Webb chuckled dryly. "Good thing our Lord and Savior wasn't in law enforcement," he said.

Once inside the hall, Rolf made for the stairs. Erin let him keep leading the way down to the basement. He pulled them down a concrete-block corridor toward a plain, solid-looking door. He stopped in front of it, scratched twice, and whined.

"This is where he went," Erin reported.

Webb stared at the label next to the door. "Server room?" he said. "That's weird."

Rolf snuffled at the base of the door. Then, abruptly, he made a one-eighty and started back the way they'd come.

"O'Reilly, get back here," Webb said. "We don't need to follow him all the way to his car. We know where he ended up. Let's see if we can figure out what he was doing here."

Rolf, meanwhile, paused at a garbage can next to the base of the stairs. He went up on his hind legs and snuffled at the opening at the top.

"That's enough, kiddo," Erin said. "Sheesh. I thought you knew better than to mess with the trash while you're tracking. *Fuss.*"

Rolf gave her a reproachful look as he returned to her hip, sullenly obeying his "heel" command.

Something in the dog's demeanor prompted Erin to take another look at the trash can. She pushed open the flap and peered inside.

"Sir!" she called. Then she put her own nose close to the trash can and gave it a sniff.

Webb hurried over. "What is it?" he asked.

She pointed. "Pizza box. Ninja Pizza. But I don't smell pizza."

"You're smelling trash cans now?" Webb inquired.

"You can learn a lot from your nose, sir," she said.

"I'm not going to argue that," he said. "The server room is locked. You stay here and watch that door and this garbage. I'm going to call a CSU guy to bag the trash, and see if I can get us into that room. I've got the feeling whatever's behind that door was worth killing for."

# Chapter 5

Erin and Rolf were stuck in the basement hallway with nothing to do. They couldn't get into the server room, and Erin knew they shouldn't touch the trash can until CSU had a crack at it. Erin didn't have access to the Departmental database, so she couldn't even look up anything about Floyd Shelton.

What she did have was a bored K-9, a rubber Kong ball, and a concrete hallway without anything breakable in it.

When Webb finally returned, almost half an hour later, he found Rolf happily bounding after the ball as Erin bounced it off floor, walls, and ceiling. The dog was having a great time. So, for that matter, was Erin.

Webb had a bespectacled young guy, a campus cop, and a CSU man in tow. The CSU technician got to work securing the garbage can. He'd dust the can for prints, then scoop up the trash in the bag in which it already rested and take the whole thing back to the lab to go over everything in a controlled environment. Meanwhile, the detectives accompanied the security guy and the kid with the glasses to the server room.

"Don't touch nothing," the guard said as he ushered them in. "There's, like, sensitive equipment in here. We're talking millions of dollars."

"He's not joking," the kid said. "This is the brains of the whole campus's computer network. Everything runs through this room."

Erin stared at row after row of mysterious plastic boxes. Bundles of fiber-optic cables snaked into the boxes. She thought about all the computers in all the classrooms, labs, offices, and dormitories, all plugged into this network. It really was like a body's nervous system.

"I don't know computers," she said.

"Neither do I," Webb said. "I'm too old."

The kid snickered. "I guess you are," he said. "I grew up with these. You barely had electricity back when you were a kid."

"Or running water," Webb deadpanned. "I had to walk to school, through knee-deep snow."

"I didn't know you got snow in Los Angeles," Erin said. "I think the only thing that's knee-deep here is the bullshit."

Webb turned his attention back to the kid. "What's your name?" he asked.

The kid grimaced. "Seymour W. Emerson," he said reluctantly. "But everybody calls me Sparky."

"I can see why," Erin said, smiling. "What's the W short for?"

"Waldo. My mom wanted to call me Ralph, but my dad said Ralph Waldo Emerson was too much. Mom always wanted me to be a writer."

"But you went into computers instead?" Erin asked.

"Yeah," Emerson said. "I figured that was where the money was."

"You figured right," Webb said. "Can you tell if anything's missing?"

"Yeah," Emerson said, scanning the room. "But it'll take some time. And you have to understand, I'm just a junior admin. I don't really run this place. But I do know what goes where."

"You figure someone broke in and swiped some equipment?" the security guy asked. "I didn't see no signs of, whaddaya call it, forced entry."

Erin knelt and examined the edge of the door. He was right. Kicking it in would have left obvious damage. So would a crowbar.

"They might've had a key," she said. A forensics team would be able to tell if the lock had been picked. The picks would've left scratches on the tumblers. But they'd have to disassemble the lock to get a good look at it, which would also take time.

"I don't notice anything obvious," Emerson said after he'd walked up and down the aisles between the servers. "Everything seems to be plugged in and running okay."

"Why would someone want to break in here, but not take anything?" Webb asked.

"You can do all sorts of things with a compromised network," Emerson said. "You can introduce viruses, set up monitoring software, you name it."

"Shelton was a street hood," Erin said. "Did he know anything about electronics?"

"Not that I know of," Webb said. "But we'll check. Mr. Emerson, I want you to do a thorough check of these systems. And I mean thorough."

"What am I looking for?" Emerson asked.

"If I knew that I'd have your job," Webb said. "And my paycheck would be a lot bigger. One other thing: who has keys to this room?"

"All the admins," Emerson said. "Plus campus security."

Webb and Erin looked at the security guard, who shrugged.

"Beats me," he said. "I'm just a little guy. I'll ask my boss."

"Were you on duty last night?" Webb asked.

"No. I came on at nine this morning."

"Where were you last night?"

"Asleep. At home." The man frowned. "What's that supposed to mean?"

"It means we can trust you," Webb said. "Assuming someone can verify it."

"My wife and kids," he said indignantly. "If my word ain't good enough for you."

Webb studied his face. "Yeah," he said. "I think it is. And I'm going to prove it. Your job, here and now, is to guard this room and Mr. Emerson. Nobody else comes in, nothing gets brought in or out. Are we clear?"

"Yeah," the guard said.

"Good," Webb said. "O'Reilly, let's bounce. It's time to touch base with the rest of the squad. Hopefully they've been spending their time well."

*    *    *

"I hate security cameras," Vic said. "I hate colleges. I hate my life. And I hate being a cop."

"That's not true," Erin said. "At least not that last part. You love wearing a shield."

"Okay," he admitted. "But the rest of it's true. Three out of four."

They were crowded into a small security office, clustered around a tiny black and white screen. Wycliffe had gone outside to give them a little more room. On the screen was a frozen image of a man wearing a baseball cap, pulled low over his eyes. He was coming out of a door that looked very familiar to Erin.

"That's the server room," she said. "In the basement of St. Augustine Hall."

Vic stared at her. "How the hell did you know that?" he demanded.

"Lucky guess," she said.

"Luck my ass," he said. "It was the mutt, wasn't it."

"Yeah. He tracked Shelton by smell."

"Okay," Vic said. "So you're saying I just wasted my time. That's fantastic."

"We need the footage," Webb said. "It's evidence. Rewind it."

"Whatever you say, sir," Vic grumbled. "Here we go. Couple minutes before one, our guy comes up to the door. He sets down the pizza box for a minute, right there on the floor, and monkeys with the door."

"Unlocking it?" Webb guessed.

"Picking it," Erin said. "He's taking too long to use a key."

"Erin's right," Vic said. "If you look close, you can see him shove the picks back in his pocket. You can't see his face, but you can see the jacket. It's the same one our dead guy's wearing, with that corny pizza ninja logo across the back. Once he's got the door open, he picks up the box and goes in. He's inside for exactly six minutes and thirty-six seconds. Then he comes out, and now he's facing the camera. Only problem is, that damn baseball cap is still over his face. You can catch a little of his chin, but that could be anybody of the right race."

"But we already know it's Shelton," Webb said.

"Maybe," Erin said.

"What do you mean?" Webb asked. "Rolf led us straight there. He's wearing the right clothes."

"Rolf was following a trail on the pizza box," she said. "But something feels weird. I didn't see a baseball cap in the delivery truck. Did you?"

"No," Webb said thoughtfully. "But what difference does that make? Maybe he ditched the hat somewhere. He might've just had it on to spoof the camera."

"Anyway, that's all I've got," Vic said. "He comes out and goes back the way he came. The camera just covers the server room door."

"Good work," Webb said. "Get a copy of the footage."

"Already did." Vic held up a thumb drive. "Where's Zofia?"

"Back at the cars, I think," Webb said. "Doing research. She's our next stop."

\*     \*     \*

"Hey, guys," Piekarski said. "Couldn't solve it without me, huh?"

"Not yet," Webb said. "Find anything?"

"Yes and no." Piekarski shifted in the driver's seat of Vic's Taurus.

Webb crossed his arms and waited.

"I checked the campus security report first," Piekarski said. "Nothing popped. It's all small potatoes. A couple kids' backpacks got swiped, someone lost a laptop in the dining hall. None of it is during our murder window."

"We know what was getting broken into then," Vic said. "We just came from there."

Piekarski held up a hand. "I wasn't finished. Guys are so impatient. I decided to look back over the past month to see whether anyone reported a burglary and mentioned pizza delivery. And I got a hit."

"God bless our database," Vic said.

"Amen," Webb said. "In the old days, back when you youngsters were in grade school, we would've had to sort through the DD-5s by hand. It would've taken days."

"Don't keep us waiting," Vic said. "What'd you find?"

Piekarski smiled, savoring the moment. "A computer lab got robbed over in Brooklyn, last week."

"Another computer place," Webb said. "That's interesting. What's it got to do with pizza?"

"Security cameras saw a guy carry a pizza up to the door. He was wearing a cap and a coat with the Ninja Pizza logo. Nobody was in the lab, so the pizza guy jimmied the lock. He came out half an hour later, still carrying the pizza, and left."

"Let me guess," Erin said. "Nothing was missing."

Piekarski gave her an odd look. "That'd be a weird burglar," she said. "The owner said he'd lost this fancy thing he'd been building. Some kind of surveillance system."

"How big was this thing?" Erin asked.

"I don't know," Piekarski said. "All I've got is the incident report. It doesn't go into too much detail. We'd have to talk to the detective who caught the case."

"Sounds like a plan," Webb said. "O'Reilly, Neshenko, hop over and see if you can talk to the detective."

"They won't have anything for us," Erin gloomily predicted. "Burglaries have a terrible closure rate. It's not even going to be on his back burner; it'll be on the floor behind the damn stove."

"Look on the bright side," Vic said. "It's not in the 116, and it's not a homicide, so we won't be talking to your buddies Lyons and Spinelli. Who's the dick on the case?"

Piekarski glanced at the computer screen. "Detective Ivanova," she said. "At the Six-Oh. Wait a second, that 'a' on the end of the last name means it's a woman, doesn't it?"

"Yeah," Vic said. He looked like he'd just taken a big bite of something sour. "Do we really have to go all the way to Brooklyn?"

"CSU is still processing evidence here," Webb said. "And Levine's going to be busy with our victim's postmortem for a while. I don't think we've got enough to occupy four cops' time at this location. Why? Is there a problem?"

"No problem, sir," Vic said through clenched teeth.

"Good. Find out what this case has to do with ours. The burglar might be our victim, or it might be our killer, but there's got to be a connection."

"Yes, sir," Erin said. "Come on, Vic. We can leave your car here and you can ride with Rolf and me. First we went to my home territory, now we're going to yours. The Six-Oh is Brighton Beach, isn't it? Where you grew up?"

"Yeah," Vic said. "Little Odessa."

"You don't sound happy about going back."

"If you'd grown up there, you wouldn't either."

# Chapter 6

"Spill," Erin said as soon as they pulled out of the parking garage. "Who's this detective, and how do you know her?"

"It could be a different Detective Ivanova," Vic said without much hope.

"But if it isn't...?" she prompted.

He sighed. "I went through the Academy with this girl, Mira Ivanova. We came from the same neighborhood, we knew some of the same people. Hell, we went to the same high school. So we hung around each other a lot. You know how it is. Every year at the Academy, a few of the graduates pair up."

"Did you?"

"Eventually, yeah."

"And it ended badly?"

"You could say that."

"Vic, I never knew you'd had another girlfriend on the Force," Erin said. "What happened?"

"We graduated together," he said. "And we both got assigned to the Six-Oh. She wanted it, I wanted to go where she was. Of course, we weren't partnered up. We were both rookies, so we got farmed out to a couple of FTOs."

Erin nodded. Field Training Officers were experienced cops whose main job was to keep their rookies alive while teaching them the ropes.

"Everything went great for a while," Vic said. "Then we had what the PC likes to call a civil disturbance."

"A riot?" Erin asked, smiling.

"Exactly. Some stupid political thing got out of hand and a few dozen idiots started smashing windows. Both our units got called in, along with some others. I was doing my job, busting perps. I'm pretty good at riot control."

"I'll bet you are," she said. "What'd you do, bounce rioters off each other?"

"Something like that. We're getting things under control, my FTO and I are wrestling with this jerk, and I hear Mira scream. I look up, and there she is, this other guy's got her by the hair and he's dragging her across the pavement."

"Didn't she have her hair up?" Erin asked. Every policewoman knew better than to wear her hair loose when working the street. It was hard enough being smaller than the average perp without giving the bad guys an easy handhold on the back of your head.

"Yeah, but she'd lost her riot helmet and the whaddaya call it, the bun, came loose," Vic said. "Anyway, it shouldn't have been a big deal, Mira's a tough girl, she's more pissed off than scared. The scream is just 'cause it hurts, getting your hair pulled like that. Her FTO's on the way to help, he's closer than I am, but that doesn't matter, because I'm not hearing another cop getting manhandled, I'm hearing my girl getting hurt."

Erin swallowed. She could see where this was going.

"I forget about the guy I'm wrestling," Vic said. "My FTO's yelling at me, I guess, but I don't even hear him. I'm already on my way toward Mira, shoving everybody else out of my way. By the time I get there, she's got things under control. Doesn't even need her FTO's help. She hauls out her X-26 and Tases the son of a bitch right in the throat, contact close, just rams the thing into his neck and triggers it off. Paramedics had to immobilize the guy so they could get the needles out without killing him. She nearly took out his jugular."

"So what's the problem?" Erin asked.

Vic shook his head. "While I'm gone, and my FTO is distracted, the guy we were wrestling gets his hands on a loose brick. He smashes my FTO right in the temple. If he hadn't been wearing his riot gear, his skull would've cracked like an egg. Even with the helmet, it's a bad concussion. Lights out for ten solid minutes. Poor guy didn't come back on duty for two weeks."

"Ouch," Erin said.

"Mira broke up with me the next day," Vic said. "She told me our thing was bleeding through into the Job and putting other people in danger. She said neither of us would ever forgive me if I got another officer killed because I was too busy worrying about her. So I put in for a transfer and got the hell out of Brighton Beach. I got into ESU, she made detective down at the Six-Oh, and that's all there is to it."

"Wow," Erin said. "When's the last time you talked to her?"

"It's gotta be five, six years," Vic said.

"Look, if you don't want to see her, I can handle this alone," she said.

"No, I'm a professional," he said. "Jesus, haven't I proved that? I'm working with Zofia now, and it's fine."

"Is it?" Erin asked.

"I'm a professional," Vic repeated, but he sounded to Erin like he was trying to convince himself.

"I'm looking forward to meeting this Mira," Erin said.

"You'll like her," he said. "She's a lot like you."

"Should I have been worried about you making a pass at me?" she replied. "Am I your type?"

Vic snorted. "That's the last thing you should've been worried about," he said. "You're too much like her. I learned my lesson the first time. Besides, she's a lot hotter than you are. I mean, a *lot*."

Erin smacked him.

\*    \*    \*

Vic paused outside the Precinct 60 station house. He stared at the building for what seemed to Erin like a very long time.

"You okay?" she finally asked.

"Yeah," he said, shaking his head to clear it. "I'm fine."

"That's my line," she said.

"Except it's bullshit when you say it," he said.

"It's always bullshit," she retorted. "We're never fine."

"That's either real profound, or the biggest load of crap I've heard in a week," Vic said.

"Philosophy is like that," Erin said. "Blame it on the TBI."

"You're gonna keep milking that traumatic brain injury, aren't you," he said. "Not that you can actually milk a brain, you understand. You'd end up with a glass full of whaddaya call it, cerebrospinal fluid."

"Yuck," she said. "Let's go see your old flame."

"Don't call her that," he groaned.

The desk sergeant directed them to the Six-Oh's Burglary unit. Erin wondered what Detective Ivanova would look like. She had an odd mental image of meeting a woman who looked and sounded exactly like Erin herself, which was nuts. Maybe the head injury really was affecting her. That was the real hell of brain damage. You didn't always know what it was doing to you.

The Burglary office was a cluttered cluster of four desks, divided by low partitions. Only one of the desks was currently occupied. A black-haired woman sat with her back toward the door, reclining in her chair and twirling a pen between her fingers.

"Excuse me," Erin said, rapping on the doorframe with her knuckles. "We're looking for Detective Ivanova."

"You found her," Ivanova said, swiveling in the chair without getting up. Her accent was solid working-class Brooklyn, with a raspy, throaty undertone that suggested she smoked more than she should. "Who wants to know?"

"Hey, Mira," Vic said. "Long time, huh?"

Ivanova blinked once, slowly. "Vic Neshenko," she said. "I heard you got your gold shield. Looks good on you."

Vic automatically put a hand to his chest, where his detective's shield hung on its chain. "Thanks," he said. "You're looking pretty good yourself."

Ivanova stood up and walked toward them. She was wearing black leather boots with a two-inch heel, but she would've been a tall woman even without them. Erin pegged her at five-eleven, long and lean. She had intense dark eyes and a jagged scar that ran the full length of her cheek. In spite of the scar, or maybe because of it, her face was truly striking. It had a model's high cheekbones and those remarkable eyes. A Sig-Sauer automatic nestled under her arm in a shoulder holster. Her own gold shield gleamed on her belt.

"I've been reading about you in the papers," Ivanova said. "You're a genuine hero. How do you like it?"

Erin didn't often get the chance to see Vic embarrassed. She couldn't help enjoying the way he flushed and mumbled something about reporters exaggerating what had happened.

"Don't let him fool you," Erin said. "He's rock solid. He's saved my life more than once."

"And I bet you've bailed him out, too," Ivanova said. "His heart's in the right place, but his balls are bigger than his brains, and he thinks with them half the time."

"You say that like it's a bad thing," Vic said, recovering himself.

"So what're you doing here?" Ivanova asked. "Taking a walk down Memory Lane?"

"It's the Job, ma'am," Erin said. "I'm Erin O'Reilly, Major Crimes. We were hoping to talk to you about a case."

"Okay," the other woman said. "But I got a condition. You call me 'ma'am' one more time and you get nothing out of me, you got it?"

"What should I call you?" Erin asked.

"Mira," she said. "For Vic's sake."

"Copy that," Erin said. "Can we talk here, or do you want to go somewhere else?"

"Here's fine," Mira said. "We got two guys out and the other two are pounding pavement, so it's just me. What can I do for the folks downtown?"

"We need to know what you have on the computer lab burglary last week," Erin said.

"The one with the pizza guy," Vic added.

"You serious?" Mira asked. "How does Major Crimes even know about that? And why do you care? That's a nothing case. Nobody got hurt. We don't even have a dollar value for the thing that supposedly got jacked."

"Somebody did get hurt," Vic said. "A Ninja Pizza delivery boy got his head caved in last night, over on St. John's campus in Queens."

"And someone wearing a jacket with the pizza company's logo broke into a campus server room," Erin said. "It might've been our victim, or it might've been somebody else."

"A server room, you said?" Mira asked. "That's interesting."

"We thought so," Vic said.

"What can you tell us about the computer job?" Erin asked.

"Just a sec," Mira said, bending over and opening the file cabinet next to her desk. "I've got the case file in here. I haven't scanned it into the system yet. We're way behind on our paperwork, if you can believe it."

"What else is new?" Vic said. Erin glanced at him, then gave him a glare. He was definitely checking Mira out as the other detective was bent over. It was a good enough view, Erin supposed, but that was no excuse.

"Here it is." Mira straightened and turned, handing them a disappointingly slim folder. It contained the inevitable DD-5 incident form, the statement they'd taken from the owner, a few other statements, some stills from the lab's security camera... and that was about it.

"You haven't exactly been burning out your cylinders on this one," Vic observed.

"Bite me, Vic," Mira snapped. "I've got thirty-nine open robberies assigned to me, and that's low. We don't get the resources you fancy Major Crimes people do. People expect goddamn miracles from us. You want to know what that pencil-neck nerd-boy said when I took his statement? He wanted me to get fingerprints, but he said his equipment was too sensitive, so we shouldn't use powder. What were we supposed to use? Thoughts and prayers?"

Vic snickered. "You never know," he said. "Those might work. Have you ever tried them?"

Mira gave him a dirty look. "I talked to the guy who runs Ninja Pizza," she said.

"Martinelli?" Erin asked.

"Yeah, that fat Italian ex-con," Mira said. "He spun me this bullshit story about how he's trying to help other cons reform."

"He told us the same thing," Vic said. "I figured he was full of shit."

"He claims none of his drivers were in the area at the time of the robbery," Mira said, rolling her eyes. "But he's got two guys on his payroll with burglary priors."

"Floyd Shelton and Bode Cross," Erin said.

"Right again," Mira said. "You've been doing your homework. Not sure what you need me for."

"What was stolen?" Erin asked.

"According to that zit-faced loser, some fancy thing he called a Trojan," Mira said.

Vic nearly choked on his own tongue.

"It's named after the Trojan Horse," Mira said, rolling her eyes. "You know, the big wooden horse? The one the Greeks used to sneak into Troy?"

"You ever think how weird that is?" Vic replied.

"Yeah," Mira said. "I always wondered why the Trojans didn't just torch the horse and call it a day. I mean, what sort of brilliant plan is that? Build a giant horse and hope the other guys are dumb enough to bring it inside?"

"No," Vic said. "I meant, naming a brand of condoms after a war where the only thing people know about it is a bunch of little guys sneaked into a place they weren't supposed to be and then spilled out and wrecked everything."

"I see what you mean," Mira said. "That is pretty funny, now you mention it."

"What was this Trojan thing?" Erin asked, trying to keep on the point.

"It's a kind of computer virus," Mira explained. "It pretends to be innocent, but it's really malicious software. It gets into your data and steals stuff, or corrupts your files, or locks up your system. There's all sorts of shit a virus can do."

"Hold on," Vic said. "I'm not a computer guy, but I know the difference between software and hardware. A computer program isn't something you have to physically carry around. You could just upload it to the Net and copy the file, couldn't you?"

"This thing is special," Mira said. "It can bypass anti-virus programs, but you have to plug it into the computer in meatspace."

Vic snorted again.

"That's a real word," Mira said. "I didn't make it up. I swear, you've got the dirtiest mind of any guy I know, and I worked Vice for a while. That's where I got this little souvenir."

She touched the scar on her cheek.

"I noticed," Vic said. "How'd you manage that?"

"I was undercover," Mira said. "Pimp with a knife. I was too good at my job. If he'd known I was a cop he wouldn't have done it. He thought I was moving in on his turf, so he signed his name on my face."

"Bastard," Vic growled. "What's this punk's name?"

Mira shook her head and smiled. "Same old Vic," she said. "You haven't changed a bit. Forget about him. I took care of my own business."

"What'd you do to him?" Vic asked.

"The surgeon was able to fix most of it," Mira said with a hard smile. "They never did find his left nut."

Vic winced.

"That reminds me," Mira said. "When do you clock out? We ought to get together, have a few drinks, catch up."

"I don't think that's a real good idea," Vic said.

"How come?" Mira asked. "We're not working the same PSA anymore. I promise, I haven't forgotten how to have a good time."

Vic cleared his throat and very deliberately avoided looking at her. "It's not you," he said. "I've got this other thing."

Mira looked from him to Erin. "Wow," she said. "You really haven't changed. Damn, Vic, didn't you learn a single damn thing?"

"What?" Vic stared at her, then at Erin, who stared back. "No! It's not that! Shit, you think I'm sleeping with *her*?"

"You don't have to sound quite that shocked," Erin said with a grin. She turned her attention back to Mira. "Vic's trying to say he's spoken for, but the other girl's not in this room."

"I see," Mira said. "Who's the lucky broad?"

"Her name's Zofia," Vic said.

"What'd you bust her for?"

"Hey, she came after me! I'll have you know, there's some girls in this city who actually want to spend time with me."

"Hmm," Mira said. She licked her lips thoughtfully. "Well, if she ever dumps you, give me a call."

"As I recall, you're the one who dumped me," Vic said.

Erin cleared her throat loudly.

"What?" Vic said.

"Can we go back to talking about the stolen Trojan horse or whatever it is?" Erin asked. "What the hell is meatspace?"

"Right," Mira said. "Meatspace was a word that techie dweeb used. He meant the real world, as opposed to the online one. The world where pieces of meat walk around. His point was, this device of his can break through any security firewall, but you have to physically plug it into the computer you're trying to crack."

"That's a stupid design," Vic said. "You can't get into government computers or big corporate ones. They've got locked doors and guys with guns guarding them."

"How about a server room at a college?" Erin suggested. "All you need is a key."

"Or a guy who's good with lockpicks," Vic agreed. "You think this heist was setting him up for the job at St. John's?"

"I can't think of another reason for it," Erin said.

"Why the pizza disguise?" Vic wondered.

"A delivery guy can go anywhere," Mira said. "Nobody asks questions."

"But everybody would know to go after the pizza guy," Vic objected. "That logo's all over the security cameras!"

"Maybe that's why our pizza guy is in the morgue right now," Erin said quietly.

# Chapter 7

"You think Shelton was a fall guy," Vic said.

"It's a theory," Erin said.

They were back in Erin's Charger, on their way to rejoin Webb and Piekarski.

"I like it," he said. "Shelton's got a record of breaking and entering. He probably knew how to jimmy locks. He hung out with other ex-cons. And now he can't answer any questions, on account of getting his brains scrambled."

"The killer would have to be somebody who knew him," Erin said. "There had to be surveillance. The other guy had to know he'd be on campus last night."

"Or he was in on it and the other guy screwed him," Vic said.

"Maybe," Erin said. "Either way, I think we need to look a lot closer at Ninja Pizza. We're going to need a list of all their employees, past and current, and cross-reference them with our victim."

"That sounds an awful lot like desk work," Vic said gloomily. "And unpaid overtime."

"Yeah," she said. "You might have to miss out on your date with Detective Ivanova."

"There is no date!" Vic said angrily. "Jesus, Erin! Did I say or do one thing, one lousy thing, to encourage her? *She* came on to *me!*"

"You're just the victim here?"

"Exactly!"

"She's not a bad looking woman, even with that scar."

"I like the scar," he said. "It makes her look like a badass."

Erin said nothing.

"I'm allowed to find other women attractive," Vic said defensively. "I'm just not allowed to screw them."

"So you've got nothing to hide?"

"Not a damn thing."

"And I can tell Piekarski all about Mira?"

"Are you crazy? Don't say a word about her!"

Erin threw him a sidelong look. "Why not?"

"Zofia's six months pregnant! She's already freaking out about everything. You've never been pregnant, have you?"

"I think I'd remember," Erin said.

"She's put on weight," Vic said. "I know, because she won't shut up about it. She says she feels all bloated and swollen like, and I quote, 'the goddamn Michelin Man, or maybe the Pillsbury Doughboy.' She already thinks I'm not gonna think she's sexy or some bullshit like that. You gotta remember, our relationship started out all physical."

"Do you still think she's sexy?" Erin asked.

"Hell yes! She's the sexiest woman in New York!" Vic exploded. "You think I care she's put on a few pounds? It looks good on her. She's got bigger... never mind what she's got. That's none of your damn business. And that's not the point. The point is I love her, and I'll still love her even if she's not feeling like... whatever. Okay?"

"You're afraid she's going to think you're looking elsewhere," Erin said.

"Yeah. She wants me in the room when the baby comes, not 'getting a blowjob from some skank in the parking lot.' That's another direct quote. So no, I'm not gonna tell her I ran into this tall, gorgeous cop I used to bang at the end of our shift back in the day. Is that so hard to understand?"

"No," Erin said. "But this is the sort of thing that leaves a guy looking pretty bad."

"I'm used to looking bad," he said. "And I'm doing the best I can here, okay? Besides, this isn't gonna go anywhere. We pumped Mira for info, we got what we came for, and that's it. I'm probably not gonna see her again for another five years."

"If you do tell Piekarski, maybe don't use the word 'pumped,'" Erin suggested.

"Good call," Vic agreed.

*       *       *

Erin, Vic, and Rolf met Webb and Piekarski at Ninja Pizza. It had been Webb's idea, but everyone else had been thinking it. There were just too many connections to the pizzeria to be ignored.

Erin shared what they'd learned from Mira, leaving out the bit about her being Vic's ex. It was a tough spot to be in, caught between the demands of the sisterhood on one hand and loyalty to her partner on the other. Erin decided to trust Vic and let him decide what to tell Piekarski in his own time.

"It's Martinelli, or Cross, or both," Webb said. "Maybe the whole business is a front."

"Pizzas out the front door, stolen goods out the back," Vic said. "Can we get a warrant to toss the joint?"

"For what?" Webb replied. "We only have one item reported stolen, and it sounds like that may not be in the perps' possession anymore."

"We should contact the University and warn them," Erin said.

"Already done," Webb said. "When I sent you to run down the burglary info, I figured there might be a connection, so I called campus security and told them to look for any unauthorized equipment in the server room. They're going over it with a fine-toothed comb."

"They ought to shut down the servers," Vic said.

"I suggested that, too," Webb said. "The security chief transferred me to the Dean. He said it would seriously disrupt their academic and research activities."

"Anyone else here seen *Jaws?*" Vic asked.

"The Spielberg movie?" Erin replied. "The one with the shark?"

"Yeah."

"Vic, I don't think anyone in America hasn't seen *Jaws*. What about it?"

"Because the Dean sounds like the mayor in the movie who won't close the beaches until the shark starts chowing down on tourists."

Webb smiled thinly. "That's not the worst comparison," he said. "But it's not our call. Anyway, we can't get a warrant based on what we've got now. The best we can do is lean on these guys and see what we can squeeze out of them. If we get Cross and Martinelli separated, we can play them off one another. If both are in on it, maybe we can flip one."

"So which one first?" Vic asked. "The fat bastard or the tattooed thug?"

"We'll do both," Webb said. "I'll take Martinelli. Piekarski, you come with me. You can watch how Major Crimes does interviews. O'Reilly, Neshenko, while we're talking to Martinelli, put some pressure on Cross."

"Oh boy," Vic said. "I call bad cop."

\*　　\*　　\*

"Welcome to Ninja Pizza," Cross said. He was still manning the counter. His smile became a little uncertain when he recognized the cops, but he kept it gamely plastered on his face. "Did you come back for another slice?"

"I assume Mr. Martinelli's still in," Webb said, walking right past him toward the manager's office. "We've got some more questions."

"Sure thing—" Cross began. Then he stopped short. Erin and Vic were standing to either side of him, watching him.

"We've got some questions for you, too," Vic said ominously.

Cross sighed. "I figured. Okay. Where do you want to do this?"

"We don't want to cause unnecessary trouble for your business," Erin said. "Is there someone who can man the counter while we step outside?"

"Sure," Cross said. He pushed open the swinging door that led to the kitchen. Erin automatically dropped a hand to the clip on Rolf's leash, getting ready to turn him loose if the man made a run for it.

But Cross just called, "Angelo! Can you get up here? I gotta go out for a few."

A moment later a small Latino in a tomato-stained apron emerged from the kitchen. He gave Erin a wink, which she pretended not to see. Cross came around the counter, grabbing his coat from a hook. It was a yellow jacket with the Ninja Pizza logo on the back.

"Where'd you get that jacket?" Erin asked as they exited the building onto the street.

"Came with the job," Cross said. He started to put his hands in his pockets. Then he paused, seeing Vic and Erin both tense. He brought the hands out again, empty, and they relaxed. Cross smiled sheepishly.

"Geez, guys," he said. "We're just having a conversation, right? I'm not under arrest, am I?"

"Do you want to be?" Vic asked.

"What for? I didn't do anything."

"I'll bet," Vic growled. "Tell me about Floyd Shelton. Everything you got!"

"What about him?" Cross said, taking a step back. Vic followed, trapping him against the wall next to the pizzeria's big plate-glass window.

"You knew him!" Vic said. "Don't bother denying it."

"Of course I did!" Cross said. "We worked together! So what? This job's legit!"

"I'm not talking about the pizza," Vic retorted. "I'm talking about the burglaries."

"I did my time," Cross said. "If you're gonna keep holding that over me, why'd you guys ever let me out of prison?"

"Not those burglaries, dipshit! The computer jobs!"

Cross blinked. "I never did any computer jobs with Floyd!"

Erin noted the specifics of the denial. "But you did jobs with him," she said quietly.

"Sure!" Cross said. "You know that!"

"Tell me about them," she said. "Refresh my memory."

Cross shrugged helplessly. "There was that warehouse back in '06, and the refinery job a month later, plus the Thanksgiving Parade thing. I pled out on all three of those. Floyd, too. That's how come we only got five years. But I've been clean since I got out, I swear!"

"Hold on," Erin said. "You and Floyd were accomplices?"

"Yeah, we used to run together," Cross said. "I got an early release, and when Floyd got out, I talked to Mr. Martinelli to get him this job."

"Did you know he was still taking scores?" Vic demanded, getting back in Cross's face.

"He wasn't!" Cross exclaimed. "He was going straight, just like me!"

"Then how come he got popped helping with another heist?" Vic asked.

"He was delivering a goddamn pizza!" Cross shouted back. "What do you want from me, huh? Floyd screwed up, sure, and he took a fall for it! So did I! And that's gonna follow me around for the rest of my life! I'm never gonna have a good, high-paying job. I could make five, ten times as much if I went back to the Life, but I'm here tossing pizza. Why? Because of my mom, if you gotta know! She's sick. Cancer. She's got insurance, but what she hasn't got is anyone to take care of her. So I gotta stay out of prison and stay out of trouble. Otherwise she'll be all alone. I know you don't believe me, because cops never do. You always assume everybody's playing you, but I'm not, and if you don't believe that, then fuck you!"

Vic actually took a half-step back, as if the force of Cross's outburst had pushed him away. "Your mom, huh?" he said after a moment. "Cancer?"

"Yeah," Cross said. "Breast cancer. They say she's got a year, maybe two. And I thought I had it rough in the can. Life's a bitch, huh?"

"Sounds like you're trying really hard to do the right thing, Bode," Erin said, using his first name to try to build rapport. "And I know that's hard, especially when you've had a bad hand dealt to you."

"You got that right," Cross said. "And I'm telling you, I had nothing to do with whatever Floyd had going. And I thought he was okay! I've known him since we was kids, and he was never the one who started nothing. It was always me, or one of the other guys, putting him up to it. But we all liked him. Nobody wanted Floyd to get hurt. It tore me up bad when he got nailed, since the Parade job was my idea. And I knew how bad his sister felt about it when he went to prison."

"Alicia?" Erin said.

"You know about her, huh?" Cross said. "He'd do anything for her. And I know she told him to keep his nose clean. No more screwing around, that's what she told him."

Erin considered the man in front of her. He seemed earnest, but liars often did. Contrary to popular opinion, there was no magic way to know if a guy was lying. Some people were better at it than others. There were no universal "tells." And Cross was right, cops didn't tend to believe the stories they were told, particularly by former convicts.

"You've got a tattoo," she said.

"I got a bunch of them," Cross said. "And I bet you guys got a list, so you can ID me. Fingerprints weren't enough, huh?"

"Three cats," she said.

"What about it?"

"Who are they?"

"The cats?"

"Who do they represent?" she asked patiently. "I know what it means. It stands for three thieves that worked together. You're one of them, Floyd's the second one. Who's number three?"

"Oh, him," Cross said. "You're talking about Robbie Black. You can ask him about Floyd and he'll tell you the same thing he told me."

"Where can I find him?"

"I've got no idea," Cross said. "Robbie was inside too, a little before us. You can't be in the Life without doing some time, you feel me? But he got paroled while we was still inside, and I lost touch with him. He ain't working for Mr. Martinelli, that's for sure. I can't see Robbie ever tossing pizzas."

"But he was your friend," Erin pressed. "You must have some idea where he went."

"Nope," Cross said. "Maybe you oughta ask your own people. His parole officer probably knows more than I do. You wanna know anything else about my ink? Every tat's got a story to go with it."

"Maybe later," Erin said.

*       *       *

Webb and Piekarski came out of the pizzeria a few minutes later, after Cross had gone back inside. Webb straightened his trench coat and nodded to the other two detectives, who fell in step beside him.

"How'd it go?" Erin asked after they'd walked most of the way to their parked cars.

"You ever see this guy interrogate someone?" Piekarski said. "What am I talking about? Of course you have. But damn! You look at him, and you think he's nothing but a tired old burnout, and then he starts talking and he makes the poor schmuck shit his pants!"

"This is your idea of a compliment, Officer?" Webb said mildly.

"Seriously, he's amazing," Piekarski went on. "He cracked Martinelli like an egg. The guy was practically crying. He gave up everything!"

"So how come you don't have him in bracelets?" Vic asked.

"He's not our guy," Webb said, shaking his head. "I put the fear of God in him, Piekarski's right about that. He swears he doesn't know a thing about the burglaries or the murder."

"He snowed you," Vic said.

"I've grilled dozens of old cons," Webb said. "He's telling the truth, I'd bet a week's pay on it."

"Then what did he give you?" Erin asked.

"One of the company jackets is missing," Webb said. "The closet at the pizzeria was broken into a couple weeks ago. The lock was intact, but it looked like it'd been jimmied."

"Maybe Cross stole it," Vic said. "He was part of the same crew as Shelton."

"Cross wouldn't need to break in," Erin said. "He'd have keys. Besides, he already had a jacket. Why would he need another? Same thing with Shelton. It must've been somebody else. I'm guessing our killer."

"Maybe," Webb said. "But then it's probably someone unrelated to the pizzeria."

Erin unlocked the Charger and slid into the driver's seat. She got into the NYPD database on her onboard computer and brought up Robbie Black's record.

"Here's our third guy," she announced. "Robert Black, age thirty-three. Went down for multiple B&Es. His MO is careful recon, followed by a quick smash-and-grab. He always tried to work it so people weren't home, but he got unlucky once. Looks like his target's son came home while he was in the middle of ransacking the guy's house. There was a fight."

"Let me guess," Vic said. "Black freaked out and beat his head in?"

"Nope," Erin said. "Turns out the kid was on the varsity wrestling team. He got Black in a hammerlock and held him until the cops got there. Dislocated Black's shoulder."

"Instant justice," Vic said. "I love it."

"The judge gave Black ten years upstate," Erin said. "He got out in seven. Good behavior. He's been on the street for the past eighteen months."

"How's he connected to the other two?" Webb asked.

"He isn't, at least not in our system," she said. "They were never convicted or even charged as accomplices. But Bode Cross gave us his name."

"To take the heat off himself!" Vic objected.

"I don't know," Webb said. "This doesn't sound like the sort of guy who'd be stealing high-tech gadgets and cracking server rooms."

"There's a connection," Erin said stubbornly, continuing to go through Black's police record. "Look! He took a bunch of classes in prison and got a degree."

"In what?" Piekarski asked.

"Computer science," Erin said.

"Now that's interesting," Webb said. "Where is this guy now?"

"According to his parole, he's working for a tech company called ChainLink Incorporated," she said.

"Do they fence stolen computers?" Vic said.

Everyone stared at him.

"You know," he said, "as in, chain-link *fence*?"

Piekarski groaned.

"Hey," he said. "If I'm gonna be a dad, I gotta work on my dad jokes, right?"

"If that wasn't so obnoxious, it'd be kind of sweet," Piekarski admitted. "But even if it's sweet, it's still not funny."

"Black's definitely a person of interest," Webb said. "But it's getting toward quitting time, which means we may have trouble tracking him down. Let's hit ChainLink in the morning and give Black a good shake. Hopefully we'll have Levine's postmortem report and CSU's findings by then."

"Does that mean we're done for the day?" Erin asked.

"You're free," Webb said. "Try not to kill anybody while you're off the clock."

"Yeah," Vic said. "Wait until you're on duty. Makes the paperwork more fun."

# Chapter 8

Erin didn't go straight home. She crossed the East River into Manhattan and drove to Bellevue Hospital. She parked in one of the police spaces in the lot, gave Rolf a chance to relieve himself outside, and went in.

Her destination was guarded by possibly the most bored member of the NYPD in the five boroughs. The Patrolman had a chair to sit in, and the inevitable thermos of coffee, box of donuts, and *New York Times*, but his eyes were glassy and his mouth hung slightly open. He was drooling just a little out of the corner of his mouth.

When he spotted Erin and Rolf, he sat up, straightened his collar, and wiped his mouth. He didn't bother asking for her identification. She'd been coming here every day, ever since the hospital had moved their patient into this room.

"Officer Ford, isn't it?" Erin said, recognizing him.

"Yes, ma'am," he said. He was very young. At first glance he looked clean-shaven, but that was because his efforts at growing a mustache had been completely ineffective.

"I would've thought there'd be someone else on this detail by now," she said. "You must want to be out there pounding pavement."

"Someone's gotta do it, ma'am," Ford said, his cheeks flushing.

"What'd you do?" Erin asked.

"What do you mean?" Ford asked.

"To get on your CO's shit list," she said, giving him a knowing look. "This is three days running you've been babysitting this hallway. If you were me, you'd be thinking about eating your gun right about now. So what happened?"

"My FTO let me drive for the first time last week," Ford said sheepishly. "I didn't even make it out of the garage. I could've sworn I had the car in reverse. I hit the pedal and rammed another Patrol unit, nose to nose. Put two squad cars in the shop."

Erin winced. "So now you're stuck here?"

"Until they finish the bodywork on both cars," Ford said. "And my FTO says I can't drive again until I grow a 'stache that looks like his. Guy looks like Sam freaking Elliott and I don't even have peach fuzz."

"There's worse things," Erin said. "Anything happen here?"

"Nothing ever happens here," the rookie said miserably. "The wife and kids come by every day. Sometimes other cops. And you."

"I'll let you get back to your crossword," Erin said. "Rolf will keep you company. Rolf, *sitz. Bleib.*"

Rolf sat next to Ford's chair and stared mournfully at Erin as she went into the room. He wanted to be there about as much as Ford did.

It was immediately obvious that people cared about the guy who was staying here. Every horizontal surface had flowers, cards, photos, and mementos on it. Pictures had been stuck to the walls wherever the medical equipment had left a blank spot. Erin saw two radios; a standard AM/FM unit and a police-band. Someone had even managed to replace the hospital's normal blinds with curtains like you'd find in a suburban home.

But none of it made Erin feel better, because in the middle of it all, saline bag dripping into one arm, electrodes on his chest and head, lay Lieutenant Philip Stachowski, NYPD. Clean white bandages swathed his head, but she knew under them was a steel plate and screws holding his skull together.

Phil had been a well-respected cop, an expert in undercover operations. His balding, bespectacled face had framed a keen mind, a wise mentor, and a true friend. He'd always been there for Erin, through the twists and turns of her unusual infiltration of the O'Malley gang, and what had he gotten in return? He'd taken a nine-millimeter slug at close range from a dirty cop, and he'd done it to protect Erin from discovery. He'd survived, but he'd never be the same again.

"Hey, Phil," she said awkwardly. "How're you feeling today?"

He tilted his head toward her with an oddly jerky motion and smiled with the left side of his face. The right side of his mouth didn't move. He raised his left hand and gave her a thumbs-up.

The neurosurgeon had said the left side of Phil's brain had been severely damaged. The worst harm, oddly, hadn't come from the bullet itself but a blood clot that had formed in the immediate aftermath. He'd been shot in Central Park during a blizzard, and the intense cold had frozen the blood from the injury. It had kept him from bleeding to death, but the result had been, effectively, a severe stroke. The right side of his body was fully paralyzed. Maybe he'd regain some use of it, and maybe not. Nobody could say for sure.

"Anything I can get for you?" Erin asked, walking to his bedside. She saw a new get-well card on the table, signed by Phil's daughters. One of them, Nora, was ten; about the same age as Erin's niece Anna. The card stood open, and the message inside just said *We miss you, Daddy*.

"'m fine," Phil said. "Happy."

Erin hated being here, hated seeing what had happened to her friend and comrade. She wished she could stay away, and hated herself for wishing it. That was a cowardly, ugly thought to have. Phil wouldn't be here if it wasn't for her. The very least she could do was visit him.

"Any news from the docs?" she asked.

"Might go sweet," Phil said. His face twisted. "No. Not sweet. Wrong. Humble?"

"Home?" Erin guessed.

He nodded. "Aphasia" was the word for his speech problems. Her brother had explained to her that aphasia was the inability to translate thoughts into the correct words. It wasn't a well understood phenomenon. Maybe Phil would end up in some medical textbook. Now *there* was a happy thought.

"That's great," she said. "I bet you're looking forward to it."

He nodded again. "Hard for Cam," he said. "All this way, every day. Easier when no rivers."

"It'll be easier when she doesn't have to come across from Hoboken all the time," Erin agreed, her heart aching. "She's a good woman."

"Best," Phil said. "Love."

"Yeah," Erin said. She'd met Camilla Stachowski. The woman was formidable, both in terms of inner strength and in devotion to her family. Erin hoped she was formidable enough. The Stachowski family had a marathon struggle in front of them, one with no endpoint.

"Enough," Phil said. "Tell me you. What's going on? O'Malley."

She had to remind herself that, however he sounded, by some freak chance Phil's mental faculties had come through largely undiminished. He might not be able to turn his ideas into words, but he was still thinking clearly. And he was still thinking like a cop.

"I've got a meeting with the Captain about it," she said. "Tomorrow. We'll figure out what we're doing."

Phil reached toward her with his usable hand. She took it and he squeezed hers.

"Have to do it," he said earnestly. "Soon."

"I know," she said. "So does Captain Holliday. But with all this..."

She gestured with her free hand toward Phil and the various medical apparatus around him.

He shook his head as emphatically as his condition allowed. "Not important," he said. "I don't master. No, not right. Don't martyr? Damn."

"You matter plenty, Phil," she said.

"Not the point," he said, his frustration obvious. "Stop making me feel good. Trying to get job done. That's important. Do the job. Then worry about me. If you have to. Don't wait. Get ready and go."

"Okay," she said. "That's what I'll tell the Captain."

"Good," he said. "Erin?"

"What?" She was still holding his hand.

"It's okay," he said quietly.

"What is?" she asked.

"Don't fame you."

"Fame me?" She felt her forehead wrinkle.

"Not your fault. Lucky."

"Yeah, I was lucky," she said, touching the scab where the same dirty cop had shot her. An inch to the side and she'd have been in the same state as Phil, or worse.

"Not you," he said. "Me. Lucky."

Erin blinked hard, trying to keep the tears from filling her eyes, knowing it was a losing battle. The man in front of her had been crippled for life and he was calling himself *lucky*? What was she supposed to say to that?

"You just keep getting better," she said hollowly.

"Keep me pasted," he said.

"I will," she promised, not bothering to correct him. Then she got out of there.

*       *       *

On the stairs on the way down to the parking lot, Erin felt a sudden wave of intense dizziness. She stumbled, put a foot wrong, flailed, and somehow managed to grab hold of the railing. There was no sensation of falling. Rather, it was as if the rest of the world had been kicked off its axis and was madly spinning around her. She clung to the railing and sank to her knees.

Gradually the feeling diminished. She became aware of Rolf, sitting on the stairs beside her. He was staring at her quizzically.

"I'm fine, kiddo," she said.

He kept staring, unconvinced.

Erin got slowly to her feet and looked up and down the stairs. They were deserted. Nobody had witnessed her mishap. She gave it a moment, waiting to see if the feeling would return. Nothing happened.

It was like being drunk off her ass, but without tasting a drop of liquor. And it had come out of nowhere. She pressed a hand to her temple and felt the blood pulsing under her skin. Her gunshot wound throbbed dully.

"Shit," she muttered.

Rolf continued watching and waiting patiently.

After a few moments more, Erin carefully walked down the remaining half flight of stairs to the next landing. Then she left the stairwell and took the elevator the rest of the way down. She didn't like elevators, but they beat falling down the stairs and killing herself.

Erin loaded Rolf into her car and drove home. The Christmas lights seemed particularly bright and glaring in the December darkness. She squinted through the windshield and tried to ignore the pounding in her head. It didn't help that she kept thinking of Phil.

She usually liked living over a pub. The Barley Corner might be the watering hole of choice for O'Malley mobsters, but the atmosphere was cheerful, boisterous, and friendly. She knew most of the regulars and they knew and liked her. The big-screen TVs were always showing some sporting event or other, the room was warm and welcoming, and it was the only bar she'd knew that stocked Glen Docherty-Kinlochewe whiskey, the finest drink on Earth.

But tonight the light and noise of the place were overwhelming. Erin just wanted to get somewhere dark and quiet. She moved through the crowd mechanically, meeting the greetings of the customers with a game smile and a wave. Carlyle was at the bar on his customary stool. When he made eye contact with her, he smiled and stood to greet her. His smile faded into concern as he looked at her.

He was only a few steps behind as she opened the door to the upstairs apartment. The door didn't have time to swing shut before he'd gotten hold of it and followed her up.

"Erin, darling?" he said. "What's happened?"

"Nothing," she said over her shoulder, unsnapping Rolf's leash. She went into the living room and let herself collapse onto Carlyle's couch.

Rolf lingered in the kitchen doorway, cocking his head. The next thing that was supposed to happen was supper. That was one of the most important occasions of the day. It wasn't like Erin to forget something like that. The Shepherd decided to stay right where he was until she came to her senses and filled his kibble bowl.

"You're white as the snow, darling," Carlyle said.

"I'm fine," Erin said, throwing an arm over her face.

He knelt beside the couch and put a hand on her shoulder. "Are you ill?" he asked quietly.

"I said I'm fine!" she snapped with sudden, irrational anger. "Didn't you hear me?"

Carlyle's face stiffened for just a moment. Then its lines smoothed out again. When he spoke, his voice was calm and quiet.

"I see you're not wanting to be disturbed just now," he said. "I've some things to take care of in my office. If you're needing me, that's where you'll find me."

Erin was already feeling bad for her outburst even before Carlyle left the room. But she couldn't make herself get up and go after him. Her whole body felt heavy and the room was spinning again. She was just tired, she told herself. All she needed was to lie down for a little while.

Rolf settled himself on his belly on the linoleum and planted his chin between his paws. After a moment, a low whine came from his mouth. He wasn't begging for food. That was beneath his dignity. He was worried about his partner.

A while later, about half an hour, Erin came back to herself enough to sit up. What had happened? She'd felt so weird. Had she taken a shot of hard drugs without realizing it? Or drunk too much?

Rolf perked up, first his ears, then the rest of his head.

"Sorry," Erin said, remembering she hadn't fed him. She stood up, then sat down again. Once the room stopped moving she tried once more and succeeded. Trailing one hand along the wall, just in case she needed to catch herself, she went to the kitchen and filled Rolf's food bowl. The Shepherd began eating gladly enough, but he paused a couple of times to give her a sidelong look, as if he was making sure she was still there.

Erin watched him eat. Then she walked slowly down the hall to Carlyle's office. The door was open. Carlyle was typing on his laptop. He glanced up and saw her in the doorway.

"You're feeling better, I see," he said, getting to his feet.

He was always such a gentleman, Erin thought. They'd have to keep the casket closed at his funeral, or his corpse would stand up politely to welcome the female mourners. The thought made her want to smile and cry at the same time.

"How can you tell?" she asked, coming in and sitting in one of the chairs to one side of the desk.

"Your color's improved," he said. "When I first saw you this evening, I feared you'd perished and your pale ghost was coming to haunt me."

"No such luck," she said.

"Are you wanting to talk about it?" he asked, pulling another chair to sit next to her.

"Can I have a drink?"

"Of course. Glen D?"

"Always."

He brought out a bottle from his private supply and poured them each a shot. It helped steady her a little.

"Is it your injury?" he asked quietly.

"I don't know," she said. "I was fine all day, but after work I went to see Phil. Afterward, I... I just went all funny in the head."

"You should tell your physician."

"No!" she said sharply. "They'll take me off active duty."

"Perhaps you ought to be," he suggested gently.

"I can't. Not now. I'm in the middle of a case."

"You're always in the middle of a case, darling."

"And we're about to put the O'Malley operation to rest. Damn it, I don't have *time* to keel over! A little dizziness is no excuse. I just got cleared for duty! If I tell the doc about it, he'll throw me back on the bench so fast my head will *really* spin!"

"You were shot, darling. In the head."

"I'm aware of that," she said bitterly. "I'm also aware how lucky I was. Lucky! Do you know, Phil said that to me?"

"He told you how lucky you were?"

"No. He said *he* was the lucky one. Can you believe that? His brains must be more scrambled than I thought."

"Perhaps," Carlyle said thoughtfully, sipping his drink. "Or perhaps he's thinking more clearly than the rest of us."

"You'd better explain that," she said, finishing her own whiskey and staring at the empty glass.

"I wasn't struck in the head," he said. "But I know what it's like to take a bullet, knowing it's likely the last thing I'll be taking in this world. It changes one's perspective a bit. When they wheeled me out of that ambulance into the hospital and I let go your hand, I thought I'd never touch it again."

Erin felt fresh tears prickling the corners of her eyes. "Don't," she said, almost choking on the word.

"Through God's grace, I'm still walking this Earth," Carlyle said, reaching out and taking her hand. "I don't deserve it, but I've been given a chance to make things right. Don't you understand, darling? For all its pains and trials, life is the greatest of gifts. The dear Lieutenant is keenly aware how close he came to losing it."

"But he can't walk! He can hardly talk!"

"He can see his wife's face and hear her voice," he said. "He can hold his children. A lesser man might be angered by what he's lost, I'll grant, but he's a good man and he's far more conscious of what he's retained."

Erin clenched her fists. "It shouldn't have happened," she said.

"But it did," he replied. "This isn't the world we should have, darling, but it's the one we've got. The world doesn't run on 'should.'"

"Yeah? Well, it should," she said, cracking a smile. "I'm sorry. For snapping at you."

"As you'd say, darling, forget about it," he said, making a fair approximation of her Queens accent and startling a laugh out of her.

"Okay," she said.

"But if these spells persist, I'm going to insist you inform your physician," he said. "I worry about you."

"Copy that," Erin said.

"Are you hungry, darling? It's going on suppertime."

She wasn't, not really, but she did like the thought of something warm inside herself. She felt cold and a little shaky.

"Irish stew," she suggested.

"I'll have it brought up," he said, reaching for the telephone.

# Chapter 9

Erin felt fine when she woke the next morning. Her vision was a little blurry when she first got up, but it cleared after a few minutes. Her head hurt, but that was to be expected. She'd been hit by a bullet, after all. It wasn't like taking a punch. And maybe she was a tiny bit dizzy on her way to the bathroom. But she was fine, generally speaking; feeling good.

All the same, she settled for taking Rolf for a short walk around the neighborhood instead of their usual morning jog. Rolf was disappointed. The Shepherd, however, like most dogs, was an optimist at heart. Maybe their quiet morning meant they were saving their energy to chase bad guys later in the day. He'd be ready.

After breakfast, Erin headed to work, leaving Carlyle asleep. He'd been up until after two, keeping his usual late hours. She wondered if that would change after they took the O'Malleys down, or if it was just the normal schedule for a New York pub owner. Maybe she ought to try to juggle her own schedule to work more nights; then they might see more of one another.

She wished the sun wasn't shining, or that there wasn't quite so much bright white snow. New York snow usually turned gray and slushy almost as soon as it hit the ground, but there'd been so much of it in the recent blizzard, it was still piled up all over town. The blinding glare wasn't doing her headache any favors. For once, she was looking forward to some indoor work.

She went straight downstairs to the morgue, where she was unsurprised to find Sarah Levine. The Medical Examiner had the mortal remains of Floyd Shelton spread out on a slab. She'd finished the invasive parts of the autopsy; Shelton's chest now sported a stitched-up Y-incision in addition to his prison tattoos.

"Don't you ever sleep, Doc?" Erin said.

"All mammals require sleep," Levine said. "Most scientists postulate that if it were not necessary for complex organisms, there would be extant examples of non-sleeping higher life forms. Since there are none of these known, we must conclude sleep is not merely beneficial but essential."

"Right," Erin said. "How much did you sleep last night?"

"I've been awake since seven-thirty yesterday morning," Levine said.

"It looks like you're done with Shelton," Erin said, changing the subject. It really was possible Levine was a vampire. "What are your findings?"

"My preliminary examination was accurate," Levine said. "Cause of death was massive cerebral trauma. The weapon was most likely a hammer with an octagonal steel head. Lack of defensive wounds suggests the victim did not anticipate or resist the attack."

"That's because he was working with the guy who killed him," Erin muttered, bending over the body to examine the tattoos.

"That hypothesis fits the available data," Levine agreed.

"What about the bloodwork?" Erin asked.

"Initial screening shows nothing unusual," Levine said. "He was neither intoxicated nor under the influence of narcotics. He appears to have been in excellent health."

"Right up until his brain got rearranged," Erin said. She was still looking at the tattoos. Specifically, she'd seen a familiar one; three cats sitting side by side. It was identical to the one on Bode Cross's arm.

"You photograph the tattoos, right?" she said.

"Correct," Levine said. "The entire body is photographed prior to the invasive portion of the postmortem examination."

"Would there be any way to tell if the victim had been using lockpicks?" Erin asked suddenly, as the thought struck her.

"How recently?" the Medical Examiner asked. For one of the few times in all their conversations, Levine looked genuinely interested. It made her face more animated, more normally expressive.

"Less than an hour before death."

Levine picked up a magnifying glass and brought it to the slab. "Statistical likelihood is that the victim was right-handed," she said, scrutinizing the fingertips of Shelton's right hand. "Tools leave impressions on the fingers. These impressions are only temporary. I see no signs of this hand having gripped fine wires, but absence of positive evidence is insufficient to support a definite conclusion."

"In other words, maybe he did and maybe he didn't?" Erin replied.

"Correct."

"What about wearing a hat?"

Levine blinked. "Please clarify."

"Do you think this guy was wearing a hat right before he died?"

Levine turned her back on the corpse and went to her computer. She brought up the photographs of the crime scene, in which Shelton was slumped behind the wheel of the Toyota. Levine enlarged one of the photos until Shelton's bloodied scalp filled the monitor. It was slightly pixelated by the magnification.

Erin wished they could enhance the image like cops were always doing on TV. Unfortunately, that was pure fantasy. The computer could only work with what it had, and the camera's resolution couldn't be improved by technical wizardry. She rubbed her eyes and squinted.

"I see no sign of flattening on the hair," Levine said at last. "What sort of hat?"

"A baseball cap," Erin said.

"Unlikely," Levine said. "It would have left a telltale ring around the scalp approximately here, unless it was unusually loose. However—"

"Absence of positive evidence is insufficient to support... whatever," Erin finished for her. "Copy that. Anything else?"

"My report is thorough," Levine said. "Would you like me to walk you through the document?"

"No, thanks," Erin said. "Have you forwarded it to Major Crimes?"

"Yes."

"I'll stop bothering you, then."

"I doubt it," Levine said matter-of-factly.

"I mean, I'll get out of your hair for now."

"You haven't touched my hair," Levine said.

"Forget about it," Erin said. "Thanks."

*    *    *

Webb, Vic, and Piekarski were waiting for Erin upstairs. Vic and Webb were wearing their coats. Webb had on his battered old fedora.

"Glad you could join us," he said.

"We're going to ChainLink, Inc.," Vic said. "That name's got a kinda nice ring to it. Want to come with?"

"Or you could stay with me and go through the CSU reports," Piekarski said glumly. "Next time I'm making Vic carry the baby to term."

Vic grinned.

"What?" Piekarski said. "You think I'm joking? What're you smiling about?"

"You said there'll be a next time," Vic said.

"Let's saddle up," Webb said. "I'm riding with O'Reilly."

"You don't like my driving, sir?" Vic asked.

"The actuarial tables already say I'm in trouble from the drinking and the tobacco," Webb said. "I don't want to push my luck. Besides, I ride with you a lot. I wouldn't want my squad to think I'm playing favorites."

"I'd never think that," Vic said. "I just assumed you wanted to keep an eye on me."

\*    \*    \*

"Why did you really want to ride with me, sir?" Erin asked as she aimed the Charger's nose south.

"You don't think I prefer your company to Neshenko's?" Webb replied.

"I think we're cops, so we spend most of our time with people we don't like very much," Erin said.

Webb smiled thinly. "I wanted to see how you're doing," he said.

"Oh, good," Erin said, rolling her eyes. "So it's an on-the-job evaluation?"

"As your commanding officer, I'm concerned," Webb said.

"Because yesterday was my first day after a medical absence?"

"Because you stopped a nine-millimeter round with your skull."

"That's not accurate, sir."

"It isn't?"

"My skull didn't stop the bullet, sir. It deflected it. The round ricocheted."

It was Webb's turn to roll his eyes. "All right, so you bounced a nine-millimeter round off your inexplicably thick skull. Is that better?"

"Much, sir."

"As long as we're picking over conversational details, I've noticed something about the way you talk, O'Reilly."

"What's that, sir?" she asked without much interest.

"You say 'sir' a lot more when you think you're in trouble."

Erin said nothing. Inwardly, she damned him and all perceptive detectives.

"I'm not going to waste time and energy arguing with you over whether you're fit for duty," he went on. "You could lose both arms and one leg and you'd still hop into the Eightball and claim you were ready to come back."

"They're doing amazing things with prosthetics these days, sir."

"Instead, I just want to get a close look at you," Webb said. "So you're right. This is an evaluation. I'm not your enemy, O'Reilly. I'd like to think I'm your friend."

"You're my commanding officer, sir."

"That, too. And that makes it my responsibility to protect you from everything I can. In addition to the criminal element, that includes members of our own bureaucracy, obstructive citizens and, incidentally, yourself."

"I'm fine, sir."

"Do you practice saying that into your mirror every night?" Webb sighed. "Some cops go months or even years between critical incidents. You collect them like baseball cards. You've been shot, more than once. You've been knocked unconscious, more than once. You've killed perps, more than once. You've been blown up, more than—"

"I get the idea, sir," Erin said sharply. "What's your point? You want me to hand in my shield, is that it?"

"My point is, *nobody* could be fine after going through all that," Webb said. "John Rambo wouldn't be fine."

"Wasn't the whole point of *First Blood* that Rambo *wasn't* fine?" Erin asked. "He was totally screwed up in the head."

"Whatever," Webb said irritably, waving his hand. "Don't worry, O'Reilly. I'm not going to bench you."

"Then why are we having this conversation, sir?"

"I know you're damaged," he said. "I'm trying to determine how deep the damage goes, and, if possible, prevent it going any further."

"Good luck with that, sir."

"If it was up to me, I'd put you on desk duty alongside Piekarski."

"Isn't it up to you, sir? As my commanding officer?"

Webb's smile was distinctly cynical. "I thought you understood the NYPD better than that after twelve years wearing a shield. It's political. Captain Holliday's got his eye on you. So does the PC. Until the current operation shuts down, we need you front and center. We have to maintain appearances. It'd be dangerous to change anything in your normal pattern, unless we have absolutely no choice."

"The Commissioner's watching me?" Erin said, fighting the urge to glance over her shoulder, as if she'd see a giant pair of eyes glaring at her from the top of Number One PP in the distance.

"The Captain briefed him on your operation yesterday evening," Webb said. "I understand you've got a meeting with the Captain later today."

"That's right, sir. At noon."

"Over lunch?"

"Yeah. If I have any appetite."

"You'd better eat something," Webb said. "Or Holliday may think your nerves are getting the better of you."

"Nobody has to worry about my nerves. I'm—"

"Fine," Webb finished for her. "Besides, I can't spare you. I've been asking, hell, I've been begging for another shield on the squad for months. They finally sent me Piekarski, which is great on paper. She's one hell of a street officer. Great rep, a list of commendations as long as my arm. Only two problems."

"I can guess one of them," Erin said.

"She can't work the street in her current condition," Webb said. "Or at least she shouldn't. And she's involved with one of my detectives, which is against protocol."

"They weren't on the same squad when they started seeing one another," Erin said. "And they're keeping things professional on the clock."

"Neshenko never keeps things professional," Webb retorted. "Even if I could put Piekarski streetside, I'd hesitate on account of him. Are you familiar with that little item from his record?"

Erin winced. She'd hoped Webb hadn't known about Mira Ivanova.

"That's right," Webb said. "I know about the incident that led to his transfer. You think I don't do background checks on my squad members? I know everything about Neshenko, and don't think I don't know about your past, either."

"I've got nothing to hide," she said, bristling.

"I know a couple of Homicide boys down at the 116 tried to shit-can your career," he countered. "The same Homicide boys, incidentally, that we talked to yesterday. And Lieutenant Keane saved your bacon, which made me wonder for a while if you were an Internal Affairs plant in my squad."

"I'm not. I can't stand Keane!"

"That's excellent camouflage for an IAB undercover," Webb said. "But don't worry about that, either. I know you aren't one of Keane's."

"How do you know that, sir?" Erin hadn't had the slightest idea all this was going on behind Webb's eyes. Speaking of camouflage, he played the part of a burned-out world-weary gumshoe so well that she constantly forgot how sharp he could be.

"Your ill-advised fling with a mid-level mob boss was a pretty good indicator," Webb said dryly. "I've been sure you weren't IAB ever since Morton Carlyle got shot in your living room."

"I'm glad that earned your trust," she said.

"Of course it didn't earn my trust!" Webb shot back. "I damn near threw you in jail, in case you've forgotten. But it did tell me a lot about who you were."

"And who is that, sir?"

"You're brave, dedicated, stubborn, reckless, smart, and foolish," Webb said. "Maybe most importantly, you're lucky. You should probably be dead a couple of times over, you know that?"

"I'm well aware," she said.

"But the thing you have to remember about luck is, it can't be depended upon," he said. "It tends to run out exactly when you need it most. I've told you to be careful too many times to think it'll stick if I say it again. So I'm going to monitor you and make sure you're functioning properly. This isn't like being a meter maid. When we have an off day on the Job, people die. I don't want it to be you, and I don't want it to be some poor schmuck you could've saved if you'd taken better care of yourself. Are we clear?"

"Crystal, sir." Erin's lips were pressed tightly together and her jaw was clenched. She was gripping the steering wheel a little too hard.

"Good," Webb said. "Glad we had this little talk. Now we need to start thinking about ChainLink Inc. and what it's got to do with our dead pizza convict. We're almost there."

# Chapter 10

To Erin's surprise, they weren't the only cops in the ChainLink parking lot. The black Taurus wasn't marked, but the low-profile flashers and spotlight were a dead giveaway. And the tall, slender woman leaning against the rear fender was familiar.

"Great," Erin muttered.

"Who's that?" Webb asked.

"Detective Ivanova," she said. "Vic must've called her. The burglary's her case."

"Good," Webb said.

"Yeah," Erin said hollowly. "Good."

Vic pulled in a few seconds behind them. The Major Crimes detectives climbed out of their cars, accompanied by Rolf. Ivanova walked over to them. She was wearing knee-high black leather boots, a snug-fitting maroon jacket, and very tight jeans. Vic was looking at her in a way Erin didn't much like.

"Good morning, Detective," Webb said, extending his hand. "Lieutenant Webb, Major Crimes."

"Mira Ivanova, Burglary," Ivanova replied, shaking hands. "So you're the one who got stuck with Vic? I've heard about you."

"Word gets around," Webb said. "We don't want to step on your toes here."

"By all means, step on them," Ivanova said. "We're not getting anywhere with this one. If you can help clear it, I'll be glad. I called ahead, so the owner knows we're coming."

The offices of ChainLink Incorporated were unimpressive, even by the low standards of underfunded tech companies. The company had rented space in a strip mall with a tattoo parlor on one side and a seedy-looking massage parlor on the other. The sign over the door had obviously been done on the cheap; Erin's dad could have knocked out something that looked better in a couple of hours in his shop.

"I'm amazed this is the first time this place has been robbed," Vic said. "Look at this neighborhood."

"Tell me about it," Ivanova said. "You know what they taught me in Vice about massage parlors?"

"Yeah, yeah," Vic said. "They're all fronts for prostitution. Everybody knows that."

"I guess nobody thought ChainLink had anything worth stealing," Erin said.

The inside of the building was no better than the outside. The carpet was drab gray, worn, and stained with what Erin hoped was just spilled coffee. Someone had brought in a couple of potted plants and had actually gotten real ones instead of plastic, but then the plants had died, either from want of sunlight or maybe just the depressing atmosphere. Now they were sitting there dried up, brown, and dead.

Erin wondered whether plants got depressed. Maybe she'd ask Levine about it. That was the sort of thing Levine might know.

The secretary was a pimple-faced kid who looked about sixteen. He was sitting behind a computer, staring intently at the screen, one hand on the keyboard, the other on his mouse, wearing headphones. Faint sounds of computerized violence filtered toward the detectives. He hadn't noticed their arrival.

Webb walked up to the desk and waited a moment. The kid finally looked up, paused his game, and pushed the headphones off his head so they looped around his neck and hung there.

"Oh, hey guys," he said. "You the cops Kevin said were coming?"

"That's us," Webb said, holding up his shield.

"Whoa," the kid said, staring at Erin and Ivanova. "You're women."

"He noticed," Ivanova said with a sardonic smile.

"I'm surprised he knows what a real woman looks like," Erin whispered, causing Vic and Ivanova to snort with badly-suppressed laughter.

"Kevin's in back," the kid said, pointing to a door. "Go on through there."

The detectives trooped through the office and found themselves in a lab. Computers were everywhere. Monitors displayed arcane and incomprehensible data. Hard drives hummed. Erin noted that, while there were over a dozen computer keyboards, there was only one chair. It had wheels, and in it sat the young man Ivanova had described, uncharitably but accurately, as pencil-necked and zit-faced. He wore thick glasses and a distracted expression.

"Kevin?" Webb guessed.

"I'm Kevin," the man confirmed. He looked right past Webb at Ivanova. "Did you get my Trojan back?"

Vic snickered.

"This is Lieutenant Webb," Ivanova said. "Lieutenant, Kevin Moore."

"And these are my colleagues, Detectives O'Reilly and Neshenko," Webb said.

Moore noticed Rolf for the first time. "Hey," he said. "Get that thing out of here."

"Rolf's a police K-9," Erin said.

"It's a dog," Moore said. "Dogs shed. I've got a clean room back there, where the really delicate stuff is put together, but I don't want hair getting in all my equipment here."

"You've got hair," Erin pointed out.

"I wear a hairnet," Moore replied. Erin saw that he was, indeed, wearing a fine mesh net on his scalp.

"We'd like to ask about the item that was stolen," Webb said.

"The Trojan?" Moore said. "I call him Odysseus."

Webb nodded. Erin, Vic, and Ivanova looked blank.

"The *Iliad*?" Moore said. "The Trojan War? Anybody?"

"Was that the guy who couldn't be killed until somebody stabbed him in the heel or something?" Ivanova guessed.

"That's Achilles," Vic said. "Haven't you ever heard of the Achilles tendon?"

"Oh, right," Ivanova said. "That makes sense, now you mention it."

Moore rolled his eyes. "Okay," he said, recalibrating his intellectual expectations. "You're thinking of Brad Pitt in the movie. The guy I'm talking about is Sean Bean."

"Gotcha," Vic said, comprehension dawning. "Hey, that's, like, the only movie he's in where he doesn't get killed."

"He lives through *Ronin*," Ivanova said.

"Not in the original script," Vic said.

"What does Odysseus do?" Erin asked, ignoring the speculation about Sean Bean's fictional mortality.

"When you plug him in, he infiltrates the system," Moore said. "I can't disclose the details, for NDA reasons, but basically he takes over the entire system, but he does it in a really sneaky way. Then he harvests all the data that passes through. He's really smart, too."

"You mean this machine can think?" Vic asked.

"Of course not," Moore said. "Artificial intelligence can't actually think, per se. Odysseus just has really clever subroutines. And he adapts to the situation as it changes. He evades antivirus software and can even co-opt it. He basically *becomes* the system."

"That's not creepy at all," Vic said, rolling his eyes. "And you built this thing why?"

"It has obvious applications," Moore said. "We expect military contracts. And the NSA—"

"I think we can see why they'd want it," Webb said dryly. "This... Odysseus. Does it work?"

"Yes," Moore said. "Except for a few little things."

"Like what?" Erin asked.

"He damages the systems he inhabits," Moore said. "I think maybe it's a feature more than a bug, but you can't take him out once he's in, not without rendering the system fatally unstable. Not without command-level access."

"So we're talking about a *deadly* computer virus?" Vic demanded. "This just gets better and better."

"It's not dangerous to people," Moore said impatiently. "Just computers."

Erin leaned in close to Webb. "We need to call the college," she said. "Right now. If they find this thing and try to unplug it, they'll fry their network."

"Good Lord," Webb said, hauling out his phone. "I'm starting to feel like we should get the Bomb Squad on this."

"Just tell me one thing," Vic said to Moore. "You're a smart guy, right?"

"I went to CalTech," Moore said indignantly. "Three point nine six GPA."

"Then why the hell would you think making something like this was a good idea?"

Moore shrugged. "Somebody was going to make it sooner or later."

"That," Vic said, "is the shittiest reason for doing something dumb that I've ever heard. And I'm a cop. We hear bad excuses every damn day."

*   *   *

"I've talked to campus security," Webb said, putting his phone away. "They know not to mess with the thing, but they're not happy about it."

"Not happy," in Webb's personal vernacular, was about one step away from homicidal rage. Vic and Erin nodded.

"What's going to happen to their network in the meantime?" Erin asked Moore.

"Odysseus is supposed to report here," Moore said, pointing to one of his computer monitors. "But he went offline about three hours after he was stolen."

"Meaning what?" Webb asked.

"Either he's been broken or he's been hacked," Moore said.

"Isn't this thing hack-proof?" Vic asked.

"He should be," Moore said. "He's state of the art. But he hasn't been field-tested. He's still in alpha development. I was planning to move to beta testing sometime this week. Not all of the security features are enabled. But it's more likely he got broken by some idiot who didn't know what he was messing around with."

"Nothing else was stolen, right?" Ivanova asked.

"Not as far as I know," Moore said.

"Then I think it's safe to say the thief knew what he had," she said. "This other computer equipment looks expensive."

"It is," Moore said proudly.

"Then a normal thief would've taken it," Ivanova said.

"How big is Odysseus?" Erin asked.

"He's about the size of a stack of magazines," Moore said.

"Or a medium pizza?" Vic suggested.

"Yeah, I guess so," Moore said.

The detectives exchanged meaningful glances.

"So, assuming our thief knows what he's got, and is able to hack into it," Webb said. "What could he do with it?"

"Anything he wants, within the network," Moore said. "Like I told you, Odysseus becomes the network. He'd have complete access, command level. Anything a systems admin can do, he can do. You name it. And the output can go wherever he directs it."

"It'd own the network," Webb said.

"Why a college?" Vic wondered. "Why not a bank?"

"Banks are pretty hard to break into," Ivanova said. "You'd have to do a lot more than get through a locked door or two."

"He wanted something with easy physical access," Erin said. "But there must be something valuable on those servers. Mr. Moore, how do we kill this thing? You said we can't just unplug it."

"You can't," Moore said. "Not without killing the network."

"There's got to be some sort of failsafe," Webb said. "A kill-switch or something."

Moore shook his head. "That's something we were planning to install," he said. "I told you, Odysseus wasn't ready for deployment yet! I can shut him down, but I need access to his data stream, and I don't have it."

"How many people knew about him—it?" Erin asked.

"He's proprietary technology," Moore said. "The details are well protected."

"As well protected as your lab?" Vic asked sardonically.

Moore flushed. "We're a tech company," he said. "Physical security isn't our primary concern."

"The bad guy wouldn't need to know all the details," Erin said. "He'd just need to know what sort of thing it was. How many people have you told you were working on something like this?"

"A few," Moore said. "Investors, mostly. I needed to raise capital."

"Of course," Webb sighed. "Where did the money come from?"

"Investors," Moore repeated.

"Names?" Webb prompted.

Moore hesitated.

"Investing in a technology company isn't illegal by itself," Webb said. "But we need to figure out how this information got to the wrong people. I'm going to need a list of your investors."

"Okay," Moore said. "But I don't want you harassing them."

"I'll keep my hands above the waist," Vic promised.

"You sure about that?" Ivanova asked. "Because as I recall—"

"I think we're done here," Webb said. "Thanks for your help, Mr. Moore."

"I'd really like my prototype back," Moore said. "Can you return him to me?"

Erin wondered how, exactly, they were supposed to do that if they couldn't unplug it. But she said nothing.

The detectives circled up in the parking lot to discuss their next move. Rolf, seeing Erin's attention fixed elsewhere, sniffed at a corner of the building and cocked a leg.

"You thinking organized crime, sir?" Erin asked Webb.

"That's exactly what I'm thinking," Webb said.

"Why is it always the Mob with you guys?" Vic demanded.

"A lot of computer crime is done by overseas criminal organizations," Webb explained.

"Yeah," Ivanova said. "It used to be individual scammers, your typical basement-dwelling geeks, but nowadays it's mostly controlled by cartels and syndicates."

"Exactly," Webb said. "This is precisely the sort of thing those guys would be interested in. Think what they could do. If they could plug it into a hospital, they could steal medical records. A bank, and they could drain the accounts. The possibilities are endless."

"But why steal it, if they already own a piece of the company?" Vic asked.

"I don't know yet," Webb said. "But if we can tie ChainLink to organized crime, it may give us our perp."

"I don't know," Erin said. "This whole burglary seems pretty small-time for it to be a Mob operation. It's one guy with a stolen pizza uniform and a claw hammer."

"It's a theory," Webb said. "I'm open to other suggestions."

"I think we should look at Robbie Black," Erin said. "The guy who used to work with Cross and Shelton."

"Absolutely," Webb said. "Find out where he is and what he's doing."

"After lunch, sir," she said.

"Oh, right," Webb said. "You've got that thing with Captain Holliday."

"Hanging out with the brass?" Ivanova said, smiling. "Brown-nosing your way to the top?"

"It's not like that," Erin said, bristling. "And neither is Holliday. He's good police."

Ivanova shrugged. "He's one of the guys upstairs," she said. "They're all assholes, even the good ones."

"I'm inclined to resent that," Webb said.

"I wasn't talking about you," Ivanova said with false innocence. "At least, not intentionally. *Are* you an asshole, sir?"

"When I have to be," Webb said, deadpan. "All right, O'Reilly, you'd better get moving. Check in with me after your meeting. Detective Ivanova, thanks for your help. We'll let you know if we need anything else."

"I live to serve," Ivanova said. "Hey, Vic, you want to grab lunch? I know a place just up the road, they do great subs."

Vic hesitated, and Erin saw him considering his options. Then he shrugged.

"Why not?" he said. "But I'm not paying for you."

"Cheapskate," Ivanova said with a grin.

"What about you, sir?" Erin asked. "You don't have a ride."

"I'll hitchhike," Webb said in a flat deadpan.

"Can he do that?" Vic asked.

"I've got a thumb," Webb said. "But I was thinking I'd use the subway."

"Careful," Vic said. "Old guys get mugged on the subway."

"If I see any, I'll keep them safe," Webb said.

# Chapter 11

The "business lunch" wasn't a thing cops usually did. For a police officer, working over lunch meant grabbing takeout in the squad car, or munching a sandwich during a stakeout, or snacking on vending-machine food during a long shift in the station house. Meeting her Captain at a restaurant was a different experience for Erin.

Holliday had selected a Mexican place four blocks from the Eightball. He'd just arrived when Erin got there, and was in the process of hanging his coat and hat on the hook outside his booth.

"Glad I didn't keep you waiting, sir," she said, sliding into the seat opposite him.

"You're right on time," Holliday said. "Thanks for making room in your schedule."

"I work for you, sir," she said.

"You work for the city of New York," he replied. He picked up a menu and scanned it. "Do you have any idea what's good here?"

"I haven't eaten here before," she said. "You picked the place. I figured you knew it."

Holliday's mustache hid most of his smile. "I figured it was safer than an Italian joint," he said. "Not many Mafia from Mexico."

"Plenty of street gangs," she replied.

"But they're not our problem right now," he said.

Erin had noticed the odd anonymity of public dining more than once during her career. The hubbub of a busy restaurant made eavesdropping on a particular conversation nearly impossible. She and Holliday could discuss anything without fear of being overheard or recorded.

"What's the situation, sir?" she asked.

He held up a hand to stall her as a teenage waitress arrived to take their order. Holliday asked for a burrito and black coffee. Erin opted for a taco salad and a Diet Coke.

"Where's your partner?" he asked once the waitress had gone.

"Which one?" she asked.

"The furry one."

"I left him in the car," she said. "It's only about thirty degrees, so he'll be fine. Shepherds don't get cold easily. He has more trouble in the summer."

"How's his health these days?"

"Rolf's fine," Erin said, a little too quickly.

"He got knocked around pretty badly a while ago, didn't he?"

"He can take it," she said.

"And you?"

She met his eyes. "So can I."

Holliday nodded. "All right. Your doctor signed off, so you're fighting fit in my book. Have you checked on Lieutenant Stachowski recently?"

"Yeah," Erin said, the word falling heavily from her mouth. Holliday heard the change in her tone and nodded.

"No change?" he asked quietly.

"Not really. I don't see any way he comes back on duty."

"No," Holliday agreed. "It's a damned shame. And we don't have the slightest idea where his shooter is."

Erin said nothing. She knew where Lenny Carter had gone, up to a point. She'd handed him off to Lieutenant Keane and the tender mercies of Internal Affairs. What had happened to him after that, she had no idea. Apparently Keane had kept Carter so tightly under wraps, his precinct Captain didn't even know about him.

"It burns me up, knowing he got taken out by one of our own," Holliday said. "It's almost enough to make me wish I'd gone into IAB myself, just so I could run that scum down."

"You're better the way you are, sir," Erin said.

Holliday smiled again. "IAB aren't the enemy, O'Reilly," he said.

"Of course not, sir," she said woodenly.

Holliday's smile vanished. "We're down to the wire," he said. "We're doing it around Christmas. I'll get you the specific timing."

"Doing what?" she asked. Then, feeling stupid, "Right. *It*."

"Affirmative," Holliday said.

"*Christmas*, sir?"

"The best time," he said. "The O'Malleys won't be expecting a major police operation during the holidays."

"It's not because of your name?" she asked, unable to resist. "Imagine the headlines: *Holiday Bust for Holliday*."

"I'd never run an operation on the basis of headlines," Holliday said dryly. "What's your schedule?"

"I'm heading upstate on the 24th in the morning to visit my folks. I'll be there overnight through Christmas, and coming back on the 26th. Is that going to work? Are we going to be able to close this thing down in one day?"

"I don't see why not," Holliday said. "The whole point is to sweep everyone up at once."

"Wow," Erin said.

"What?" Holliday asked.

"It's just... after all these months, to think it'll actually be over," she said. "In just a few days. It's a weird thought."

"It's hard to come back after a long undercover stint," Holliday said. "If you need to talk to someone..."

"I know where Doc Evans's office is," she said. Jim Evans was the Eightball's psychiatrist. Erin had been seeing him off and on about her nightmares and post-traumatic stress, so he certainly wasn't a stranger to her.

"After it's over, and the paperwork has been processed, I want you to take a week," Holliday said. "Maybe two."

"Time off?" Erin asked. "Mandatory?"

"I'd prefer you do it voluntarily," he said. "But I think you need it. Take some time and figure out where you're standing. Think where you are now and where you want to go."

"I'm not going anywhere, sir."

Holliday leaned forward slightly. "Think carefully about that," he said. "If this goes smoothly, you're going to be in the spotlight."

"I like the shadows better," she muttered.

"I'm serious," he said. "You're going to pile up a stack of commendations as thick as the Patrol Guide. There may be medals awarded. You can practically write your own ticket."

"I wrote plenty of tickets in Patrol," she said. "Nobody was ever happy I wrote one."

"Do you want Lieutenant Webb's job?" Holliday countered. "Or mine?"

Erin blinked. "Webb's a good Lieutenant, sir," she said. "And you're a good Captain. I don't want to push either of you out."

"You're not pushing anybody out," he said patiently. "But Webb and I aren't young men, and we're not the only Lieutenant and Captain in the NYPD. If you want your own squad, you can probably get it. If you want higher command, you can put your foot on the first rung of that ladder."

"You mean that?" she said. "Me? A Captain?" It was a very strange thought.

"Why not?" he replied. "Not right away, of course. You'd have to go one step at a time. You're an exceptional street officer, O'Reilly. You've got great instincts, you're smart, and I'm not sure you know what fear is. You've proven you can handle complicated cases involving multiple officers. You've also shown you're damned near incorruptible. If you're asking whether you've got what it takes, I think the answer is 'yes.'"

"What about Rolf?" she asked.

"What about him?" Holliday was bewildered by the question.

"What happens to him if I get promoted?"

"He's an NYPD K-9," Holliday said. "Standard practice is to keep the K-9 and handler together for the dog's working life. However, if you were promoted to a desk assignment, I assume he would be paired with a new handler in Patrol."

Erin swallowed hard. The waitress chose that moment to place her taco salad in front of her, but she was suddenly not at all hungry. The thought of losing Rolf, not to an injury or death but to bureaucratic bullshit, left her feeling like she'd swallowed a chunk of cold concrete.

"He's not a pet, O'Reilly," Holliday said softly. "You know that, don't you? He's a piece of NYPD equipment, purchased with City funds, maintained by the City and for the City."

"He's more than that, sir," she said.

"I know you have a bond with him," Holliday said. "And he's a good dog. I understand how you must feel about him."

"Do you, sir?" Erin retorted sharply. "If you did, you wouldn't even think of taking him away from me."

Holliday nodded. "I see," was all he said.

"Is that why you asked me here? To give me career counseling?"

"I asked you here to tell you our timetable," he said. "I don't have to remind you to keep this information absolutely secret. If I were you, I wouldn't even tell Morton Carlyle ahead of time."

"He can keep a secret," she said.

"I know that. But the more people who know, the more likely something is to slip. You know that as well as I do."

Erin nodded unhappily.

"How's your salad?" he asked.

"It's fine," Erin said with no enthusiasm whatsoever. She hadn't touched it.

\*     \*     \*

According to his parole officer's reports, Robbie Black worked tech support in a Brighton Beach travel agency. The agency's name was Far Horizon Journeys. Before driving all the way south to Little Odessa, Erin decided to drop in at the Eightball. She was only a few blocks away and it would give her a chance to see how Piekarski was doing.

She found the other woman in Major Crimes, staring at evidence reports. Piekarski looked glum. Erin couldn't blame her.

"I bet you can't wait to get out of the office," Erin said.

"My feet are swollen," Piekarski said. "At least, that's how they feel. I can hardly see them. Whoever had the idea of carrying babies in their bellies ought to be Tased right in the nut-sack."

"I think you're talking about God," Erin said. "Maybe you shouldn't get in a Taser fight with a guy who throws lightning bolts."

"Goddamn patriarchy," Piekarski muttered. "Maybe that's why people figure God's a man. Because if He was a woman, He wouldn't put us through all this shit. March can't come soon enough. I know I won't get any sleep after the little guy's born, but it'll be better than lugging him around inside me. You thinking of having kids?"

"Maybe," Erin said.

"Don't."

"My mom says it's the most wonderful feeling in the world."

Piekarski rolled her eyes. "Really? Because I've heard it hurts like a son of a bitch. I've got your miracle of childbirth right here. Speaking of royal pains, where's Vic?"

That was a question Erin didn't really want to answer. "He's having lunch across the River," she said. "It turns out he knows the detective who's working the ChainLink burglary."

"Oh, right," Piekarski said. "He used to be stationed in Brooklyn. He and this other guy are swapping old war stories, huh?"

"Something like that," Erin said, disliking the evasion but not knowing what else to say. "Anything good in the CSU reports?"

"They've got a bunch of hair and fibers from the delivery truck," Piekarski said. "Which might be useful, except that the trucks get swapped around all the delivery guys. We're going to need elimination samples from everyone else who works at Ninja Pizza, and that's assuming none of them is the killer."

"Bode Cross is one of our suspects," Erin reminded her.

"Yeah, I know," Piekarski said, cocking her head toward the whiteboard. Cross's name was prominently featured. "Our victim still had his wallet, and the cash from some deliveries, so we can probably rule out robbery."

"I figured," Erin said.

"But he didn't have his phone," Piekarski went on.

That got Erin's attention. "What?"

"No phone. I guess it's possible he wasn't carrying one..."

"No way," Erin said. "A delivery guy is always going to have a phone on him. CSU's sure it wasn't in the car?"

"I've got a full inventory of everything that was in the cab. No phone."

"I'm guessing there was something incriminating on it," Erin said. "Can I see the inventory?"

"Help yourself." Piekarski rotated her monitor toward Erin. "I'm going to run to the little girls' room. That's another thing about being preggers. I have to piss every five minutes. They say kids get on your nerves, but this one prefers to get on my bladder. I swear, he's going to be a tap-dancer."

While Piekarski visited the restroom, Erin scanned the list of every item that had been recovered from the Toyota. The car keys had been in the ignition, which made sense. There was no point in stealing those and leaving the car. CSU had found the car's registration in the glove compartment, along with a flashlight and a phone charger that plugged into the cigarette lighter. None of it was out of place. At least the charger suggested a phone should have been present.

"Anything?" Piekarski asked, rejoining her.

"Just another thing that wasn't there," Erin said. "A baseball cap."

"What do you think that means?" Piekarski asked.

"I think it means the guy on the security footage isn't Floyd Shelton," Erin said. "It was somebody else who stole a Ninja Pizza jacket and broke into the server room. But that doesn't make any sense, because Rolf tracked Shelton from the dorm to the server room. And only one guy shows up on tape."

She sat down and rubbed her temples, which was a bad idea. The bullet wound on the side of her head sent a bolt of pain straight through her skull.

"You're sure Rolf tracked him properly?" Piekarski asked.

"Rolf doesn't make mistakes," Erin said indignantly. "Not with his nose. I gave him the pizza box and he tracked the guy's scent straight there."

"So it had to be Shelton," Piekarski said. "I guess the killer swiped the cap for some reason. Maybe it had the other guy's DNA on it. Maybe he'd worn it himself and thought it might have his hair in it."

"If he was going to be that careful about DNA evidence, he would've torched the Toyota," Erin said. "Or at least poured bleach all over it. No, I'm missing something. You know what my dad says?"

"Old-timey wisdom?" Piekarski guessed.

"He says assumption is the mother of all screw-ups," Erin said. "If something seems impossible, it's because you're assuming the wrong things."

"I don't think we're making very many assumptions," Piekarski said doubtfully.

"No," Erin said. Then she snapped her fingers. "Just one."

"What's that?"

Erin was on her feet. "We're assuming Shelton's the one who delivered that pizza to the dorm," she said.

"Of course he did," Piekarski said. "I mean, who else could it have been?"

Erin was already on her phone, calling Webb.

"Everything go okay?" he asked.

"Yeah," she said. "Listen, sir. We have to show that kid at the dorm, what's his name, Overholtz, a picture of our victim."

"Why?" Webb asked.

"Because I don't think that's who he paid for the pizza," she said. "I think it was our killer."

"Explain."

"The pizza delivery was a cover," Erin said. "I think Shelton picked up his killer and brought him to the campus in the car. Then Shelton hung out in the parking garage while the killer delivered the pizza and broke into the server room."

"That seems awfully complicated," Webb said. "But from what I'm getting, you think he was setting Shelton up as a fall guy?"

"That's what I think," she said.

"Where are you now?"

"I'm at the Eightball with Piekarski. I'll head south in a minute. I figured as long as I was in the neighborhood I'd check in with her. My next stop is Far Horizon Journeys. It's a travel agency."

"In Brighton Beach," Webb said. "I know. I've seen Robbie Black's PO's reports, too. What's your ETA?"

"Call it thirty or forty minutes."

"I'll meet you there."

# Chapter 12

The sound of the siren cut through the December air. Blue and red lights flashed in Erin's rearview mirror. The low whine of an unhappy dog came from somewhere next to her ear.

She blinked and looked around. What the hell had happened? Where was she? Her hands were wrapped around the wheel of her Charger. A car accident? She didn't see any other stopped vehicles. The Charger appeared undamaged. She felt the throaty purr of its powerful engine through the floor. But she was pulled over to the curb, the car idling in Park.

A rapping on the driver's-side window made her jump. She whipped her head around to see what it was. Her brain felt like it lagged just a little behind the rest of her head, sloshing inside her skull with a liquid, nauseating pain.

An NYPD Patrol officer stood outside her door, every inch the stereotypical cop, from the peak of his dark blue cap down past his aviator sunglasses, body armor, and equipment belt to the tips of his shiny black shoes. His left hand was poised to knock on her window again. His right was at his belt, conveniently close to the butt of his sidearm.

Erin rolled down her window, her mind doing cartwheels. "Officer?" she said.

"Have you been drinking, ma'am?" the cop asked.

"What? No!"

*Had* she been drinking? The headache felt an awful lot like a hangover. And she couldn't remember how she'd gotten here.

"Do you know why I pulled you over?" he asked.

"No," Erin said again. "Listen, Officer, I—"

"License and registration, please," he said.

Rolf abruptly thrust his head through the hatch between the front seats and began barking ferociously.

"Holy shit!" the cop exclaimed, stumbling back and grabbing for his gun.

"Stand down!" Erin snapped, finally getting her thoughts in some sort of order. "He's a police K-9! I'm a detective!"

The Patrolman gave her a wary look. "ID," he said. "Slowly." His pistol was in his hand now, though it was pointed at the pavement.

Erin unclipped the gold shield from her belt and held it up. "O'Reilly," she said. "Major Crimes. Shield four-six-four-oh. Didn't you run my plates when you pulled me over?"

She already knew the answer to that. If he had, the Charger would have been flagged as a Department-issued unmarked police car. It also would have been designated as a K-9 vehicle, so he wouldn't have been so shocked when Rolf staked out his turf.

"No, ma'am," the cop said. "Sorry."

His voice had lost its authoritative edge. He sounded young and suddenly uncertain. He took off his sunglasses, revealing a boyish face absent the slightest hint of facial hair.

"What's your name, Officer?" Erin asked.

"Denholm, ma'am."

"How long have you been out of the Academy, Denholm?"

"Six months, ma'am."

"Where's your partner?"

"Out sick," Denholm said. "Flu. Geez, I'm really sorry to hassle you like this. It's my first week riding without my FTO. He's got a lot more years on the Force than I do, but like I said, he's sick and we're shorthanded so here I am."

"Officer?"

"Yes, ma'am?"

"Why *did* you pull me over?"

Denholm blinked. "You really don't know?"

Erin held onto her patience, reminding herself this kid was just a rookie, and she'd once been one herself. "That's why I'm asking, Officer."

"You were all over the road, ma'am," he said. "I picked you up just south of the bridge. I could've sworn you were drunk, or maybe asleep at the wheel. You were weaving like crazy, over the line and back. You were gonna hit someone if I didn't do something. Are you okay, ma'am?"

"Yeah," Erin said automatically. "I'm fine. Just tired, I guess."

Denholm nodded. "You take care, ma'am," he said. He turned and walked quickly back to his Patrol car. He climbed in, turned off his flashers, and pulled around her.

Erin watched him go. So did Rolf. The K-9's hackles were up. He liked other cops most of the time, but he hadn't liked the way this one had sauntered up to their car like he owned it. Rolf had felt the man's aggressiveness. Now that he'd put the rookie in his place, the Shepherd started to calm down.

Erin glanced at her GPS. She was in Brooklyn, just south of the East River. She had no memory whatsoever of crossing the bridge. The last thing she recalled was aiming her car south.

She was scared. Denholm had made some mistakes and done some stupid stuff. He should have run her plates before getting out of his car. For all he'd known, she might have been a wanted felon, armed and dangerous. Come to that, she *was* armed; in addition to her Glock nine-millimeter and her snub-nosed .38 backup piece, she had an AR-15 rifle in the car. And Denholm had walked up on her in his fancy sunglasses and spit-shined shoes with no backup and not a care in the world. If she'd been a bad guy, she could have wasted him on the spot.

But for all that, he'd been right to pull her over, and he shouldn't have let her go like that, without even a warning. She knew why he'd done it. He was a rookie, at the start of his career. The last thing he wanted to do was hassle a Major Crimes detective. That was the sort of thing that could get a cop reassigned to perpetual foot-patrol traffic duty. But she'd been driving impaired. Even if it was just fatigue, she'd been a danger to herself and to everyone else on the road. He should have given her a breathalyzer, or at least done the fingertip test to see if her pupils twitched. It shouldn't have mattered that she was a cop.

And that wasn't the worst of it. She'd had an honest-to-God blackout in the middle of the day, wide awake, while driving. Denholm wasn't going to report her. He wouldn't dare. She'd seen plenty of kids like him, all bravado on the surface, boiling with insecurity underneath. It took time for a cop to grow into the uniform. But whether he reported her or not, she needed to get herself right.

Erin was trying not to admit it, even to herself, but she was more than scared; she was terrified. Something was wrong with her head. Maybe the doctors could fix it and maybe they couldn't. Words ran through her brain, frightening words: *dementia, early-onset Alzheimer's, blackouts, traumatic brain injury, amnesia.*

"I'm fine," she insisted, but she knew she wasn't.

Rolf snorted in the direction of the departing Officer Denholm. Then he nosed Erin's ear. He could tell something wasn't right with his partner, but he didn't know what. It was making him anxious.

"A week," she promised. "I just have to keep going another week. Then I'll take some time and figure this out."

She gave herself a few more minutes, waiting to see if anything else happened inside her head. Nothing did. She felt okay, except for a lingering headache. Then, with definite misgivings, she put the car back in gear and went to meet Webb at Far Horizon Journeys. She drove a lot slower than usual.

*       *       *

Webb was halfway through his third cigarette when Erin arrived. The butts of the first two lay in the gutter at his feet. He was staring at Far Horizon Journeys, thinking and sucking down smoke.

If Erin had expected a glamorous, exotic facility, she was in for a letdown. The travel agency was wedged into a seedy strip mall very similar to the one which housed ChainLink Incorporated. In this case the agency sat between a bail bondsman and a payday loan joint.

"Did you have a pleasant drive?" Webb asked as she and Rolf joined him on the sidewalk.

Erin gave him a sharp look, but apparently he was just making small talk. He hadn't heard from Officer Denholm. "I'm here," she said.

"So I see," Webb said.

"Where's Vic?" she asked.

"At the Six-Oh, looking over burglary reports with Detective Ivanova. He thinks there might be some sort of pattern we can link to our guy."

"Copy that," Erin said, hoping that was all they were looking over. Vic was a good guy, she told herself. He was devoted to Piekarski and they had a kid coming. No way would he step out on her. Not a chance.

"Are you okay, O'Reilly?" Webb was looking at her funny.

"Don't worry about me, sir," she said. "What do we know about Far Horizon?"

"Besides the obvious?" he replied, gesturing toward the building. "What do you see?"

"I see a bunch of businesses that prey on lower-class schmucks," she said.

"And a travel agency," he said. "Doesn't that strike you as a little odd?"

"You think it's a front, sir?"

"Massage parlors are fronts for brothels, payday loans are fronts for loan sharks, and travel agencies are fronts for smuggling," Webb said dryly. "Since we're in Little Odessa, that means Russian Mafia."

"That's a little cynical, don't you think?"

"I'm not paid to look on the bright side of human nature," he said. "And neither are you."

"Do we have anything linking Far Horizon to Russian mobsters?"

"Nothing definite. I'm planning to have Piekarski run their financials. Robbie Black isn't Russian, is he?"

"I don't know many black Russians. But he works here, and he's connected to Shelton and Cross, so I guess we'd better talk to him."

The lobby of the travel agency reeked of cheap cigarette smoke, so thick even Webb's eyes started watering. Rolf snorted irritably and twitched his nose. The carpet was stained, worn, and incredibly ugly. A few posters of Russian cities hung on the walls. Behind a desk sat a black-haired, skinny young woman with a cigarette smoldering in her hand. She wore bright crimson lipstick and a red blouse, top two buttons unfastened to show the upper portion of a tattoo on her chest.

The woman looked the detectives and dog over. "You want a trip to Russia?" she asked.

"We're here to talk to Robbie Black," Erin said, showing her gold shield. "We're with the NYPD."

"No shit," the girl said, unimpressed. "I never would've guessed. You sure you don't want to book a flight? The Caucasus is real nice this time of year. Beautiful mountains, snow, and lots of cheap, good-looking girls. Your buddy there looks like he could really stand to get laid."

"If I want STIs, I can get them from local girls without the jet lag," Webb said. "Mr. Black, please?"

"Okay, okay. Keep your shirt on." The girl picked up the phone on her desk, an ancient model from the early '90s, and punched a number. After a moment she said, "Yeah, there's a couple cops up front. They want to talk to Robbie. And they got a dog with them."

After a moment, she hung up. "He'll be right here," she told them.

"Or he'll be running out the back door," Erin told Webb in an undertone.

"If he is, we'll find him," he said placidly. "The man's a paroled felon. He knows if he jerks us around, we send him straight back to prison."

Rolf watched Erin attentively. He always hoped the perps ran. Chasing them down was one of the best parts of his job.

But the K-9 was doomed to disappointment. A few moments later, the door at the back of the room swung open and a dark-skinned guy walked through it. He looked to be about Erin's age, and would have been good-looking if not for the prison ink decorating his neck and the gaunt, hollow-eyed look of a habitual heroin user. He was wearing jeans, a T-shirt, and a surprisingly expensive-looking leather jacket.

"Robbie Black?" Webb said.

"That's me," the guy confirmed. "What do you want?"

"We'd just like to talk to you for a little while," Webb said. "We've got a few questions for you."

"Do we have to do it here?" Black replied.

"Of course not," Webb said. "It's a little cold out, but we can step outside."

Once they were out on the concrete again, Erin paid extra attention to Black. She didn't think he'd run or attack them, but it was always best to be prepared. She watched his hands. Cops never liked it when people put their hands in their pockets, even on cold days. Pockets were where knives and small guns lived.

"Look," Black said. "It's not cool, you guys coming to my place of work like this. Are you trying to get me fired? I lose my job, it violates my parole."

"And you don't want to go back upstate, do you?" Webb replied.

"Of course not," Black said. "I did my time, okay? And I can't talk long, I've got work to do."

He was awfully twitchy. His eyes were all over the place and his muscles were jittery. Either he was really nervous or he was looking for his next heroin hit. Possibly both.

"Drug use is a violation of your parole," Erin commented.

"You a Narc?" Black demanded. "You got a drug dog there?"

"We're Major Crimes," Webb said. "I'm Lieutenant Webb, this is Detective O'Reilly."

"I've got nothing to say to you," Black said.

"Floyd Shelton," Erin said.

"Who's that?" Black replied.

Webb shook his head. "That's the problem with bad liars," he said. "A good liar will tell the truth most of the time, in case we already know some of it. A bad one just denies everything, like a two-year-old with his hand in the cookie jar."

"We already know you know Floyd," Erin said. "You worked with him and Bode Cross. Remember the refinery job and the Thanksgiving Parade?"

She was bullshitting him, but he didn't know that. His eyes darted between her and Webb. He licked his lips. In spite of the cold December air, a thin sheen of sweat showed on his forehead.

"Okay, yeah, I knew him back in the day," Black said. "I thought you meant, had I talked to him recently? Like, since I got out. And I haven't. I'm not supposed to associate with other cons. I've got no idea where he is, or what he's doing. And whatever it is, it's got nothing to do with me."

"Floyd's dead," Webb said bluntly. "Someone beat his head in, night before last, and left him in a parking garage."

Black licked his lips again. "Damn," he said. "That's harsh. I don't know nothing about any of that."

"Do you own a hammer, Mr. Black?" Erin asked.

"A what?"

"A hammer," she said. "Like for pounding nails."

"No."

Webb sighed. "Again with the lies," he said. "Of course you have a hammer, Mr. Black. Everybody owns a hammer. Has it ever occurred to you that telling us the truth might be your best option?"

Black said nothing. Clearly that thought had not been foremost in his mind.

"What's the shape of your hammer's head?" Erin asked.

"Huh?" Black said.

"The head of the hammer you don't have," she said patiently. "The part you hit nails with. What is it shaped like?"

"It's shaped like a hammer, lady," Black said.

"You're a smart guy, Mr. Black," Webb said. "You got a degree in computer science while you were in prison. So drop the idiot act. Where were you, night before last, between the hours of midnight and three in the morning?"

"I was home," Black said. "In bed. Asleep."

"Alone?" Erin asked.

"Yeah, I was alone."

"So nobody can vouch for your whereabouts?" she pressed.

"Nobody was watching me," he said. "Does anybody watch you sleep, lady? Jesus. I meet with my parole officer, just like I'm supposed to. I hold down a steady job. I piss in a cup every month, so he knows I'm clean. He's had guys search my apartment twice. What else do I have to do? You want to put on a glove and do a body-cavity search right now? Want me to drop my pants and spread 'em?"

"No thanks," Erin said. "What do you do for Far Horizon?"

"Tech support. I keep their computers upgraded and stuff."

"It seems like kind of a dinky little company to need full-time tech support," Webb said.

"Screw you, man!" Black snapped. "I've got criminal convictions. It's not like I can just grab a job with some Fortune 500 company downtown. I had to take what I could get. The pay's okay, the bennies suck, but I could do a lot worse."

"How did you find this job?" Erin asked.

"I know a guy who knows a guy," Black said.

"These folks are Russians," she said.

"Yeah, so? I'm Russian," Black said.

"Really?" Webb asked.

"On my mom's side," Black said. "Not that it's any of your business. Now, if you've got nothing else to ask me, I'd like to go back and see if I've still got a job. Goddamn cops."

He spat on the ground at Webb's feet, turned, and stomped back inside, slamming the door.

"That was a little uncalled-for," Webb said. He didn't sound particularly upset. If saliva was the worst body fluid a cop got on him during his shift, it was a quiet day.

"No it wasn't," Erin said. "He was making a point."

"The same point a thousand macho hoods have made," Webb said.

"No," she said again.

Webb raised an eyebrow. "Explain."

"That wasn't for our benefit," she said. "It was for anybody else who was watching. You're right, sir. This place is a front. It's being run by mobsters."

Webb nodded. "Right. And he couldn't afford to look like he was cooperating with the police, so he had to be belligerent. I'm getting too old for this. They say the wits are the first thing to go."

"Your wits are fine," she said quietly. "I'm the one who's been hanging around mobsters all the time. I'm used to them."

"What do your gangland instincts tell you?" he asked. "Is Black our guy?"

"I don't know," she said. "But I think we need to look closer at Far Horizon."

"Funny thing about horizons," he said, smiling thinly. "No matter how fast you go, you can never get to them. They just keep retreating into the distance. But you're right. Let's go to the Six-Oh and scoop up Neshenko. Then we'll figure our next move."

# Chapter 13

They found Vic and Ivanova in the Precinct 60 Burglary office. They were at Ivanova's desk, looking at her computer, their backs to the door. Ivanova was sitting down. Vic was leaning over her. He had his hand on her shoulder.

It was just a hand, Erin told herself. That didn't mean a thing. Plenty of guys would clap a hand on a coworker's shoulder. It was a friendly gesture, one that said they were all on the same team.

She didn't like making excuses in her head. Not for Vic. It made her feel confused and suspicious and dirty.

Webb cleared his throat loudly. He'd also noticed the gesture.

"Good afternoon, *tovarisch*," he said.

"He doesn't speak Russian, does he?" Ivanova said, spinning her chair to face the newcomers.

"Just what I know from old spy movies," Webb said.

"I figured," she said. "Your accent could use some work, Lieutenant."

"So could Sean Connery's in *The Hunt for Red October*," Vic said. "A Russian with a Scottish accent? Seriously?"

"He's playing a Lithuanian, not a Russian," Ivanova said.

"Okay, a Scottish Lithuanian then," Vic said. "It makes just as much sense."

"I'm providing you with a convenient conversational segue," Webb said. "We have reason to believe Far Horizon Journeys is a front for the Russian Mafia."

"God damn it," Vic growled. "I thought we took care of those guys."

"We dealt with one gang of human traffickers," Webb said. "Did you really think those were the only Russian gangsters in New York?"

"A guy can hope," Vic said.

"What've the *bratva* got to do with this case?" Ivanova asked.

"We don't know yet," Webb said. "First things first. Did you find any additional burglaries?"

"No," Vic said. "I mean, we've got plenty of burglaries, but nothing that ties in with that pizza place. I really thought Martinelli was using a gang of ex-cons to pull jobs for him. Like maybe he'd have his pizza guys case the joint ahead of time, then send in his crew a day or two later. But we haven't got any reports of places that've been hit ordering Ninja Pizza around the time they got taken down."

"It was worth a shot," Webb said. "Now, on to the... what did you call them?"

"*Bratva*," Ivanova said. "Or you can say Mafiya, with a 'y' between the 'I' and the 'a.' It means 'brotherhood.'"

"I swear, all those gangster groups call themselves that," Vic said. "Aren't the Triads the same way? It's all 'Brother Yang' and 'Brother Wong' and whatever."

"I wouldn't know," Webb said mildly. "I'm from the LAPD. Out there, we'd say, 'Forget it, Jake. It's Chinatown.'"

"We really ought to get together for movie nights as a squad," Erin said. "Sometimes I think we learned half our shit from pop culture when we were growing up."

"That's a great idea," Ivanova said. "I'll bring the popcorn."

"Getting back to the *bratva*," Webb said patiently. "I know they run prostitution, from that gang we broke up a little over a year ago. What else are they into?"

"You name it, they do it," Ivanova said, shrugging. "Anything that makes money. Besides the trafficking there's drugs, gambling, guns, hijackings, computer crime, old-fashioned muggings."

"Computer crime?" Erin asked, half a beat ahead of Webb and Vic, who'd both opened their mouths to chime in.

"Yeah," Ivanova said. "That's not my department, but I know they do it. I think it's mostly credit card fraud and identity theft these days. There's big money in that data."

"The sort of data you could access through a college database, maybe?" Erin suggested.

"I can definitely see why the Mob would be interested in a gadget like Odysseus," Webb said. "But if they were investing in ChainLink, why bother burglarizing the place? They'd be able to get at the thing legally while attracting less attention."

"These guys don't think like that," Vic said. "They don't give a crap if something's legal or not and they aren't patient."

"We've got a computer science guy with a criminal record, a connection to the victim, and possible links to the Russian Mob," Webb said. "I'm starting to like Robbie Black for this."

"Let's get a warrant and search his house," Erin said.

"For what?" Webb asked. "We think the device is plugged into the campus servers."

"How about a computer that's receiving the data from Odysseus?" Erin replied.

"That's a good thought," Webb said. "But Black's smart enough not to have a computer just sitting in his basement. Or if he has it, it'll be heavily encrypted. We'll need hackers from Homeland Security or some such organization and they'll take two months breaking into the thing. In the meantime, we can't charge Black and he walks."

"Why not do it the old-fashioned way?" Ivanova suggested. "Physical surveillance. Slap a tail on him and see where he goes."

"That's not a bad idea," Webb said. "But we're pretty short on warm bodies. Besides O'Reilly and Neshenko, all I've got is Piekarski, and she's not supposed to be in the field."

"Limited duty?" Ivanova asked. "She get hurt in the line?"

"She's got a temporary health consideration," Webb said dryly.

Erin stared at Vic and Ivanova, realizing Vic hadn't told the other detective about Zofia's pregnancy. She could feel her paranoia hardening into suspicion. It was a familiar feeling, one she'd had about dozens of perps over the years, and she'd learned to listen to it.

"Let me talk to my CO," Ivanova said. "He hates those Mafiya bastards. I'll bet he'll get me on a temporary detail with you, along with a couple other plainclothes officers. Would that help?"

"That'd be perfect," Webb said. "You folks at the Six-Oh know the area better than we do."

"Speak for yourself," Vic retorted. "I grew up here. I fit in like OJ's hand in that glove."

"I thought the glove didn't fit," Ivanova said.

"So he claimed," Vic said.

"That trial was more than twenty years ago," Webb said. "And don't remind me. I was in LA at the time, working Patrol. I know more than I want to about it."

"Were you in the car chase?" Vic asked. "The white Bronco?"

"There's about nine thousand officers in the LAPD," Webb said. "There were only a dozen cars in the chase. What do *you* think?"

"It would've been neat to be a part of history like that," Ivanova said. "Did you ever bust any movie stars?"

"I am so very done talking about this," Webb said. "Let's talk surveillance. We'll need two officers on duty at any time, and that's the absolute bare bones. We can't do revolving tails, we don't have the manpower. O'Reilly, you and Neshenko get back to Far Horizon and sit on it. Discreetly. What time is it?"

"A few minutes past three," Erin said.

"Assuming Ivanova gets permission for herself and two others, that'll mean we've got two more shifts available," Webb said. "Even if Black works late, that should be enough. I'll relieve you at eight with one other cop. Ivanova will take over with another at midnight if necessary. Make sure you've got everyone's cell numbers so we can all keep in touch. The Mob guys might have police scanners, so let's stay off Department radio frequencies."

"What're we looking for?" Erin asked.

"Find out where he goes, who he talks to, what he does," Webb said. "The main thing we need to know is whether he's got a base of operations somewhere away from home."

"He could just be working out of that travel agency," Vic pointed out.

"If he's not in it for himself," Webb said.

"You think he's freelancing?" Vic asked. "That's risky. They'll kill him for that."

"I don't know what to think," Webb said. "That's why we're still developing information. Get moving. And leave your car keys. I'll take the Taurus."

"My car?" Vic demanded in outraged tones.

"The NYPD's car," Webb corrected him. "You're riding with O'Reilly and her K-9."

"And if you're extra good, I'll let you ride up front," Erin said. "Otherwise you're going in back with Rolf. We'll put the bite sleeve on you and he can chew on your arm while I drive."

"Reminds me of family trips when I was a kid," Vic said.

"I didn't know you had a dog," Erin said.

"I had a kid brother," he said.

\*   \*   \*

"You know why women shouldn't be cops?" Vic asked.

"Why do I have the feeling you're about to spout some macho bullshit?" Erin replied.

They were in Erin's Charger, parked half a block from Far Horizon. Erin felt awfully conspicuous. She wished they had Piekarski's old squad with them, especially their shit-brown rusted-out van. That old thing looked about as far from a police vehicle as anything with four wheels and an engine could. The Charger wasn't marked, but a sharp-eyed crook would spot the telltales. The spotlight on the rearview mirror and the ferocious K-9 in the rear compartment were dead giveaways.

"Stakeouts," Vic said.

"Are you saying we don't have the patience?" she demanded.

"I'm saying you can't piss in a paper cup the way guys can," he said. "You can't stay on station as long without bathroom breaks."

"You seem pretty fond of female cops," Erin said.

"Just what do you mean by that?" he asked.

"I'm noticing a pattern forming here. I guess I'm lucky you haven't made a pass at me."

"Yuck!" he exclaimed.

"You know how to make a girl feel beautiful," Erin said, scowling.

"It doesn't matter how good-looking you are," he retorted. "I don't think of you that way. You're like my kid sister."

"Vic? How old are you?"

"Thirty-four."

"I'm older than you!"

"What's your point?"

"You've got a habit of getting cozy with your female partners."

"Okay, first off, Zofia wasn't my partner when we got together. We weren't even posted to the same house, for Christ's sake! And it was *her* idea!"

"What about Mira?"

"What about her? She wasn't my partner either! Weren't you listening when I told you about her? I don't screw the lady I ride with!"

"And I'm eternally grateful you don't."

"Am I that ugly?"

"Smelly and bad-tempered, too." She said it with a straight face.

"So are you," he shot back.

"I can't help the smell," she said. "That's mostly Rolf. But now what? Mira comes back in the picture and the two of you are all over each other."

"That's not true!" he said hotly.

"Oh, my mistake," Erin said. "I must have imagined your hand on her back."

"That wasn't what it looked like!"

"When a guy says it's not what it looks like, it's pretty much always exactly what it looks like."

"So you're a relationship therapist now?"

"I'm a detective. I read body language."

"Read this." He showed her an expressive finger on his right hand.

"You seem a little touchy," she said.

"You seem to think I'll jump anything with boobs and a shield. What difference does it make to you anyway? Have I ever tried to put the moves on you? Have I ever been anything but respectful?"

"Respectful?" she echoed. "Vic, you're the least respectful guy I know. You're insulting and rude and belligerent."

"Yeah," he said. "But I'm like that to everybody. It's totally gender-neutral."

"You've got a kid on the way," she said.

"Thanks for reminding me," he said, dripping with sarcasm. "I'd forgotten."

"You can't screw around on Zofia."

"I'm not!"

"You weren't flirting with Mira?"

"No! Maybe she was flirting with me, but I can't help that!"

"Of course you can! You can shut that shit down!"

"This from the model of appropriate dating behavior," he said. The sarcasm was getting heavier, if that was possible.

"Say what you like about Carlyle," she retorted. "But I've never cheated on him."

"Read my lips!" he shouted. "I'm not cheating on Zofia!"

Rolf started barking. His hackles were up and his teeth were showing.

Erin turned in her seat. "Easy, kiddo," she told him. "*Platz.*"

Rolf sullenly lay down, glaring at Vic.

"You take it easy, too," she told Vic. "Don't blow our cover."

"Right," he said. "Because we're practically invisible here. Look, Erin, I'm not screwing around here. I had lunch with Mira. That's *it*. We used to have a thing back in the day. We're working together. So what? It's not going anywhere now."

"She wouldn't mind if it did," Erin said. "I saw the way she was looking at you. Vic, I know you're a basically good guy. I want to help you stay that way."

"You're saying you don't trust me?"

"You're at a critical moment in your relationship," she said. "Zofia's about to give birth. You're going to be a dad, and maybe you're not sure how you feel about that. And I'm guessing you're not getting laid right now."

"Ain't that the truth," he said gloomily. "Zofia's not feeling too great. She says she's all bloated and swelled up, and she can't get in the mood. She says it's because of the hormones and shit. I think it's because she isn't running vertical patrols with SNEU anymore. The action's what gets her jazzed up. And she thinks I don't think she's attractive anymore. Which is not true, by the way."

"And now you're spending a lot of time with your tall, shapely, definitely-not-pregnant ex," Erin said. "And you don't see why Zofia might feel threatened by that?"

"But nothing's going on!"

Erin grabbed his shoulder. "Don't you get it?" she snapped. "That doesn't matter! Nobody cares what's really happening! All anybody ever cares about is what they *think* is happening! If Zofia stops trusting you, do you have any idea how hard it's going to be to get that back? Even if nothing ever happens between you and Mira?"

"I'm innocent," Vic muttered sulkily.

"And no innocent man ever went down for a crime he didn't commit," Erin said. It was her turn to lay the sarcasm on thick.

There was a long, awkward pause. Rolf, chin resting between his paws, let his eyes roam back and forth between the two detectives. He had no idea what was going on.

"What do I do?" Vic finally asked. "So I don't give Zofia the wrong idea."

"Tell Mira about her, for starters," Erin said. "All of it. Not just that you're dating, but you're living together with a kid on the way. Why didn't you?"

"I dunno," he said, but his eyes slid away from hers and he became very interested in the fingernails on his right hand. "I didn't think it was relevant."

"I'm a woman, Vic."

"I'd noticed."

"We can tell when a guy's available," she said. "If a guy's interested, he gives off one set of signals. If he's spoken for, he gives off another. You've been giving Mira the wrong signals. That's what you need to stop."

"I don't know how."

"Of course you do. Stop playing dumb, Vic. I swear, you're as bad as Robbie Black. Both of you are pretending to be morons. If you stop fantasizing about this other lady, you'll suddenly find out she's not that into you anymore. Like magic."

Vic looked up. "Thank God," he said.

"It's really not that hard," Erin said.

He held up a hand. "That's not what I mean," he said. "Thank God we can stop talking about this. Our guy's on the move. Look."

Vic was right. Robbie Black had come out Far Horizon's front door. He glanced up and down the street. Then he pulled out a set of keys and got into a sedan that was parked near the building.

"Showtime," Erin said. "Let's see what he's up to. Pay attention. I'll remind you how women do police work."

# Chapter 14

"You're getting too close," Vic said. "Give him some room."

"I don't want to lose him," Erin said. Black's car was an off-white Nissan, extremely forgettable. It also had a low profile, which could be a problem if a van or SUV got between the detectives and their target.

"He's gonna make us," Vic said.

"No, he's not," Erin said. But she eased back a little, letting Black get a bigger lead.

As police chases went, this was a pretty slow-paced one. But that was the point. If they spooked Black and he decided to bolt, they'd have to choose between high-speed pursuit and letting him get away. Neither option was a good one. Catching him wasn't the point; they needed to know where he was going. Besides, it was against NYPD policy to chase a perp's car through city streets unless he posed an immediate threat to civilians. The chances of an innocent getting hurt were just too high.

The slow pace didn't mean it wasn't tense. Erin's muscles were clenched tight, her hands gripping the wheel. She and Vic both knew the success of their case might depend on how well she followed Black. But Vic's advice wasn't helping.

"Speed up!" he said. "That jerk's gonna slip through that light! Step on it!"

"Damn it, make up your mind!" she snapped. "If you're going to be a backseat driver, I really will stuff you in there with Rolf."

She skated through the light just as it flicked from amber to red. If that intersection had a traffic cam, she might be getting a ticket in the mail in a couple of weeks. At the moment that didn't seem very important.

Black pulled over immediately after the light. Erin cursed under her breath. There was neither time nor space to stop behind him, and even if there had been, he could hardly help noticing them. She kept going, scanning the street ahead for a parking spot. Luck was with her; another driver was just pulling away from the curb. She slipped neatly into the recently-vacated space and put the car in Park.

"What's he doing?" she asked.

Vic's eyes were glued to the rearview mirror. "He's getting out," he reported. "Don't worry, this guy's a dumbass. He's not even looking at us. He's going into a convenience store. What do you think he's buying?"

Erin shook her head. "I have no idea, Vic," she said. "Does it matter?"

"It might," he said.

"Yeah," she agreed. "Cases break on little details."

"Five bucks says he comes out with a pack of smokes," Vic said.

"I'm betting a can of Coke or an energy drink," Erin replied.

"You're on," he said. "And the cigarettes? Sobranie Black."

They waited.

A few minutes later, Black came back out. He had a Diet Coke in one hand and a pack of cigarettes in the other.

"Diet Coke, not regular," Vic pointed out.

"Those look like Camels, not Sobranies," Erin retorted.

"I guess it's a wash," he said.

Black got back in his car and started driving. Erin let him get half a block ahead. Then she followed again.

"I guess we could be a little more obvious," Vic said. "You could put on the flashers, maybe hit the siren."

"Shut up," she said. "We're fine."

But Erin wasn't at all sure of that. She tried to drive casually, not attracting attention, but she was very conscious of all the things that marked the Charger as a police vehicle. There was no way Black hadn't spotted them. He was leading them a merry little chase. Corky Corcoran had once told her the story of how he'd noticed a police tail on the way to pick up a delivery of some illicit merchandise. Rather than try to lose the tail, he'd made a leisurely tour of no fewer than twelve clubs and bars, none of them affiliated with the O'Malleys. He'd made a point of talking to several people in each joint. At two of them, he'd gone around back after leaving and laid hold of empty beer cases, which he'd loaded into his car, pretending they were heavy. The end result had been an enormous amount of work for the NYPD's Organized Crime Task Force for no gain whatsoever.

Corky had thought the story was hilarious. Erin hadn't thought so at the time, and she was even less inclined to see the humor now.

"How do we know if we're blown?" she asked.

"If the bad guy starts shooting at you, that's usually a pretty good sign," Vic said. "Or if he floors it and goes screaming off into the distance."

"Thank you for those blindingly obvious insights."

"Forget about it. That's why I'm here."

Black showed no signs of making a run for it or of taking the scenic route through Brighton Beach. He drove conservatively, obeying traffic laws. After about fifteen tense but uneventful minutes, he pulled over next to a self-storage facility. The building was a big blue cube with an 800 phone number in block letters almost as tall as Erin herself.

"Okay, I like this," Vic said. "I like it a lot."

"Me, too," Erin said. But she couldn't go in after him. That would tip off the most oblivious crook in the world. She drove past, wishing she could see which unit was his. She went around the corner and parked, leaving a line of sight to the lot entrance.

"Now what?" Vic asked, as Erin unbuckled her seatbelt.

"Here," she said, handing over her keys. "You follow him when he leaves. I'll stay on site with Rolf. We'll see if we can track him to the right unit."

"And then?" he prompted. "Illegal search and seizure?"

"We'll see what we can do," she said.

"If you taint the case, Webb's gonna be pissed," he said.

"Don't worry about me," she said. "I'm the model of proper procedure."

"Yeah," he said. "You're the one they talk about in the Patrol Guide as an example of what *not* to do. Just promise me one thing."

"What's that?"

"If you run into any of those *bratva* bastards, don't get in a fight until I get a chance to join in. I hate those punks. They give Russians a bad name."

"I promise not to start any fights without you," she said.

\* \* \*

Erin could swear the Brighton Beach sidewalk felt different than Manhattan's. Even through the soles of her shoes, her feet felt right at home. The part of her that was her father's daughter was sure Brooklyn and Queens were where she belonged, hanging out with the working stiffs south of the East River.

Rolf hopped eagerly out of his compartment, ready for action. He was a little confused that Erin hadn't put on his vest. The black Kevlar told the dog he was working, and warned the bad guys to watch out. But his human partner didn't want them looking like cops, so the vest stayed in the car. Not that Rolf was likely to be mistaken for anything but a well-trained police dog, but that was humans for you.

Erin needed to give Black time to come and go, so she decided to walk Rolf a quarter mile or so down the street, keeping out of sight. Vic would let her know when their suspect was on his way. Then she'd be able to investigate the storage facility. She watched Rolf sniffing a fire hydrant, deciding whether it was worth marking or not.

Just as she thought of Vic, her phone buzzed in her pocket. She fished it out and saw his name on the screen. Rolf took the opportunity to water the hydrant.

"Is Black already moving?" she asked.

"No," he said. "I just thought you'd like to know, another car just pulled in."

"It's a self-storage place, Vic," she said, a little annoyed. "People are allowed to go in."

"I had eyes on the driver," he said. "I didn't like the looks of him."

"How many people do you like on sight?" she couldn't resist asking.

"I'm serious," he said. "I grabbed your binoculars out of your glove compartment and got a real good look at him. He's got tats on his knuckles. Russian prison ink, I'd bet on it."

"Copy that," she said, feeling a rush of excitement. "I'm going to see if I can get eyes on Black. Either he's meeting people here, or they're following him. Either way, something's going down. I need to know what."

"Careful," Vic said sharply. "These guys are no joke."

"I was in the same gunfights you were," she reminded him, walking briskly back toward the storage building.

"Hang on," he said. "I'm coming with you."

"You're staying with the car," she shot back. "We still need to follow Black if he leaves."

"You're not going in there with no backup!"

"No," she said, glancing down at Rolf. "I'm not."

"God damn it, Erin, I—!"

She hung up on him mid-sentence and considered the tactical situation. The storage facility would be like all of its type; a maze of hallways, all of them identical, lined with lockers. She saw a security camera outside the door, but didn't attach any importance to it. Half the time those things weren't even running, since some wiseass had done a study that showed the camera itself was a deterrent to theft and the grainy footage was practically useless anyway.

She got to the corner of the building in time to see three hard-faced Eastern European types going in. One was wearing a nice black leather jacket, the other two had on track suits. She didn't know why Russian gangsters liked those so much, but it seemed to be their thing. She'd have to ask Vic about it, assuming he was still talking to her after this blew over. One of the track suit guys was carrying a black briefcase.

Erin gave them a thirty-second head start, then followed. She didn't recognize them, which meant they probably didn't know her by sight either. Maybe, if they did notice her, they wouldn't immediately assume she was a cop.

Some of these facilities had a locked outer door, to keep thieves and vagrants out, but this one was unlocked. Fighting down the thought that it was a little too easy to get in, Erin opened the door onto a plain concrete hallway. She didn't see any Russians, nor anybody else.

"*Such*," she said quietly.

Rolf snuffled at the concrete, immediately picking up the nice, fresh scent of the three guys who'd just passed through. He started pulling Erin straight ahead. When they came to an intersection, he angled left.

The scrabbling of his claws on the concrete and the jingle of his collar were terribly loud in that enclosed space. Erin started wondering whether it was really such a good idea to be in here without human backup. Sound wouldn't carry outside the building, even gunfire. Why had she insisted Vic stay outside? Good tactics, or something else?

Pride would be a damn stupid reason to die. Erin reached for her phone.

Before she'd had the chance to bring up Vic's number, she heard a voice ahead. It was a man, speaking Russian. He sounded impatient and angry.

"I don't speak Russian, buddy," Robbie Black replied. "And relax, Yuri. Everything's fine."

"Is not fine," Yuri said in accented but recognizable English. "We have cops. They cover you like fleas on dog."

"*Fuss*," Erin hissed quietly to Rolf, calling him back to her hip. The dog obeyed immediately, looking up at her and wagging his tail. She thumbed a quick text to Vic, the two words *bad guys*. Then she crept closer, tucking her phone in her pocket and pushing her coat flap back to clear her Glock.

"I got rid of them," Black said. "And they don't know anything."

There was a short pause. Erin took a few careful steps, setting each foot down softly, breathing shallowly.

"Is all set up?" Yuri finally asked.

"Yeah," Black said. "Look. It's in here."

Erin reached the next corner. The echoes made it hard to tell, but she figured the voices weren't more than fifteen yards away. She waited and listened.

"It wants password," Yuri said.

"Yeah, obviously," Black said. "And I want my money. Once I'm out of here, with the cash, I'll call you with the password. Then we both get what we want."

"That was not deal."

"Well, it's the deal now," Black said. "What, you thought I was just gonna hand you this thing? On trust? Where's my damn money?"

"Is all here," Yuri said, with a hint of amusement. "You want to count?"

"No, I trust you that far," Black said sardonically. "Okay, you take the computer, I'll take the case, and we're done."

"Not quite," Yuri said. "I think you give us password now."

"Bite me, Yuri," Black said.

"How do we know this has what you say?" Yuri demanded. "Ivan, shoot him. Low down, so he bleeds slow. Then we talk. After, we call doctor. Maybe."

*Oh, shit*, Erin thought. This was one of those questions they taught in ethics class at the Police Academy. Three bad guys, at least one with a gun. Those were bad odds. But she couldn't just stand there and let them torture Black, even if Black was also a bad guy. She could just imagine what Phil Stachowski would say. Or her father.

Erin whipped out her Glock and came around the corner, pistol in one hand, Rolf's leash in the other. "NYPD!" she barked. "Hands up!"

She saw one of the track-suited guys standing outside an open storage locker. He blinked at her in astonishment, and for a second he started raising his hands in reflex. Then his eyes hardened and he snatched at something in his waistband.

"Don't!" she shouted, but she already knew he wasn't going to stop.

Every cop hated this moment, the split-second decision when you had a perp in your sights and you thought he was going for a gun, but you weren't a hundred percent sure. You hadn't actually seen the weapon yet. A decent person would hesitate, should hesitate, but every fraction of an instant gave him a better chance to put you down. If you were right, you had no choice. But if you were wrong, you could kill a man for no good reason.

Erin waited. She had to see the gun, had to *know*. The man's hand went inside his windbreaker. Erin's finger curled around the trigger of her pistol. She started tightening, giving a smooth squeeze. Her sight was centered on the middle of his sternum. Her gun barrel was as steady as if she'd been aiming at a paper target on the range. The distance was less than ten yards, practically point-blank.

Two gunshots rang out, echoing from the concrete so they seemed to come from more than one direction. The goon spun in surprise, his hand coming out with a revolver in it, but it wasn't pointed at Erin and he wasn't looking at her anymore. The shots had come from inside the locker. A man gave a breathless cry of shock and pain.

Erin made her decision. *"Fass!"* she snapped. He'd given her an opening, a chance to not kill him.

Ten yards was nothing to Rolf. He was already poised, spine tense, legs bent. He covered the ground in two leaping bounds. The man saw the dog coming out of the corner of his eye and started to turn back their direction.

He didn't make it. Rolf hit him like an oncoming subway train, knocking the man clean off his feet. The guy's head made a cracking sound when it hit the concrete floor, like somebody had whacked him with a brick. He skidded, Rolf's teeth latched onto his gun arm, the K-9 on top. The revolver spun across the hallway.

"You in there!" Erin shouted. "Throw out the gun! Then come out with your hands in the air! I will shoot you!"

For about two seconds, the only sounds were Rolf's enthusiastic growls and the dazed moans of the guy he was biting. Then two men charged out at Erin.

She very nearly fired in reflex, but she recognized that one guy was holding the other, carrying him, and the other guy was dead weight in his arms. Human shields weren't chivalrous, they weren't nice, but they were effective. The goon's torso was covered by the body of his hostage. His head and legs were visible, but they were moving fast, and it was a lot harder to shoot a guy in the leg than Hollywood made it look. A headshot was similarly chancy.

Erin shifted her aim up and pulled the trigger. It was a good snapshot, but not quite good enough. The bullet ripped a channel along the side of the man's face, tearing open his cheek. The sudden shower of blood looked almost black in the blue-white fluorescent lights. The man twitched his head to the side as if he'd been stung by a bee, but he kept coming. There was no time for a second shot.

He piled into Erin, leading with the body he was carrying. The poor bastard in his arms, of course, was Robbie Black. All three of them went down in a tangle. Erin's head smacked into the floor, exactly the same way Rolf's target's had.

A firecracker went off in Erin's skull. She was vaguely conscious of white, blinding light that seemed to be coming from inside her eyeballs. She couldn't hear, couldn't see. On some level she knew there was pain, intense pain, but it was waiting somewhere quiet, lurking. Any moment it would spring up and grab her with teeth sharper than Rolf's.

There was a weird floating sensation, like lying on a waterbed. Nothing seemed to matter very much. She wasn't unconscious, not exactly; she just didn't care. Her thoughts wandered dreamily, disconnected from one another. She blinked, slowly, and the white light faded, leaving a glowing afterimage on the inside of her eyelids.

She was lying on her back, staring up at a face. It was an ugly face, pockmarked and scarred, hair cropped close to the scalp. The man had shark eyes, like black marbles. He was grabbing at her, trying to get his hands around her throat. Erin knew, on some deep level, that she ought to stop him, but couldn't remember why.

His hands closed around her windpipe. His lips were moving, saying something, but she had a funny buzzing in her ears and couldn't make it out. She tried to draw in a breath and couldn't. Her chest heaved weakly. Her vision started going gray and fuzzy around the edges.

The man on top of her was only a little more than a shadow now, but she could still see his dark, gleaming eyes. He was grinning at her. He had a gold tooth in the middle of his mouth. That gold was the last spot of color in Erin's world. She tried to lift her hands and push him away, but those hands suddenly seemed to weigh a tremendous amount.

The weight on top of her shifted slightly. The man's head tilted. He was looking at something else above Erin's head. Something big swung into her dimming field of view. It looked like a very large shoe on the end of a very large leg.

The shoe connected with the man's face with a crunch Erin didn't hear, but could feel by the way the guy's whole body went abruptly rigid, then almost immediately completely limp. The crushing grip around her throat slackened and disappeared as the man was launched clean off her. He hit the corridor wall, then the floor, and lay very still.

Erin didn't want to get up right away, so she didn't. She just lay there, breathing.

Another ugly face came into view. It was the face of a Russian thug, a heavy face framed by a blond buzz-cut. The nose had been broken more than once and had set crookedly. But it was a face she knew, one she loved as much as she'd ever loved any of her brothers.

"Jesus, Erin," Vic said. "Are you okay?"

His voice seemed to come echoing down a long, dark subway tunnel, but she understood it. She carefully shaped her lips around her answer, speaking one slow word at a time.

"I told you to wait in the car," she said.

"It's a good thing I'm an insubordinate son of a bitch," he said. "You tell me bad guys are in here and you expect me to twiddle my thumbs? Stay right there. I'll call a bus."

Erin ignored him. The urgency of the moment was coming back to her now. She struggled to sit up. Her effort wasn't very effective.

"Three of them," she told Vic.

"No problem," he said. "We got three bad guys here. One's been shot, I nailed another, and your dog's chewing on Number Three."

"No," she said. "Three, not counting Black. Four total."

"Shit," Vic said. "Where'd the other guy go?"

Erin shrugged, which was a mistake. Pain came roaring into her head, pain so bad it was nauseating. She rolled weakly onto her side just in time. Vomit boiled up her throat and spattered the floor.

"Forget it," Vic said sharply. "You don't move. Not an inch, you understand? You're hurt."

"I'm fine," she mumbled, tasting sour bile and spitting to try to clear her mouth. "Just banged my head."

"This the same head that took a bullet a few days ago?" Vic asked. "Look, I gotta take care of this guy. He's bleeding out. And we need that goddamn ambulance. So you lie there and let me handle this."

Lying on the floor didn't actually seem like such a bad idea. When she tried to move, the world had a nasty tendency to keep going after her head had stopped, giving her a feeling of vertigo. Erin decided Vic was probably right. There was a reason she didn't want a doctor looking at her head, but she couldn't remember what it was.

Time got slippery for a little while. Vic told her Rolf was still gnawing on one of the guys, and asked if she'd get him to stop so he could cuff the poor bastard. Erin told Rolf what a good boy he was. In response, Rolf licked her face. Then the dog sniffed at the prior contents of Erin's stomach with great interest, but he was indeed a good boy and left the stinking pool untouched.

The storage building was pretty well soundproofed, so the sirens weren't audible until the first Patrol units were practically at the door. A bunch of uniformed officers showed up. Then some paramedics arrived and one of them came over to talk to Erin. He shined a flashlight in her eyes and asked her a bunch of stupid questions about her name, date of birth, and who the current President was.

"We'd better get you checked out," the EMT said.

"You just did," Erin said.

"At the hospital, ma'am," he said.

She shook her head, feeling her brain sloshing around. "I'm fine," she said.

"Just to be on the safe side," he said. "You could have a brain bleed."

"Vic?" she called.

"What?" Vic replied. He'd been helping a Patrol officer slap a bandage on the arm of the guy Rolf had bitten, since the medics were busy with more serious injuries.

"Help me," she said.

"I'm not gonna bust you out of the hospital," he said. "You could have something that needs attention."

"Take care of Rolf," she said. "If they make me stay at the hospital, get him home, would you?"

"Home? You mean that dive bar you live over?"

"The Barley Corner's not a dive," she said. She was already feeling better. The proof was how irritated Vic was making her.

"Sure, I'll look after him," Vic said. "But I'm coming with you until I know you're okay. So's the dog."

"Left pocket," she said, flicking her eyes toward her jacket.

Vic knelt beside her. "What am I looking for?"

"Rubber ball," she said. "Reward toy. Rolf's a good boy. He deserves it."

"Damn right he does," Vic said, and in his eyes was that curious mixture of toughness and softness that made Vic who he was. "I'll tell Webb where you are. And that Irishman you hang out with."

"The last guy got away," she said.

"We'll get him," Vic promised. "Soon."

# Chapter 15

"Ms. O'Reilly, you really need to be more careful," Doctor Mifflin said. "You can't keep hitting your head."

"Yeah," Erin agreed. "I'll remember that next time I have a Russian thug running at me with a human shield."

"I'm not joking," Mifflin said. "Concussions are cumulative. Keep this up and you're going to have all sorts of problems."

"I know," Erin said. "Disorientation, memory loss, nausea, memory loss, trouble with speech functions, memory loss..."

Vic snickered. He'd insisted on accompanying Erin to the hospital, leaving Patrol units to secure the scene. Normally he would have had to take his prisoners to the nearest police station, but of the three guys they'd picked up at the self-storage, one had been shot in the gut, one had a new set of holes in his arm courtesy of Rolf's teeth, and the third was getting his jaw wired back together by Erin's brother. Thus, it made perfect sense for Vic to stay with Erin and make sure the perps got proper medical care at the same time.

Mifflin didn't laugh, didn't even crack a smile at Erin's weak joke. "The MRI doesn't show any significant subdural hematoma," he said.

"Translation: you'll live," Vic said.

"But you've suffered another concussion," Mifflin went on. "Your current neurological state is not unlike that of a football player or boxer who's been repeatedly concussed."

"You know, she got punched in the head by a boxer once," Vic said. "Funny story."

"How many times have you been knocked unconscious, Ms. O'Reilly?" Mifflin asked.

"I don't remember," Erin said sourly. "No more than a few."

"That's a few too many," Mifflin said. "According to your medical records, this is the third time you've been admitted to Bellevue for significant head injuries. When I cleared you for duty, this wasn't what I had in mind."

"I didn't do it on purpose!" Erin snapped. "I don't go around banging my head on things just to make more work for you, Doc. Believe it or not, I don't enjoy this either."

"Listen to me," Mifflin said, tilting his glasses down on his nose so his eyes met hers uninterrupted. "If you keep this up, *you are going to die*. If you're very, very lucky, you may only suffer long-term physical impairment. Do you understand me?"

"Copy that," Erin said, looking away.

Rolf, sitting next to the examining table, nosed her hand. He rested his chin in her palm and stared up at her. His tail swished back and forth across the floor.

"Have you experienced any symptoms?" Mifflin asked. "Light sensitivity? Drowsiness? Unconsciousness?"

"No," Erin lied. If she told him the truth, he'd tell Webb and Holliday, and they'd bench her. No doubt about it.

"Hmm," Mifflin said, tapping his chin. "If you were a professional football or hockey player, that bullet wound would be a career-ending injury."

"Do many football or hockey players get shot in the head?" Vic asked.

Erin and the doctor ignored him.

"I'm okay," Erin insisted. "I just got knocked around a little. It happens. Listen, Doc, I can take a break soon, but not just yet. I've got something important to take care of first."

"More important than your health?" Mifflin asked.

"Right now, yeah," she said. "It is."

"You're putting yourself in danger," he said.

"I do that every day," she said.

"You might've noticed we carry guns around," Vic interjected.

"No more getting knocked on the head," Mifflin said. "I mean it. You deal with drug addicts in your line of work, I imagine?"

"Sometimes," Erin said.

"You know how with a street dose of coke or, God help you, fentanyl, the next hit you take could be your last?"

"Yeah."

"I'm telling you the next hit you take could be your last."

Erin nodded and hid her wince. She really wished her head would stop doing that painful sloshing thing. She kind of wanted to throw up again, but didn't want to do it in front of the doctor.

"When can you take some time off?" he asked.

"Soon," she said evasively. She was pretty sure Mifflin wasn't on the O'Malley payroll, but she wasn't taking chances. "By New Year at the latest."

He sighed. "That'll have to do. I don't suppose I can convince you to take the rest of the day off?"

"Sorry," she said. "We have to bounce."

"Medical school, residency, and a respected reputation as a neurologist," Mifflin said. "Why did I bother? You're going to do what you're going to do."

"I promise not to blame you if I die," Erin said.

*    *    *

"Doctors are all dumbasses," Vic said as they walked toward the lobby.

"My brother's a doctor," Erin said.

"I rest my case."

"You might be on his operating table one of these days."

"God spare me. Are you really feeling okay? You didn't look so good when that guy had you down."

"I just got knocked dizzy for a second," she said. "Good kick, by the way."

He smiled. "Yeah, I thought so. I don't get to kick perps in the face very often."

"It was solid," she said. "If you'd been in the World Cup, and his head had been a soccer ball, you would've scored a goal."

"Nobody chokes out my partner," he said. "I would've shot him, but if I'd aimed low I might've hit you and if I'd aimed high your mutt was in my background, so I didn't have a clear field. I guess it's better this way. He's still alive."

"But he's not answering questions," she said. "Sean Junior's a good surgeon and he's smart, whatever you say, but you broke that guy's jaw in three places. He won't be saying anything for weeks."

Vic grinned. "I could take up kung fu."

"I think your technique is a little too street-level for that."

"He wouldn't talk to us anyway," Vic said. "You know what those *bratva* guys are like. They're more scared of their buddies than they are of us, and they're full of that brotherhood-of-criminals bullshit. The guy your dog chewed up won't say more than his pal, and his mouth works just fine. Doesn't matter. We've got their prints running through Interpol. If they're in the system, which they will be, we'll have names by the time we get back to the Eightball."

"They've got prison tats," Erin agreed. "So that means they've been printed and they're on file somewhere, probably in Eastern Europe."

"Exactly," he said. "If we're real lucky, they'll have a known associate who matches the description of some punk seen leaving a Brooklyn self-storage unit with a laptop under his arm."

"Two of the guys are called Yuri and Ivan," Erin said. "I heard them talking."

"Oh yeah, that narrows it down," Vic said, rolling his eyes. "That's like a couple American thugs named Bob and Joe."

"Do we have footage from the storage security cameras?" she asked.

"Mira's on scene," he said. "She'll know. CSU's gonna take a while processing everything."

"Hey, I have a question about the Russian Mob."

"Fire away."

"What's the deal with the track suits?"

Vic laughed. "Oh, those? That's because of Communism."

Erin didn't get the joke. "Explain?"

"See, in the early Nineties, the only way you could get Western goods in Russia was through the black market," he explained. "Sneakers, track suits, that sort of thing. The only guys who had them were smugglers, or people who knew smugglers. Mobsters. So if you saw a guy walking around in Adidas stuff, you knew he was connected. It became kind of a uniform, a whacked-out status symbol. Sort of like Italian suits on Mafia guys, only with less class."

"Gotcha," Erin said. "I always wondered about that."

"I'm a fountain of knowledge," Vic said.

"And bullshit," she said.

"Yeah, that too," he said, unperturbed.

"The only question is whether these guys are working with Far Horizon or if they're part of some other group," Erin said.

"We won't know that until we figure out who Far Horizon represent," Vic said. "*Bratvas* aren't like Mafia families. It's not like there's just five of them. There's all shapes and sizes. And you're right, we didn't get rid of them last time. Fighting these guys is like playing Whac-a-Mole."

"So *that's* why you hit him on the head," Erin said.

"I just wish I'd had a big mallet," he said. "We heading back to the Eightball now?"

"Not quite yet," she said. "I want to talk to one of the prisoners."

"Are you kidding? I just told you, they're not gonna talk."

"Not those two. Robbie Black."

"If he's able to say anything," Vic said. "Two bullets in the stomach can make some guys go a little quiet. You think he'll say anything?"

"I think his Mafiya pals are already trying to kill him," she said. "So he's got nothing to lose."

*       *       *

Seen through the window in the hospital door, Robbie Black looked terrible. His skin was the same color as his bedsheets and had a waxy, wet quality like a half-melted candle. A handcuff bracelet tethered him to the bed, but it was entirely unnecessary. The only way Black was going anywhere was if someone wheeled him out. Even then, a Patrol officer was hanging out at the door.

"You Major Crimes guys gotta stop putting perps in the hospital," the uniform said when Erin and Vic flashed their shields at him. "My captain's using Bellevue as his shit detail.

Guys who screw up end up sitting on their thumbs, wasting their time here."

"Like poor Officer Ford," Erin said. "I heard."

"Meaning you're a screw-up," Vic said.

"I didn't say that," the cop said indignantly.

"You didn't have to," Vic replied. "I'm a detective. I know things."

"Besides," Erin said. "We didn't shoot him."

"Right," the cop said, rolling his eyes. "I guess I get paid either way. Just try not to let him die, okay? He clocks out on my watch, I gotta fill out the paperwork."

"This is what I like about New York," Vic said. "The empathy and compassion."

"I'm surprised those words are even in your vocabulary," Erin said and opened the door. "Rolf, *sitz. Bleib.*"

The two detectives walked over to the bed and looked down at Black, who didn't move. A few moments passed.

"He's not dead," Vic said at last. "Those machines wouldn't keep beeping if he was."

Erin leaned forward. "Hey, Robbie?" she said.

"More..." Black murmured. His eyes stayed shut. His jaw was clenched so tightly she could see the rigid muscles running all the way up the sides of his skull. A vein stood out on his forehead.

"More?" Erin echoed. "More what?"

"Morphine."

"You've got the button in your hand," she said.

"Doesn't work," Black said.

"That's because you're already full of the stuff," Vic said. "You ought to be so high you're flying."

"Hurts..."

"I'll bet it does," Erin said, glancing at the chart clipped to the foot of the bed. "You're lucky, Robbie. Looks like neither bullet hit anything vital. You've got two holes in your liver, but the doc patched you up and you ought to make a full recovery."

Black's eyes opened to slits. "Lucky?" he growled. "You think I feel lucky right now, *suka*?"

"I'm not your bitch, Robbie," Erin said. He'd used one of the very few Russian words she knew. "I thought you didn't speak Russian."

"You pick up some stuff," he said. "On the street."

"I'll bet," she said. "And I'm not the one who hurt you. That was your business associates. Ivan, Yuri, and that other guy they hang around with."

Black said nothing. His thumb worked restlessly on the morphine button, clicking it repeatedly and fruitlessly.

"They screwed you," Erin said. "They were going to torture your password out of you. There's no way you were ever going to see that money. It's over, Robbie. We know everything. We know about Floyd Shelton, Odysseus, your laptop, all of it."

"Good for you," Black said through his teeth. "Is that why you came here? To gloat?"

"I thought you might want some payback," she said. "These guys aren't your friends. Once they had what they wanted out of you, they would've put two more in your head and left you in that storage locker."

"Nobody would've found you until the smell leaked out into the hallway," Vic added.

"And they're not your only problem," Erin said. This next thing was a guess, but she figured she'd throw it out in front of him and see what happened. "What do you think your boss at Far Horizon's going to do when he finds out you've been dealing behind his back?"

That got a reaction. Black flinched. He could put on a tough-guy act when he was facing police and prison, but the Russian Mob was something else.

"How did you hear about Odysseus?" she asked. "At work? I know you know about it. No point denying it."

"*Nogti* asked me about it," Black muttered.

"Who's Nogti?" Erin asked.

"It's Russian," Vic said. "It means 'Fingernails.' I bet I can guess why."

"He's a real tough guy," Black said. "They say when he was in jail, in Siberia, if you crossed him he'd take out your eyes with his fingernails."

"Sheesh," Vic said. "That wasn't gonna be my guess. Why the hell would you screw a guy like that? Are you nuts?"

"You got approached," Erin guessed.

Black nodded.

"Who came to you?" she asked. "Someone inside your *bratva*, or an outsider?"

"Another *bratva*," Black said. "Yuri the Squid."

"I love these nicknames," Vic said. "What's his real last name? Kalmar?"

"As in calamari?" Erin asked, surprised. "I didn't know that was Russian."

"Vatutin," Black said. "Yuri Vatutin. He's a fixer. Gets things for people. Don't know who he's working for. He came to me and told me what he wanted. He knew about the Trojan and had a job offer."

"How'd he know about Odysseus?" Erin asked.

"Beats me," Black said. "Guys like him hear things."

"What was the offer?"

"He wanted to hack into the St. John's network," Black said. "A hundred grand. Cash."

"Why?"

"Something about some kid's dad."

"Which kid?" Erin asked.

Black shook his head. "No way. Not without protection."

"Protection?" Vic said. "Like the armed officer we've got outside your room right now?"

"We're your best bet," Erin said.

"Vladimir Ludovic's son," Black whispered.

"Hold on," Vic said. "I don't think I heard you right."

"You heard me," Black said.

"This is all over some college brat?" Erin asked, confused. "What happened, did he flunk Chemistry 101 and you're going to change it to an A?"

"No." Black looked like he really wished that was true. "They want to break into Ludovic's files."

"Oh, shit," Vic said. "What's the matter with you? Have you got rocks for brains? Did you get dropped on the head as a baby? Have you got brain damage or something?"

"What gives?" Erin said. "Who's Vladimir Ludovic?"

"Don't worry about her," Vic said to Black. "She's not from Little Odessa. She doesn't know."

"Vic..." Erin said.

"Ludovic's one of those Russian oil guys," Vic said. "A billionaire. That's billionaire with a B. And he's in with the Russian government, too. He's minister of something-or-other. Oh, and he's seriously connected with organized crime."

"Rich, powerful, *and* a professional criminal," Erin said. "Nice. What information is Odysseus looking for in the St. John's system? What's Ludovic got in there?"

"Account info," Black said. "He's paying for his kid's education out of one of his bank accounts. A secret one, with a ton of cash in it."

"What did Floyd Shelton have to do with this?" Erin asked. "Why bring him into it?"

Black didn't answer.

"That's easy," Vic said. "Think like a bad guy, Erin. Imagine you were about to do something to piss off one of the most powerful men in Russia. A guy who can reach out clear across the Atlantic and crush you without even lifting a finger. What's the first thing you'd want?"

"A fall guy," Erin said. She stared hard at Black. "That's why you swiped the delivery jacket. And you roped Shelton into driving you to the campus the first time he had a delivery there. You knew the police would investigate as soon as the device was discovered, but we weren't really the ones you were worried about. You didn't want Ludovic's people tracing this back to you. But this way, if people came around asking questions, all anybody would remember was a guy in a Ninja Pizza jacket. And if they looked deeper, they'd find Shelton was the guy on that delivery."

"And Shelton would be conveniently dead," Vic said. "In a mugging gone wrong. Jesus, he was your friend! I don't believe this!"

"No honor among thieves," Erin said. "How did you get him to go along with it, Robbie? Did you offer him a cut? Were you always planning on killing him afterward?"

"I'm done talking," Black said. "You come back, you do it with a lawyer. And if the DA wants a deal, it better come with witness protection."

# Chapter 16

Webb looked up as Erin, Vic, and Rolf walked into Major Crimes. He gave them a slow once-over, paying particular attention to Erin.

"Everything all right, O'Reilly?" he asked.

"The doc let me go," she said.

"Good. We've got the prints from the guys at the self-storage. Piekarski?"

Piekarski was at her computer. "We've got positive IDs on both the perps you put in the hospital," she said.

"Let me guess," Vic said. "One of them's Yuri Vatutin?"

Piekarski gave him an odd look. "No," she said. "Ivan Alexandrov and Misha Kazakov. That was an interesting guess, though."

"I guess Vatutin's the one who got away," Vic said.

"Don't look at me," Erin said. "I was holding onto one of them and Rolf had the other."

"Yeah," Vic said. "You had a great grip on his hands with your neck. I don't think that hold's ever gonna be popular with the Patrol guys. I'm the one who rearranged his face."

"The preliminary report from the hospital says Alexandrov's jaw was shattered," Webb said. "Was that really necessary?"

"Shattered is a strong word," Vic said. "It's broken, sure, but only in three places."

"How many breaks would you need before you'd call it shattered?" Webb asked.

"It's not an exact science," Vic said.

Webb shook his head. "Go on, Piekarski," he said.

"They've got links to Russian organized crime," Piekarski said. "Both of them have long criminal records in Russia. It's not clear how they got into the US. They work for a guy called the Squid, but his real name is—"

"Vatutin," Erin said.

"How do you know?" Webb asked.

"Robbie Black told us."

"You talked to him?" Webb asked. "And he didn't lawyer up?"

"Nope," Vic said. "And he spilled everything. I guess the morphine and death threats made him talkative."

Webb rubbed his temples. "Please tell me you didn't drug our suspect and threaten to kill him in order to get a confession," he said wearily.

"He already had the drugs in him," Vic said indignantly. "And we didn't say we'd kill him. Vladimir Ludovic's gonna kill him. That's completely different."

"But he did kill Shelton?" Webb asked.

"Definitely," Erin said. "He wanted Shelton to take the heat for the server room job."

"Did he tell you why he planted that gadget?"

"To get access to the college's financial database," she said. "Vatutin hired him to hack Ludovic's bank accounts."

"The oil baron?" Piekarski asked.

"Yeah," Vic said. "You know him?"

"I just did a web search," she said. "He seems like a pretty powerful guy. Apparently he's the Russian Minister of Finance."

"And his son goes to St. John's," Erin said. "According to Black, there's some sort of slush account he's using to pay the kid's tuition. The kid might know more."

"Good idea," Webb said. "O'Reilly, I'd like you to run down to the college and talk to Ludovic Junior."

"Is that his name?" Erin asked.

"How do I know?" Webb shot back. "I assume you can ask the Registrar for his name and dorm. While you're there, check in with campus security and see how they're coming with rooting out that Trojan. And follow up with our victim's sister. It sounds like he was involved in this somehow."

"Sir, isn't the case closed now?" Vic asked. "We've got our guy. Black killed Shelton."

"We've got a confession obtained while the suspect was seriously wounded and under the evidence of narcotics," Webb said. "Any halfway decent lawyer will get it thrown out of court. We've also got a larger conspiracy and at least one perp still on the loose. I want hard evidence."

"If we can get Black's laptop, that'll be our evidence," Erin said.

"Vatutin will get rid of it," Vic predicted.

"Not on your life," she said. "It's got his payday on it. As long as there's any chance of hacking into it, he'll keep it close. We find him, we can tie the computer to Black, and the computer to the server room."

"And the server room to the pizza murder," Webb said. "Find that computer."

"Just one problem," Erin said. "We have no idea where Vatutin is."

"Neshenko, get to Little Odessa and start asking questions," Webb said. "Move fast. Check any freelance black-hat hackers you know of. Liaise with the Six-Oh."

"Copy that, sir," Vic said.

"What about me?" Piekarski asked.

"You're doing great work," Webb said. "You and I will stay here and keep grinding behind the scenes."

"I hate being behind the scenes," Piekarski muttered, and for a moment she sounded exactly like Vic.

*     *     *

The drive across the East River was depressingly familiar. Erin wondered whether cops or long-haul truckers spent more time behind the wheel, then decided she didn't really want to know. She called Carlyle en route.

"I'm going to be working late tonight," she said.

"Everything all right, darling?" he asked.

"Yeah. We put a couple Russian mobsters in the hospital and we're trying to sweep up the rest of them. Same old, same old."

"Russians?" he asked sharply.

"Yeah. Hey, does the name Yuri Vatutin mean anything to you? They call him the Squid."

"I'll talk to Corky and have him call you back," Carlyle said. "Be careful of these lads."

"You don't need to tell me. I've tangled with Russians before. I'll let you know when I'm on my way home. Don't wait up."

He chuckled. Both of them knew perfectly well he'd be awake until after midnight, whether she was home or not. Gangsters and pub owners kept ridiculous hours, and he was both.

"I love you, darling," he said.

"I love you, too," she said. "And there's something we need to talk about. Don't worry, it's nothing bad. But you deserve to know. I'll tell you tonight."

"Grand. Ta, darling."

The rest of the drive was uneventful, but she paid closer attention than usual to the road and the surroundings. She still didn't know quite why she'd had her blackout and really didn't want it happening again. She could tell her doctor, her commanding officer, even herself she was fine, but that didn't make it true.

Her head ached and she had a little trouble focusing her eyes sometimes, but that might be just fatigue. She wondered whether coffee would help. It might just make the headache worse. She decided to go cold turkey for now.

Once on campus, she met Frank Wycliffe. He looked frazzled.

"I'm glad you're here," he said. "We found the device, but nobody knows what to do with it. We've got a guy from the company that made the thing, some kid named Moore, but he says it'll screw up the whole network if we unplug it. And it may not matter anyway, from a data-protection perspective, because the bad guys have had plenty of time to copy whatever they want. For all we know, everything's already been uploaded to some overseas server. It's a huge mess. We don't even know if the data in our system's been corrupted. Transcripts, personal health information, credit card numbers, donor information, you name it, all of it could be floating around out there looking for the highest bidder. Please tell me you've got some idea who did this."

"We've got him in custody," Erin said.

Wycliffe's eyes lit up. "That's great news!" he exclaimed. "So everything's safe?"

"Not exactly," she said. "He had a computer linked to the Trojan, and that's in the wind. It's password-protected, and the guy who has it doesn't know the password, but he might be able to hack into it. I don't know; I'm not a computer geek."

Wycliffe's face fell again, but he clenched his jaw. "Okay," he said. "What do you need from us? You name it, you've got it."

"I need to talk to Vladimir Ludovic's son."

"Lev?" Wycliffe was surprised. "What for?"

"We think his dad was the target of the attack."

"This just gets better and better," Wycliffe sighed.

"Why am I the only person who'd never heard of Ludovic?" Erin asked.

"I didn't know who he was before his son enrolled," Wycliffe said. "But when a billionaire's boy is a student, campus security knows about it. He's got a bodyguard with him, a hardass his dad sent over from Russia. We thought kidnapping was the thing we needed to worry about, not this cyber-bullshit. I'll take you to his dorm."

Wycliffe led the way to Sullivan Hall. He used his access card and took the elevator to the third floor. Erin and Rolf attracted some looks. Erin heard students talking about a potential drug bust. They didn't know Rolf wasn't trained for narcotics work, but she didn't bother correcting them. It was a decent cover story.

Wycliffe stopped in front of a room from which loud music emanated. He rapped on the door with his knuckles. Getting no response, he did it again, louder.

"Hey, come in, man!" someone shouted from inside. "It's open."

The security guard opened the door. A wave of music and smells rolled out into the hallway, making Rolf's nose twitch and Erin's eyes water. Incense was the strongest odor, but she caught an undercurrent of marijuana. Despite what generations of college kids thought, incense didn't fully mask the smell of weed.

Erin took one step into the room and was stopped short by a cold-eyed young man. He wasn't very large, but muscles rippled under his tight black T-shirt. His hair was buzzed short and he had scars on his cheek and the side of his neck. Tattoos peeked out from under both sleeves. The careless efficiency in the way he moved, the impression he gave of violent energy just under the surface, reminded her so strongly of Ian Thompson that she found herself wondering if he had a cousin at St. John's.

The young man's eyes roved up and down Erin's body, but not the way most guys' did. He wasn't looking at an attractive woman; he was sizing up potential threats. He saw the gun at her hip, the dog on her leash, and she was pretty sure he'd noticed the bulge at her ankle where she kept her backup piece. His hand was behind his back, gripping something in his waistband.

"Whoa," Erin said, her own hand going to her Glock. "Hands where I can see them, buddy."

"Take it easy," Wycliffe said. "This is Detective O'Reilly. She's with the NYPD. Don't start anything you can't finish."

"I'm just here to talk to Lev Ludovic," Erin said. "I don't want trouble."

Another kid came up behind the first one and flung an arm around his shoulders. "Hey, what's going on, Vanya?" he asked in good English, with a slight accent. "We got a problem?"

Vanya said something in Russian, without turning his head or taking his eyes from Erin.

"That's okay," the second kid said. "You worry too much, buddy. Come on in. I'm Lev. Don't worry about Vanya, he's just doing his job."

Lev Ludovic had an open, friendly face and very bright blue eyes. His pupils were constricted in spite of the dim light. He was stoned; Erin would have bet twelve years' street experience on it.

"Hi, Lev," she said, offering her hand. "Erin O'Reilly, NYPD Major Crimes. I'm not on the Narcotics squad. Rolf is an explosives-detection and Patrol dog."

Lev looked blank. Then he laughed. "Oh, the grass?" he said. "Yeah, nobody cares about that. It's fine. You want a joint?"

"No thanks," she said as politely as she could, fighting down her own incredulous laughter. This was the first time in her career she'd actually been offered drugs immediately after identifying herself as a cop.

"A drink, then?" Lev couldn't have been a day older than nineteen.

"I can't," she said. "I'm on duty."

"In Russia, the police drink all the time," Lev said, laughing again. "Some of them keep vodka right there in the police car with them. You know, you're not bad looking. We've got lady cops in Moscow, but between you and me, the men are much prettier. You could party with us if you want."

"Thanks," she said dryly. "I need to talk to you about something. You're not in any trouble."

"Trouble?" he echoed. "Why would I be in trouble? I don't understand America. Everything is great here, but you all just worry, worry, worry all the time! I'm telling you, smoke a joint or two and you'll feel a whole lot better about everything."

"This is about your father," she said. "Is there somewhere we can talk?"

"Come on," he said, motioning her to follow him. The dorm unit was a suite. They were in a living room, populated by Lev, Vanya, another young man, and two coeds. One of the coeds was wearing only a pair of jeans and a bra, but didn't seem to care. The girls were on a couch, passing a joint back and forth.

Lev took Erin into the bedroom. The smell in here was, if possible, even stronger. Pinup posters decorated the walls. Lev sat down on one of the mattresses and patted it next to him. Erin pretended not to notice and remained standing. Rolf sniffed at the sheets, snorted, and shook his head.

"What about my father?" Lev asked.

"He's paying for your education," Erin said.

"Yeah," Lev said. "Isn't it great? Hey, I know I seem like a slacker, but I'm getting excellent grades. All As, except Biology, and that's an A-minus."

"How is he paying for it?" she asked.

Lev looked at her as if she was some sort of moron. "American dollars."

"I know that," she said. "But it's coming out of an account."

"Oh, yeah," he said, laughing again. "That's mine. At least it is once I turn twenty-one. And I really need to get an A in Economics before he'll let me handle it, that's what he says."

"How much money is in that account?" Erin asked.

He shrugged, suggesting the exact amount didn't matter. "Thirty or forty, I guess," he said carelessly.

"Thirty or forty what?" she asked. He couldn't mean thirty thousand; that wouldn't pay for a college education these days.

"Million," Lev said. "I know it's not so much, but it's better than nothing, right?"

"Forty million dollars," Erin said hollowly. "And this all becomes yours?"

"In another two years," Lev said. "Then I can buy whatever I want. I think I'll get a Porsche, or maybe a Ferrari. What do you think? German or Italian? They both make great cars, better than Russian. Better than American, even."

"You could buy something useful," she said. "Assuming there's any money left in the account."

"Hey, I won't spend it all," he said. "I'm young and crazy, but I'm not stupid."

"That's not what I meant," she said. "Bad guys are trying to get into your accounts, Lev. If they do, forget about the Ferrari. You're not going to have enough for a used Chevy."

Lev thought this was pretty funny for a few seconds. Then, when Erin showed no sign of joining in his laughter, he sobered up a little.

"You mean that?" he asked.

"They've got your account info right now," she said.

"That doesn't mean anything," Lev said. "It's just numbers. They can't do anything without the passwords."

"Are these passwords saved on the network?"

"I guess so."

"They own the network," she said. "They can see everything."

"Oh," Lev said. "That's bad, huh?"

"It's bad if you like Ferraris," Erin said.

"I better call my dad," Lev said.

"Before you do, how many people know about your special account?" she asked.

"Practically nobody," the kid said. "I mean, I only tell a few people. People I trust."

"Like a cop you just met a few minutes ago?"

"You're a cop," he said. "Besides, you've got a nice ass."

"And that makes me trustworthy?" Erin asked.

Lev grinned.

"Let me guess," Erin said. "You only tell your closest friends, plus any hot girls you're trying to impress."

"Yeah."

"So we can assume pretty much everybody on campus knows about it."

"Well... yeah."

"Great. Just great. Thanks for your cooperation."

"Hey, you're not leaving, are you? We're going to have a party later. Music, pizza, vodka, some of the best weed you ever smoked. You want to come? Relax a little? It'd be good for you."

"I think a cop would put a damper on things," Erin said tactfully. "Have fun and stay safe. But I wouldn't recommend ordering from Ninja Pizza."

# Chapter 17

Erin heard Alicia Shelton's baby screaming as she and Rolf approached the door of Unit 118. Erin knocked extra loudly so the woman inside could hear.

After a few moments, the screaming came closer and the door opened to reveal Alicia, baby in her arms. She looked even worse than the last time Erin had seen her. The woman's hair was all over the place and to judge from the shadows under her eyes, she hadn't slept a wink.

"Oh, it's you again," Alicia said.

"Sorry to disturb you, ma'am," Erin said. "I was hoping I could have a little more of your time."

"Sure, come on in."

The apartment was much the same as before, but someone had provided an arrangement of lilies that now decorated the dining-room table. Alicia motioned Erin to the living room, where Erin sat on the love seat. Rolf settled onto his haunches beside the couch and awaited instructions.

"Sorry about my kid," Alicia said. "He knows I'm upset, so it don't matter what I do, he just keeps screaming."

"Forget about it," Erin said. "Do you know a man named Robbie Black?"

"Robbie Blackjack? Yeah, I know him."

"Why do you call him that?"

"On account of that's what he used to do when he was growing up. He'd sneak up behind guys and whack them on the back of the head. He used a sock full of marbles."

"Ouch," Erin said.

"Then he'd grab their wallet and take off. He's a born crook. Floyd used to hang around him sometimes."

"And Bode Cross?"

"Him too. The three of them got into all kinds of trouble together. It was the best thing Floyd ever did, getting clear of Robbie. Bode wasn't so bad, not after he got out of prison, but Robbie's bad right through."

"Have you seen Robbie recently?" Erin asked.

"You mean, since he got out?"

"Yeah."

"I did, yeah. He came by about a week ago, wanting to talk to Floyd. I told him to take a hike. He said he had an offer for Floyd, a good one."

"How come you're only telling me this now?" Erin asked.

Alicia shrugged. "It didn't come to nothing. And I didn't want you thinking bad about Floyd. I told you, he was done with all that shit. Robbie only talked to him a couple minutes. When Floyd came back in, he was upset. Like, real pissed off. I asked him about it and he said not to worry, everything was gonna be fine. I asked if Robbie had put him up to something else and he said no."

"He was lying to you," Erin said gently. "He was probably trying to protect you."

"Yeah, I been thinking about that," Alicia said. "And here's what I figure. Robbie tried to rope Floyd into some sort of crazy plan. He wouldn't play ball, so Robbie said if he didn't go along with it, Robbie would beat the shit out of me or something. But then maybe Robbie didn't want to share. Is that what happened? Did he kill Floyd over loot?"

"He killed him," Erin said. "But it wasn't exactly out of greed. He wanted Floyd to take the fall for the job he was doing."

"You can't arrest a dead guy, huh?" Alicia said with bitter humor. "And you guys woulda bought it, too. Why not? Floyd was a con. You'd just figure he got in with the wrong guys and got screwed, or else he got mugged."

"We found Blackjack," Erin said. "And we know he did it."

"So what? You came here to get a pat on the back? I don't like cops. You threw Floyd in prison."

"I came here to build the case to put Robbie Black behind bars for the rest of his life," Erin shot back. "Thanks to you, we can tie him to Floyd even if he walks back his statement. But I don't think he will."

"Why not?"

"We're not his biggest problem. His partners tried to screw him the same way he screwed Floyd."

"Good," Alicia said spitefully. "I hope they rip out his balls."

"They tried. He's in the hospital with two bullets in his stomach."

"Good," Alicia said again. "Who was he working with?"

"Russian mobsters," Erin said. "He's half-Russian. I guess he linked up with them in prison. We're still figuring out the connection. I don't suppose you know anything about that?"

"Me? I told you, I don't want nothing to do with Blackjack. He can kiss my fat ass! I don't know nothing about him or his buddies."

The kid had kept squalling through the whole conversation, finally calming down slightly toward the end. But Alicia's anger set him off again. The shrill screaming sent waves of pain through Erin's fragile skull. She felt her pulse pounding in her brain, like knuckles on the door.

It took a moment for her to realize the knuckles were real. Someone was knocking on Alicia's front door.

"Just a sec," Alicia said. She stood up, carrying her kid, and went to the door. "Yeah, yeah, hold onto your panties. I'm coming."

Erin heard the door click open. Then Alicia said, "Who're you?"

A heavily accented voice replied, "We want to talk about your brother. The dead one, yes? We come in and we talk."

"Get lost," Alicia retorted. "I won't even need to call the cops. They're—"

Whatever she was saying was cut off by a loud crash. She'd engaged the chain lock, but those weren't built to withstand a heavy blow. The door flew open, the chain snapping in two. The edge of the door caught Alicia and sent her sprawling. She somehow kept hold of her baby as her own head smacked into the linoleum of the entryway.

Erin was on her feet before she realized what she was doing. "*Fass!*" she snapped at Rolf. Even as the dog sprang toward the door, teeth bared, she snatched out her gun.

A pair of thugs spilled through the doorway. They'd expected a helpless civilian with a baby in her arms. They'd had no idea a cop and her K-9 were also inside. An absolutely priceless look of stunned surprise was stamped on the first guy's face at the sight of ninety pounds of highly-motivated German Shepherd coming straight at him. Rolf hit the man at about thirty miles an hour. The guy went over backwards, bouncing off the wall on his way to the floor.

"Freeze! NYPD!" Erin shouted, but the second man was a little quicker to react than his buddy. He dove for the ground, wrapping his arms around Rolf from behind and trying to wrestle the dog off his comrade.

"Shit!" Erin said under her breath, running toward the melee. She couldn't chance a shot. She'd hit the guy on top, sure, but the overpenetration would stand a good chance of nailing Rolf too. The dog had the first man under control, jaws clamped on his arm, but the other one had Rolf in a headlock and was trying to lever his mouth open. He was swearing in Russian. Alicia's baby was wailing. Alicia herself didn't move.

Erin raised her hand and brought the butt of her pistol down on the back of the top guy's head. The Glock was an excellent firearm, accurate and reliable, but its frame was made of light plastic polymer. It had been designed to shoot bullets, not to be used as a club. It was better than a fist, but not much. The weapon glanced off the man's skull with a dull thud.

She wished for her Patrol gear. She still had a Taser, which was sitting in her car. She didn't have pepper spray or a nightstick. As the man's head swung up and around to see what had hit him, she let him have it with another blow from the pistol butt. It caught him square on the nose. She felt cartilage crunch under the impact. The blow jarred the gun and it went off with an enormous noise and flash.

*Slam-fire*, she thought distractedly. The Glock wasn't supposed to do that. You could drop them out a third-story window onto concrete and they shouldn't go off. Maybe she'd write a letter of complaint to the manufacturer. A smoking cartridge casing spun through the air, a flash of brass in the corner of her field of vision.

The thug let go of Rolf and twisted around with surprising speed, grabbing her wrist with his left hand and forcing her gun-hand up and away from his head. He swung at her with his other fist. Erin caught his right wrist with her left hand, stopping the punch before it could connect.

They froze that way for an instant, straining against one another. Their faces were only inches apart. Blood streamed from the man's nose. His eyes were watering from the pain, but it wasn't slowing him down one bit. Erin was on top, with gravity on her side, but the man under her was bigger and stronger than she was. He'd break free in a second or two.

The thing to do was head-butt him, drive her forehead right into his freshly-broken nose. But what would that do to her own head? She thought of Doctor Mifflin. *The next hit you take could be your last.*

Sensing her hesitation, the man bared his teeth and twisted her arm. Pain shot up past her elbow as he bent her limb. He said something through gritted teeth, but it wasn't in English and Erin didn't care what he was saying anyway.

Caution didn't win fights. Aggressive action did. Erin shoved her fears to one side and drove her forehead into the middle of his face. She felt the hot splash of blood on her brow. His grip loosened. As he went momentarily slack, she levered herself up, planted a knee, and came down again, letting her full weight fall behind her kneecap as it rammed into his crotch.

The results were everything she could have hoped for. His eyes bulged like they'd pop right out of his head. A whistling wheeze of pain left his body along with all the breath in his lungs. He let go of her and his fingers clenched into fists. He tried to curl into a ball, which the position of her body prevented, and settled for writhing helplessly on the linoleum.

Erin rolled to one side and came up to a kneeling posture, leveling her gun. "Don't fucking move!" she snarled. "Or I'll blow your goddamn head off!"

At that moment, he might have considered a bullet to the head a mercy. She wasn't sure he even heard her. He'd managed to turn onto his side and partially curl. One hand was between his legs, cupping his battered equipment. The other was over his face. Blood was streaming through the fingers of that hand, spattering Alicia's floor.

Erin put up one of her own hands and felt warm, sticky blood on her forehead. She was alarmed for a moment, until she remembered it wasn't hers. Rolf still had hold of the other guy. The K-9 had all four feet braced and was tugging and thrashing, throwing his weight around. His unfortunate victim couldn't do much except scream, so that was what he was doing.

Alicia groaned and sat up, still holding her kid. She looked around in bewilderment. "What...?" she began, then stopped.

"Call 911," Erin ordered. "Give them your name and address. Tell them you've been attacked in your home, and there's an officer and a K-9 on scene, plus two bad guys. Do it now."

Alicia nodded her understanding and got shakily to her feet. She fumbled out her cell phone and dialed.

"Who the hell are you guys?" Erin demanded. "What are you doing here?"

She got no answer.

*     *     *

"NYPD!" a man shouted, rattling off Erin's favorite four syllables. "We're coming in!"

"NYPD Major Crimes!" she replied. "I'm in here, weapon drawn. Don't shoot me!"

There was a short pause. Then a pair of Patrol officers came around the doorframe, guns out and ready. Erin had her Glock in one hand and her gold shield in the other, holding them up. The last thing she wanted tonight was to get blown away by friendly fire.

"O'Reilly?" one of the cops exclaimed.

"Paulson!" she said, recognizing him. Alicia Shelton lived in the 116's Area of Service. Erin had known most of the uniforms in the 116 when she'd served there. Paulson was a good man, one of the best; a former Army Ranger who'd helped with the collar that had gotten her promoted.

"Who're these mopes?" Paulson's partner asked, taking in the messy scene in the entryway. Rolf had finally released his target, but the Shepherd was giving the guy a look that clearly communicated how eager he was to take another bite. That man's sleeve was shredded and his arm wasn't much better. Between that and the other guy's broken nose, there was an awful lot of blood on the floor.

"Russian mobsters," Erin said.

"What're you doing down here?" Paulson asked as he efficiently rolled the broken-nosed man onto his belly and cuffed him.

"I was interviewing a victim's family," Erin said. "Then these assholes showed up."

"And you showed them the error of their ways?" Paulson asked. He didn't smile often, but one corner of his mouth quirked slightly upward. "I remember Rolf. You want us to haul these guys to the 116 and you can collect them later?"

"That'd be great," she said.

"What's the charge?" the other uniform asked.

"Breaking and entering, assault, and resisting arrest for starters," Erin said.

"How bad are you hurt?" Paulson asked.

"I'm not," she said.

"You're bleeding." He pointed to her face.

"Oh, that? It's his."

"You broke his nose with your head?" Paulson said, impressed. "Classic."

"No guns," the other officer reported after frisking the two men. "Got knives, though. Nasty ones."

"All knives are nasty," Erin said absently. She was thinking now, trying to puzzle things out. She'd be talking to Webb in a minute or two and needed to figure what she'd tell him. What were these guys doing here? It couldn't possibly be a coincidence. But how did the Russians know about Floyd Shelton? And if they knew he was involved, was he really an innocent patsy, or had he been in it with Robbie Black?

Her headache was back, and she didn't think it was because she'd bounced her skull off a Russian goon.

# Chapter 18

"You're lucky I live in Brooklyn," Webb said. "It's only a short drive over to Queens. You're also lucky I don't have a life to get interrupted by your... what's the word the Irish use?"

"Shenanigans, sir?" Erin guessed.

"That's the one."

Webb didn't actually seem any more put out than usual. He looked tired and grumpy, but he always looked tired and grumpy. If anything, Erin thought he was taking things in better stride than he might.

"I didn't know this was going to happen, sir," she said.

"What if you had?" he replied.

"I would've had half a dozen uniforms waiting in the room with me," she said. "Along with Vic and maybe an ESU team."

"You handled things pretty well on your own," Webb said, looking around the apartment. "Who are these guys?"

"*Bratva*," she said.

"Is that a guess?"

"No, sir." Erin had spent the time before Webb's arrival running them through the NYPD's database. "Fingerprints are a match for Boris Nechayev and Pavel Trukhin. Both were born overseas. I already put out the request to Interpol for their records, but they're in our system too. Repeat violent offenders. They're muscle for a local boy."

"Let me guess," Webb said. "Yuri Vatutin?"

"The Squid himself," she said.

"So they were after you?"

"No."

"Are you sure?"

"They didn't even know I was here," she said. "They wanted to interrogate Alicia Shelton about her brother."

"Is she involved?" Webb was surprised.

Erin had been wondering the same thing. "I don't think so," she said. "But Vatutin doesn't know that."

"You think Vatutin thinks Ms. Shelton has the passwords to Black's computer," Webb said.

"That's exactly what I think."

"But she doesn't?"

Erin shook her head. "She hates Black and hates that her brother was involved with him. Black would never share anything with her."

"Then what were the Russians thinking?" Webb pushed his fedora back and scratched his head.

"It's a hail Mary," she said. "They need the password. It's worth thirty or forty million to them."

"*Million?!*"

"Plus whatever else they can get from the St. John's servers," she said. "They can probably grab some other valuable data while they're at it. But Vladimir Ludovic's account is the jackpot."

"You're telling me they've got a computer worth tens of millions of dollars, if they can only open it?" Webb said. "And they tried to torture the password out of Black instead of just paying him what, a lousy hundred grand?"

"That's Mob guys for you," Erin said. "These guys make millions of dollars and they'll stiff a restaurant on a fifty-dollar dinner tab. They won't pay for a single thing they don't have to."

"Being stingy cost them this time," Webb said with grim satisfaction. "Without Black's info, that computer is nothing but a really expensive paperweight. That's unless they can hack into it."

"I doubt it," she said. "Black's an IT professional, remember? He knows how to protect his own files, and he knows these are valuable. I'm just surprised he didn't try to get more money out of them. Maybe that was his plan the whole time, to tempt them and then drive up the price."

"Seems suicidal," Webb said. "But there's so much backstabbing going on here, it wouldn't surprise me. Where's Ms. Shelton now?"

"At the 116, giving her statement," Erin said. "She was a little reluctant, but I got her to accept NYPD protection."

"Good," Webb said. "Have you got solid people on her?"

"I used to work the 116," she reminded him. "I know these guys. They're good police... except Lyons and Spinelli, of course. She and her kid will be fine."

"As long as we get that damned computer," Webb said. "As soon as we have it, the bad guys won't have any use for her and they'll leave her alone."

"My thinking exactly, sir."

"But that still leaves us with the problem of not knowing where the laptop is," Webb sighed. "I checked with Neshenko on my way over. He and Ivanova have been pounding pavement in Little Odessa all evening. From the sound of it, they've been having as much fun as you have, but they're coming up empty. And I'd be extremely surprised if the guys you bagged have anything to say. Do you have any ideas?"

"Just one."

"That's one more than I have," Webb said. "What are you thinking?"

"There's only one person who knows the passwords," Erin said.

"Robbie Black," Webb said. "But even if we get him to tell us, they're useless without the computer."

"I don't care about the passwords," she said. "We don't need them. But Vatutin does. All we need to do is put Black somewhere Vatutin can get at him. Then we'll have Vatutin."

"You want us to string Black out as bait," Webb said. "That'll be tricky. He's hospitalized with severe internal injuries, in case you've forgotten."

"And the Squid and his people know that by now," Erin said. "They've already thought about busting into Bellevue and they've decided against it."

"How do you know?"

"Because if they hadn't, they'd be up there instead of down here scaring the hell out of Alicia Shelton. And if they'd hit the hospital we'd have heard about it."

Webb nodded. "Do you have a plan?"

"We transfer him," she said. "South of the river, to a Brooklyn hospital. Tonight. We make up some medical reason or other. I've got it! Alicia Shelton got a knock on the head in the fight."

"Did she?"

"Yeah, maybe a mild concussion. She's fine. But the bad guys won't know that. We'll move her to Mount Sinai Hospital over in Brooklyn and say Robbie Black's insisting on being in the same hospital as her. Then we make sure it leaks onto the street."

"It'll help convince them those two were working together," Webb said. "Vatutin will think he'll want to talk to her to find out what she told his guys. But I still don't think Vatutin will attack a hospital. And we'd rather he didn't, even if we're waiting for him. Do you really want ESU shooting it out with gangsters in the middle of an ER?"

"Of course not," Erin said. "We leak the plan. Then we drive an ambulance down from Bellevue on an obvious route, nice and slow. They'll think Black's inside."

"A Trojan horse," Webb said. "Clever."

"The name of that goddamn piece of hardware gave me the idea," she admitted.

"And instead of a beat-up hood in the back, it's full of ESU guys in full tac gear," Webb said.

"That's the plan, sir."

"What about Alicia Shelton?" Webb asked. "This could put her in more danger."

Erin winced. "Yeah," she admitted. "It might. Can we put a couple officers on her?"

"Good idea," he said. "I think this may be worth trying. It'll take some time to set up. I'll need to make some calls. We can stage out of the Six-Oh. Get over there and hook up with Neshenko. We'll need Ivanova too, plus whatever manpower she can scrape together on short notice. And keep the cards close to the chest. We don't want the real story leaking, or Vatutin will duck and cover and this whole thing will be a waste of time."

"Copy that, sir."

"One other thing. How do you know Vatutin himself will show up?"

"I don't. But he was at the self-storage, and I'll bet he was right outside the Shelton apartment until our guys showed up with lights and sirens. He wants Black and he wants that code. Plus, after this screw-up I think he'll want to take personal charge."

"You're making assumptions, O'Reilly."

"I'm thinking like a gangster, sir."

"I suppose you've gotten good at that," Webb said sourly. "All right, I think it's our best bet. Did you get yourself checked out?"

"Me? Why?"

Webb pointed to her face. Some of Nechayev's blood was still drying on her forehead.

"I keep telling people, it's not my blood," she said.

"You're sure you're not hurt?"

"I'm not some fragile doll, sir."

"Obviously," Webb said. "Or you'd be in pieces by now. I'd take it as a personal favor if you could avoid getting hit in the head again, just for the next day or two. My squad's already short of warm bodies."

"You're all heart, sir," Erin said.

*    *    *

It was a little past eleven when Erin, Webb, and Rolf arrived at Precinct 60 in Brooklyn. The station was doing its usual nighttime business of drunks, hookers, drug dealers, and generic jerks. The Major Crimes detectives skirted a nasty four-way brawl in the lobby between a pair of prostitutes—one male, one female—a pimp, and a squad of cops. It looked like the uniforms had the situation under control, though the male prostitute was putting up one hell of a fight.

"Vic would've waded in and cracked their heads together," she commented as they headed toward the Burglary offices.

"Would you like to?" Webb asked.

"I've already gotten my bell rung once tonight," she said. "Didn't you just tell me to stop taking shots to the head?"

They found Vic, Ivanova, and three more detectives hanging around Ivanova's desk. Ivanova was holding an icepack against her temple. Vic's knuckles were skinned and there was a swelling on his cheek that promised to be one hell of a bruise.

"You've got blood on you," Vic said to Erin.

"You should see the other guy," she replied. She'd tried to wipe her face off, but apparently she'd missed a few spots.

"What'd you do to him?"

"Broke his nose with my Glock, then hit it again with my head."

"Nice," Ivanova said with deep approval.

"How about you?" Erin asked.

"We've been making inquiries about the Squid," Vic said.

"Inquiries?" Webb asked, looking pointedly at Vic's damaged fingers.

"I've been asking emphatic questions," Vic said.

"I've got some contacts in Little Odessa who sometimes know what the *bratva* are up to," Ivanova explained. "But one of them was on some pretty strong shit and he got confused."

"Coked out of his mind," Vic said. "His two functioning brain cells decided we were trying to arrest him and he went nuts. He was just a little guy, but he got some good hits in. I had to bang his head on the first thing I could find in order to quiet him down."

Erin couldn't resist asking. "What was the first thing you found?"

"The curb."

"It worked," Ivanova said. "He got real quiet."

"So I'd imagine," Webb said. "He's not dead, is he?"

"Society's not that lucky," Vic said. "We dropped him at the Mount Sinai ER. He should be fine. I mean, as fine as he was before."

"We know Vatutin is operating in Brighton Beach," Ivanova said. "But we haven't got a specific location. People are scared of him. They're also scared of that other guy, Nogti. He's asking questions too, and his people got there ahead of us."

"Anybody show up minus their eyeballs?" Erin asked.

"Not yet," Ivanova said. "But it's only a matter of time. The Squid's gone to ground if he's got half a brain."

"He's still making moves," Webb said. "That's why we're here. Are these folks solid?"

Ivanova held up a hand, forestalling the angry protests from all three of her guys. "We're tight," she said. "I'd trust any one of them ahead of you, Lieutenant. No offense."

"None taken," Webb said placidly. "We're laying a trap and I'll need your street contacts. We have to get the word out that Robbie Black, AKA Blackjack, is going to be moved to Mount Sinai later tonight; let's say four o'clock in the morning. He'll be traveling by ambulance from Bellevue, one Patrol officer escorting him. I want every shady operator who might work with Vatutin to know this by one AM at the latest."

"Why's Black being moved?" Vic asked.

"He's not," Erin said.

Vic grinned. "Gotcha," he said. "I call shotgun in the ambulance."

"We're not riding to a soccer game in Mom's minivan," Erin said. "You can't call a seat."

"Both you and O'Reilly are too conspicuous," Webb said. "And Vatutin may have seen both of you at the self-storage. I'll ride up front in an EMT's uniform. We'll have another plainclothes officer driving."

"Good idea, sir," Vic said. "You look like a total pushover, so it'll put the bad guys off their guard."

"Was that a compliment or an insult, Neshenko?" Webb asked.

"Whichever you prefer, sir," Vic said.

"The two of you will team up with ESU," Webb said. "And you'll do as you're told. Now I need to liaise with them."

"So who did you and Rolf beat the shit out of?" Vic asked, once Webb had gone off to make his phone calls and Ivanova and her detectives had left to spread the word on the street.

"A couple of the Squid's guys," Erin said. "They thought Alicia Shelton might be able to get into Black's computer."

"Can she?"

"No."

"Figures. I think the Squid's gonna hide. He'll squirt ink and swim away. That's what squid do, isn't it?"

"I have no idea, Vic. But he wants the password before he runs. It's worth thirty million to him."

"You figure he'll bite on our bait?" Vic wondered. "Do squid even have teeth?"

"I think they have beaks. Like parrots." Erin was remembering an old movie adaptation of *20,000 Leagues Under the Sea* she'd seen on TV as a girl.

"Okay, do you think he'll peck?"

"He'll have to," she said, hoping it was true. "I'd better go wash my face so people stop thinking I'm bleeding to death."

"Keep it dirty," he advised. "You look like a badass."

"That's funny," she said. "Because I feel like a used piñata."

He snickered. "I thought the Irish had hard heads," he said.

"We do. Otherwise I'd be dead by now."

Vic's smile faded. "Are you okay?" he asked. "Your head, I mean."

"I'm fine," she said sharply.

"Say that often enough, you might believe it," he said. He glanced around, making sure they were alone. "Uh, Erin... about that other thing. You were right."

"Glad to hear it," she said. "What other thing?"

"Mira. After we took care of that drugged-up punk, we were checking our injuries and it got a little weird."

"Weird how?" Erin asked.

"You know how you can be hanging out with someone and it's totally innocent and then, all of a sudden, it's not?"

Erin remembered a moment with Carlyle that had started as a conversation and ended with an unplanned kiss. "Yeah," she said.

"It was just like the old days," he said. "It felt good, being there with her. Simple. Uncomplicated. And she was feeling it too. She said we had a little time and could go back to her place."

"Vic, tell me you didn't," she said.

"I didn't!" he said, sounding as surprised as defensive. "But I wanted to. I could practically taste it."

Erin made a face. "Word choice," she said.

"You've got a seriously dirty mind," he said. "That wasn't what I meant."

"It wasn't?"

"Okay, maybe it was. So sue me. Anyway, she said there'd be no strings, just letting off some steam. But there's always strings, aren't there?"

"Yeah."

"I didn't even kiss her," he said. "And that woman was really asking to be kissed."

"How noble of you," Erin said. "You want some sort of award? For being baseline decent?"

"Shut up," he said. "Jesus. I'm trying to apologize. You warned me and I didn't step on the brakes at the start, when it would've been easy."

"What did you tell her?"

"I told her I had a pregnant girlfriend and if that wasn't true, I'd tear her clothes off with my teeth right there in the car and we'd bounce it so hard we'd wreck the suspension."

"Wow," Erin said. "That's an image that'll follow me into my nightmares."

"Okay, those weren't my exact words, but that was the general thrust of it."

"Again with the word choice."

His grin resurfaced. "I did it on purpose that time."

Erin rolled her eyes. "How'd she take it?"

"Better than I thought," Vic said. "She said Zofia's one lucky girl."

"She is," Erin said.

"Nah," Vic said. "I'm the lucky one. I don't deserve her."

"Say that again," Erin said.

"Why?"

She took out her phone. "Because I want to record it and send it to Zofia."

"Bite me, O'Reilly. Record *that*."

# Chapter 19

"I don't like this," Lieutenant Lewis said.

"It'll be fun, sir," Vic said.

The ESU Lieutenant scowled. "Ambulances should be noncombatants. Neutral."

"I'm pretty sure they're supposed to be on our side," Vic said. "I saw a movie once where a medic said he was neutral. Then the bad guys shot him in the head."

The ESU squad chuckled grimly and continued checking their gear. They'd met up with the detectives in the Bellevue Hospital basement, hoping to go unnoticed.

"I wish we knew where the ambush would happen," Lewis went on. "Then we could have Twig give sniper cover."

"If we knew where the bad guys were, we wouldn't need to pull this in the first place," Erin replied. She glanced at her watch. It was three-thirty. She'd been awake more than twenty hours and was cruising on caffeine and residual adrenaline.

"They'll be watching the hospital," Webb said. He started passing out windbreakers that said FDNY in big white letters across the back. The ESU squad were already wearing body armor emblazoned with the New York Fire Department's initials. It was a sad commentary on the twenty-first century that paramedics and firefighters had their own bulletproof vests.

"No helmets," Lewis reminded his men. "We want people to think we're medics."

"Nobody here but us EMTs," Officer Parker said, working the action on his assault rifle. "Us armed-to-the-teeth EMTs. First we shoot 'em, then we fix 'em."

"Carnes, you're driving," Lewis said. "Parker, Madsen, Hopper, you're in back with Neshenko. Neshenko, you're posing as a cop for this exercise."

"Posing?" Vic retorted. "I *am* a cop!"

Webb handed him a Patrol jacket and hat. "You're pretending to be Black's escort," he explained.

"Great," Vic muttered. "I'm the one they'll shoot first."

"Hopper, you'll ride on the stretcher," Lewis continued. "Only until we're in the ambulance. We'll have your face covered. That way they'll see two medics, a cop, and a patient loaded in back if they've got eyes on the door. The rest of us will be in a chase car, trailing you a block back."

"That's pretty far away if things go sideways," Webb said.

"Can't be helped," Lewis said. "Any closer and we'll be too obvious. Twig, O'Reilly, and I will be in that car."

"What about Rolf?" Erin asked.

"He rides with us," Twig said. He scratched Rolf between the ears and received a noncommittal look in response.

"We're assuming they'll try to stop the bus," Lewis said. "They need Black alive if they want him to talk, so we don't have to worry about bombs or rocket launchers."

"Rocket launchers?" Webb said. "This is New York, not Baghdad!"

"That's the Russian Mob for you," Vic said. "They have access to military equipment. We'd better expect automatic rifles, maybe worse shit. And they'll have armor, too."

*Brain Damage*

"We still need to give them a chance to give up," Lewis said. "You know the rules and you know the drill. We're the good guys. Let's try to act like it. As I was saying, we're guessing they'll make a move on the bus, probably when we're close to Mount Sinai."

"Why wait?" Parker asked. "Why not nail us the second we leave Bellevue?"

"They'll need to transport Black to wherever they plan to question him," Erin explained, seeing what Lewis was thinking. "And they'll have to assume someone will call it in. They won't want to drive far, and we know they're based in Brighton Beach."

"How would you do the stop, if you were the bad guys?" Webb asked Lewis.

"Blocking car across the street," he said. "Pick the narrowest bottleneck possible. Then have an assault element come up from behind. Pop the doors, neutralize the medics and the officer inside, snatch the subject, and exfiltrate. That's why we're bringing up the rear. We should be in position to hit their assault team from the back."

"They'll try to run once they see it's a trap," Erin predicted. "If they do, Rolf and I can sweep up any stragglers."

"Any questions?" Lewis asked.

Nobody spoke up.

"All right," Lewis said. "Let's saddle up. Remember to watch your background and don't shoot unless you have to. They might deserve it, but that's not up to us to decide. But if they want to shoot it out, put them on the friggin' blacktop. You copy?"

"Copy that, sir," the team chorused.

"And everyone goes home at the end of the night," he added.

"Amen," Parker said.

*    *    *

Ten minutes later, Erin and Rolf were sitting in a black GMC Yukon. Twig was behind the wheel. Lewis was in the passenger seat. They were half a block from the hospital, waiting for the ambulance. Nobody was talking. The atmosphere was tense, like the air right before a thunderstorm.

The radio crackled to life. "We're rolling," Webb said.

"Copy that," the ESU Lieutenant said. "We see you."

Erin laid a hand on Rolf's shoulder and felt the dog quivering with excitement. Somehow, even without speaking English, the K-9 always knew when action was coming.

The ambulance drove slowly, only the headlights illuminated. EMTs didn't use their flashers unless they were on the way to a call, or rushing a critical patient back to the ER. The bus headed for Brooklyn, untroubled by the relatively light predawn traffic.

"Just drive nice and easy," Lewis said. "Remember, Carnes isn't trying to shake you. Give him plenty of following distance."

"This is just like Driver's Ed back in high school," Twig grumbled. "You even sound like Mister Puppy."

"I can't possibly have heard you right," Erin said. "Did you say you had a driving teacher named *Puppy*?"

"Yeah," Twig said. "And he was the grumpiest son of a bitch in the world. You know what the first thing he said to me on my first behind-the-wheel was?"

"Don't dent the school car?" Lewis guessed.

"Look at my daughter again and I'll kill you?" Erin suggested.

"He told me to put the car in gear," Twig said. "I'd never been in the front seat of a Ford Escort before, okay? So I took a couple seconds looking for the gearshift and this asshole says,

'You just failed your driving test.' Before I'd even started moving."

"Did you?" Erin asked.

"Did I what?"

"Fail your driving test?"

"Three times," Twig said. "I didn't look both ways, I rolled through a stop sign, and I took out some cones parallel parking."

"And now you're driving us into a probable ambush with the Russian Mob," Lewis said. "I don't know about you, O'Reilly, but I feel safe and secure."

"If it'll make you feel better, I can rear-end the ambulance," Twig offered.

"What part of following distance did you not understand?" Lewis shot back.

"Is your Lieutenant as much fun as ours?" Twig asked, glancing at Erin in the rearview mirror.

"More," she said. Her headache had subsided, possibly suppressed by the massive amount of caffeine in her system. Or maybe she was just too tired to feel much pain. She tried not to worry about it. Just a few more days, she told herself, and she could take a nice long break. She should probably be on medical leave. One more big effort; that was all. Then Evan O'Malley and his goons would be behind bars, she and Carlyle would be safe, and everything would be fine.

They made it over the East River without incident. Erin, unaccustomed to riding in the back seat, stared down at the black water. She'd heard somewhere that bridges were a metaphor for big changes or decisions, and crossing one meant something had happened and you wouldn't be the same afterward. She decided whoever had thought of that hadn't lived in New York. Twenty-one bridges linked Manhattan to the rest of America, and that wasn't even counting the tunnels. What did tunnels represent, metaphorically speaking? She had no idea.

Lewis picked up the radio handset. "You good up there?" he asked.

"All clear," Webb replied. "Everything's quiet."

"Copy that," Lewis said. "Sing out if anything looks funny."

"We copy," Webb said.

Erin suddenly remembered that she hadn't called Carlyle. "Shit," she murmured. She should've been home hours earlier, or at least let him know how she was. Now it was after four in the morning, and even he ought to be in bed. If he'd been really worried, she decided, he would have called her. But she still felt bad.

"What?" Lewis asked sharply.

"Nothing," she said. "I just forgot to tell my boyfriend I'd be later than we thought."

"It's tough dating a cop," Lewis said. "But this way you know if he's a keeper."

"He's a keeper," she said.

"What's he do for a living?" Twig asked.

"He runs a pub."

"Do you drink for free?"

"Yeah."

"Awesome." Twig gave her a thumbs-up. "I think I'll marry a nice plump Italian girl someday, a girl who owns a pizzeria. Then it's all tomato sauce and pepperoni for the rest of my life."

"Just steer clear of Ninja Pizza," Erin said. "They've been having trouble with their deliveries lately."

The radio came to life again. "This is Webb. No sign of any trouble. We're almost at the hospital."

"Copy that," Lewis said. "Looks like this might be a washout."

The little convoy had turned off Flatbush onto King's Highway and was just a few blocks from Mount Sinai. Erin could see the hospital's lighted entrance. A couple other ambulances were idling outside.

"What do you want to do, sir?" Twig asked.

"Lieutenant Webb, play the game all the way to the end," Lewis said into the radio. "Carnes, park the bus with the others. We'll debark and circle up once we're all inside. Then we'll figure what to do next."

"Copy that, sir," Carnes said.

"Damn," Erin said quietly. "I really thought they'd go for it."

"Feeding intel onto the street is chancy," Lewis said. "Maybe the bad guys didn't get the news in time. Maybe they couldn't coordinate their response quickly enough. Maybe they just got cold feet. It's not like—"

Lewis's comparison remained incomplete. Carnes had swung his borrowed ambulance around and was backing it toward the ER entrance. At that moment, one of the other ambulances lurched into motion, cutting him off from view. Lewis snatched up his handset again.

"Carnes! Eyes front!"

Then the other idling ambulance T-boned the ESU bus, slamming into it directly on the driver's side door. Even from half a block away, Erin heard the squeal of tires and the shrieking crash of metal on metal. The ESU ambulance slewed sideways from the force of the impact, sliding until the tires jammed against the curb.

Even before the two vehicles stopped moving, the back doors of the one that had rammed Carnes swung open. Four black-clad men in ski masks sprang down and ran toward the rear of their target. They were carrying assault rifles.

"Go!" Lewis snapped at Twig, who was already flooring the pedal. The Yukon's wheels dug into the highway.

Erin pulled her Glock and got ready. She squinted, trying to follow the unfolding action. Carnes was pinned in place, his door crumpled in on him. She couldn't tell if he was hurt or not. Webb was moving. He had the passenger-side door open and was heading toward the rear of the ambulance on the opposite side from the bad guys. He was holding his .38 Special. The stubby little revolver looked like a toy next to the rifles the goons were sporting.

Lewis keyed the police-band radio, sending his next message to everybody who could hear him. "10-13, Mount Sinai Hospital!" he shouted. "Multiple active shooters outside, automatic weapons. All units, converge!"

The gunmen vanished from Erin's view, screened by the ambulance that had boxed in the ESU vehicle. Then Twig spun the wheel and brought the Yukon to an abrupt halt, just a few yards short of the crash.

Erin already had her seat belt unbuckled. She yanked the door handle and slithered out onto the street, Rolf right behind her. Lewis sprang down, rifle in hand. The three of them took cover behind the Yukon, looking for targets.

Someone shouted something out of Erin's field of view. There was a rattle of rifle fire, muzzle flashes lighting the night behind the ambulance. Webb thrust his revolver around the back of the ambulance and fired twice at something Erin couldn't see. The passenger in the blocking ambulance hopped out and took aim at Webb's back with what looked like a shotgun.

Erin stepped onto open blacktop, aiming her Glock at the gunman. "NYPD!" she yelled, but he didn't even turn and she didn't have time to wait for him to do the sensible thing. She drew a bead on his center of mass and pulled the trigger.

The Glock didn't fire.

Her brain didn't process what had happened, so she pulled the trigger two more times. The gun made a dry clicking sound, but that was it.

The shotgun roared. Webb fell forward on his stomach.

Before Erin could do anything else, before she could fully process what she'd just seen, Lewis's rifle cracked three times. The shotgunner spun halfway around, the gun falling from his hands, and he hit the pavement. Then Erin was running toward the shootout, Rolf loping beside her. She saw the window on the blocking ambulance was open, most likely so the bad guys could see and hear better. She also saw the driver's eyes, peering at her from the shelter of a black ski mask. He was shifting in his seat, probably trying to draw a handgun.

"Rolf!" she shouted, pointing to the window. "*Fass!*"

This was a maneuver K-9s practiced, but she hadn't really expected to use. Rolf sped up. Without breaking stride, he sprang up and forward, clearing the last bit of ground between him and the ambulance. He plunged straight through the driver's window into the face of a very surprised Russian, leading with his teeth.

Half Rolf's body was inside the vehicle. His hind legs and tail protruded, feet scrabbling at the metal, tail lashing eagerly. Snarls and muffled cries came from inside.

Twig was out of the car now, closing in from Erin's right. Lewis was covering them with his rifle. He didn't fire again, lacking a clear target. A few more shots crackled from the back of the ESU ambulance.

Erin hesitated between going to Webb's aid and helping Rolf. "Officer down!" she shouted, pointing to Webb.

"I got him!" Twig replied, peeling off and sprinting toward the downed Lieutenant.

Erin circled the blocking ambulance to the passenger door, which still stood open. By the light of the dome lamp she could see Rolf struggling with the driver. The dog was getting the better end of the exchange. The man had a gun in his right hand, a pistol, but Rolf had the guy's forearm in his teeth and wasn't letting go. The ninety-pound weight of the dog across the man's chest and legs was pinning him in his seat, but the perp was fighting as well as he could.

Erin slid into the passenger seat and shoved the muzzle of her Glock against the side of the man's head, just in front of the ear.

"Drop it, or I blow your brains out!" she barked.

The Glock had failed to fire three times in a row, and probably wouldn't work if she tried a fourth time, but her target didn't know that. He opened his fingers and let his pistol fall to the floor.

"I give up," he said thickly, getting the words out with difficulty. It was hard to talk while being bitten by a massive, ferocious dog.

The shooting had stopped. "Clear!" someone called. Erin closed her eyes for a second in sheer relief. That was Vic's voice and he sounded okay.

"Sound off!" Lewis yelled.

"Carnes," said the ESU officer, still a little dazed from the crash.

"Hopper."

"Parker."

"Neshenko."

"Terwilliger. Webb's down, but he's breathing. I don't see blood."

"O'Reilly," Erin said. "Somebody call for a—"

She stopped short. She'd been about to request an ambulance, but that was absurd for a couple of reasons. First, they had three of the damn things right there. And second, they were directly in front of a hospital. The docs could just wheel a stretcher out to them.

Erin still had a perp to deal with. She secured him by the simple expedient of handcuffing him to the steering wheel, threading the chain through the wheel. She told Rolf he could let go. The Shepherd slid back out the way he'd come, landing on the street. He sat there, tongue hanging out, jaws curled in an unmistakable grin. Then Erin took the car keys and left the guy where he was. He'd need his arm looked at, but he wouldn't bleed to death so it wasn't urgent.

She tossed Rolf his rubber Kong ball, which he caught before it could hit the ground. The K-9 sank to his belly and commenced some serious chewing. Erin jogged toward her downed commanding officer.

To her astonishment, Webb was sitting up without assistance. He had one hand on the small of his back and a grimace on his face, but he was conscious and looked about as good as he usually did. Twig was kneeling next to him, a hand on his shoulder.

"Are you okay, sir?" she asked, hurrying to Webb's side.

"It's finally my turn to tell you I'm fine," Webb said, giving her a strained smile. "That's a pleasant change of pace. Lower back pain is normal for a man my age. As you New Yorkers say, forget about it. What happened?"

"You took a twelve-gauge shell from behind," Erin said. "I thought you were dead."

"Vest must have taken most of it," he said. He shifted painfully. "How does it look?"

"You're lucky you weren't wearing your trench coat," she said. "FDNY's going to be pissed you tore up one of their windbreakers. But I don't think you're bleeding."

"Just some road rash on my knuckles," Webb said, looking ruefully at his hands.

Vic rushed around the ambulance. "Lieutenant!" he said. He had such an open, frightened expression on his rough, brutal face that Erin felt a sudden lump in her throat.

"Careful, Neshenko," Webb said. "People will start thinking you care."

Vic stopped and looked him over. "Geez," he said. "You scared me. Here I was thinking you'd been *shot*. I look worse than you after a night of drinking."

"Anyone else hurt?" Webb asked.

"None of ours," Vic said. "We had a couple stupid assholes who wanted to fight, so Parker blasted them. I think one's still alive, but he's got a bunch of holes. The other one's done. The two smart ones dropped their guns and put up their hands. We've got them cuffed around back."

Sirens blared on all sides. Blue and red lights flashed on King's Highway as the first Patrol units began to arrive.

"Typical," Vic muttered. "Reinforcements showing up the minute we don't need them."

"We certainly do need them," Webb said. "We've got a crime scene with a bunch of perps to control." He put out a hand. Vic clasped it and hoisted the older man to his feet without apparent effort.

"Let's get their masks off and see who we've got," Vic said. "And one of them better be the asshole we want."

# Chapter 20

"This is an unusual situation, isn't it?" Vic said, grinning.

"I'll say," Erin said.

Webb sighed. He was sitting on an examining table at Mount Sinai, his shirt off. His back showed a roughly circular pattern of welts.

"Looks like he got his ass kicked at paintball," Vic said.

"Good news, Mr. Webb," the doctor said. "No broken bones, and I don't think you've cracked any ribs. You'll probably be sore for a couple of days, but that's all. I can write you a prescription for Vicodin."

"No thanks," Webb said. "I'll just treat it with Aspirin and booze."

"That's very on-brand for you, sir," Vic said.

"Are we done here?" Webb asked the doctor.

"Yes. Let us know if you have any unusual symptoms, particularly chest pain or trouble breathing. You're very lucky."

"That's the first word that comes to mind every time I look in the mirror," Webb said dryly.

"Now, if you'll excuse me, we're unexpectedly busy this morning," the doctor said. He left the room.

Webb picked up his undershirt and carefully pulled it over his head. Then he gingerly poked his arms through the sleeves of his outer shirt and started buttoning it.

"What a wimp," Vic said. "I'd swear you haven't been shot with a shotgun before."

"I haven't," Webb said.

"How much have you had to drink tonight?" Vic asked. He had on a serious frown now, feigning deep concern. "Because they're gonna put you on the Breathalyzer."

Webb gave him a look. "You're enjoying this reversal of our usual circumstances, I imagine," he said.

"Like you wouldn't believe," Vic said. "But you have to think what you're gonna say to the Captain. After all, you've been in more than one officer-involved shooting. There's this one, the one last year... hey, that was Russians, too! You got something against my people, sir?"

"Only a few specific ones," Webb said, still glaring at him.

"And what about those Colombians on the cargo ship?"

"Are you coming anywhere near a point?"

"And then didn't you waste a guy in Los Angeles a few years back?"

"Neshenko?"

"Yes, sir?"

"Shut up."

"I'm just trying to help, sir."

"Don't."

"Give it a rest, Vic," Erin said. "We've all shot guys. You know how it feels."

"Yeah," Vic said. "I was just trying to dispel some of the tension. Did you actually take either of those punks down, sir?"

"I hit one of them at least once," Webb said thoughtfully. "But he was already taking fire from the guys inside, so I have no idea how much good it did. What about you, Neshenko?"

"This is a little embarrassing," Vic said. "But I don't know if I got any hits. I've got no excuse, they were standing right there, but I got knocked over when that asshole rammed us and I dropped my M4. I got my Sig out and squeezed off a couple rounds, but Parker did most of the damage. He held onto his rifle and I gotta say, he's good. You, Erin?"

She took out her Glock and stared at it. "I didn't fire a single shot," she said. "I pulled the trigger, but it misfired."

"Let me see it," Vic said, holding out a hand. She gave him the gun. He carefully ejected the magazine and worked the slide. The chamber was empty. He looked at her with a raised eyebrow.

"I think I see your problem, Detective O'Reilly," he said. "You didn't chamber a round."

"Bullshit," she said. "My piece went off earlier tonight, when I was fighting those thugs at the Shelton apartment. It was loaded then and it was loaded now."

Vic was shaking his head before she finished. "Jesus, Erin, don't you know anything about guns? This is the same piece you used to pistol-whip the guy, isn't it?"

"Yeah. So?"

"Was that before or after you fired it?"

"Before."

"And did you hit him with the barrel or the butt?"

She thought back. "I clubbed him with the grip," she remembered. "That's when it went off. Slam-fire."

"Thought so," he said. "You must've jarred the magazine and knocked it out of alignment. When it went off, it cycled but it didn't feed the next round into the chamber. You'll want a gunsmith to take a look at this before you try to shoot it again."

"Damn," Erin said. "I'm really sorry, sir."

"Sorry?" Webb echoed. "Why?"

"That guy wouldn't have shot you if I'd checked my gun properly," she said. "Jesus Christ, I could've gotten you killed!"

"But you didn't," he said, threading his tie through his collar and knotting it. "Don't sweat it, O'Reilly. It was a gunfight. Things happen fast, and small factors make for big, permanent outcomes. They say baseball is a game of inches, don't they?"

"Yes, sir," she said.

"Gunplay is a game of millimeters," he said. "Learn from this. And next time you feel the need to use your sidearm as a club, make sure you check it afterward. Carefully. Don't worry, I won't write you up for it. Besides, you grabbed our main target."

"Rolf did most of that," she said. The driver of the blocking ambulance had turned out to be none other than Yuri Vatutin, AKA the Squid. Rolf had badly lacerated his forearm. Vatutin was currently being treated down the hall, under heavy guard.

The K-9, sitting on the floor beside Erin, stared up at her and worked his jaws. His Kong ball squeaked wetly.

"Oh, for crying out loud," Webb said. "Take the win, O'Reilly, and stop arguing. That's an order."

"Yes, sir," Erin said.

"And stop fretting over me," he said. "I've had two wives, and neither of them was looking at me like you are now. Neshenko, you and I need to turn in our guns and go through the post-shooting red tape. O'Reilly, your malfunctioning sidearm is a blessing in disguise. Since you didn't discharge your weapon, you won't have to worry about modified assignment or any of that rigmarole. You can keep working the case without any interruption. I assume the ambulance Vatutin was driving was the one they intended to use as their getaway vehicle."

"I'd say so, yeah," she said. "The other one certainly wasn't drivable, and they must've known it'd get wrecked."

"Then I want you to take a look at the one that's intact," he said. "I have a feeling there may be something in it we'll want."

"Go on," Vic said. "I'll babysit the Lieutenant."

The street outside the hospital was cordoned off by yellow police tape and an awful lot of NYPD blue-and-whites. Cops were everywhere. Erin had to show her gold shield to three different guys before she was able to get to the ambulance. CSU hadn't arrived to collect evidence yet, so the pavement was littered with shell casings, broken automobile glass, and bloodstains.

Rolf trotted beside her, still proudly carrying his toy. Erin normally would have taken it away from him by now, but she figured he'd earned it.

Nobody was quite sure how Vatutin's guys had gotten their hands on the ambulances. There'd be an investigation at the hospital. At the moment, Erin didn't care. She pulled on a pair of disposable gloves, told Rolf to stay on the ground, and climbed into the back of the ambulance.

At first glance, nothing looked out of place. She saw a stretcher and a bunch of medical equipment. Then she noticed that what she'd taken for a defibrillator was actually a set of jumper cables, hooked up to a car battery. The alligator clips glittered, throwing back the flashing emergency lights. And most ambulances didn't come with a set of dental picks, or a pair of pliers, or a blowtorch.

She took out her phone and called Webb.

"What now?" he asked wearily.

"They were going to interrogate Black right here in the ambulance," she reported. "They were going to torture him."

"How do you know?"

"Dental tools, jumper cables, blowtorch."

There was a brief, appalled silence.

"I see," Webb finally said.

"They would've wanted to know whether he was telling the truth," she went on. "And that means the computer's probably here somewhere. Vatutin wouldn't have wanted to be far away from it."

She found it in one of the equipment cabinets, just a plain laptop, plugged into a portable charging unit, waiting for someone to put in the right information.

"Got it, sir," she said triumphantly.

"Is it the same one from the storage unit?" Webb asked.

"I think so."

"Don't let it out of your sight. It's worth…"

"Thirty or forty million dollars," she said. "I know."

\*　　\*　　\*

The sun was coming up by the time Erin, Rolf, Vic, and Webb finally left the scene of the foiled ambush. The Mount Sinai doctors were still trying to save one of the mobsters Parker had shot. The other one of Parker's targets and the guy Lewis had nailed hadn't been so lucky. They were cooling in the hospital morgue, where the nocturnal Doctor Sarah Levine was doing the postmortem examinations. Yuri Vatutin was in better shape. Rolf's teeth had torn some muscle in his arm, nothing permanent. He'd have plenty of time to recover while awaiting trial.

The only police casualties were Webb and ESU Officer Carnes. Webb's bruises were more an annoyance than anything, but Carnes was banged up worse. The crash had fractured his collarbone and left him with a mild concussion. He'd be under observation at the hospital for the rest of the day. The remainder of the ESU squad was hanging around the lobby to make sure he was okay.

The Major Crimes detectives hitched a ride north in the prisoner transport van, which also contained Vatutin and his uninjured buddies. The Squid hadn't said much since he'd been taken in; the only information Erin had learned was the Russian word for lawyer: *advokat*. He'd definitely be needing a good one.

Even after they got back to the Eightball, they weren't anywhere close to done. They needed to process the prisoners and get them safely into holding cells. Then there was the paperwork; mountains of the stuff. Use of Force reports, arrest reports, accident reports, and of course the ubiquitous, infamous DD-5s.

"When did my shift end?" Vic asked, around ten o'clock.

"Five," Erin said. "Yesterday afternoon. 1700 hours. Why?"

"Just wondering," he said gloomily.

"What are you complaining about?" Webb asked. "You've got donuts and Mountain Dew. You've got a roof over your head. All the necessities of life."

"Thanks for the donuts, sir," Erin said. Webb had made a run to the local Krispy Kreme as soon as they'd gotten the Russians stowed.

Vic grunted.

"Don't be like that," Piekarski said. "It's not so bad. At least you got some action." She was the only one who seemed anywhere close to fresh and rested. But then, she'd been home in bed while the rest of them were shooting it out with gangsters in Brooklyn.

"Not the right kind of action," Vic grumbled.

"Well, I'm glad of that, too," she said. "Seeing as how I wasn't there."

"If you're trying to make me feel better, it's not working."

"Sourpuss," Piekarski said. "You get really grumpy when you're doing paperwork. Look, if you want to get out from behind that desk, we need to run the case files down to the archives. I could use an extra pair of big, strong hands."

"Sure," Vic sighed, getting up and helping load file boxes onto a cart. He and Piekarski disappeared down the elevator to the basement.

Erin's phone rang. She saw an unidentified number. For most people, this meant telemarketers. For her, it meant gangsters.

"O'Reilly," she said in her most noncommittal tone.

"Erin, love," an Irishman said. "Is that any way to talk to a mate?"

"Corky," she said. "Is this important? I've had a really long night."

"A mutual friend asked me to inquire about a lad called the Squid and to tell you what I learned," Corky said. "But if you're not wanting to know, I'll take my vital information and leave you be."

"What is it?" she asked.

"His name's Yuri Vatutin," Corky said. "He's working for some particularly nasty lads overseas, rivals of a lad you might have heard of. A bloke name of Ludovic. Anyway, word on the street is that he's about to make a big move. He's engaged a gang of hired guns and muscle, former Russian military types. Whatever's happening, it's going down soon."

"Corky," she said. "Forget about it."

"Erin, I know you don't always take me seriously," Corky said. "But don't extend that casual attitude toward these fellows. They're unpleasant and they're dangerous. Don't laugh this off, or you'll likely regret it."

"Corky, we've got Vatutin," she said. "He's in a holding cell downstairs from me as we speak."

"Oh," he said, deflating.

"But if it makes you feel better, you were right," she said. "He was up to something, it did involve a bunch of thugs with guns, and it was big. You'll hear about it soon, on the street or in the news."

"Would this have something to do with all those lights and sirens in Brooklyn a few hours ago?"

"It would."

"Is there anything else you're needing from me?"

"Not right now. But thanks. I do appreciate it."

"I suppose I'll hang up the phone, then, and have a good stiff drink as some compensation for my nightly labors."

"It's not even noon!" she protested.

"It's five o'clock somewhere," he replied more cheerfully and hung up.

Erin shook her head. She was still holding her phone, so decided it was as good a time as any to let her boyfriend know she was still alive.

"It's good to hear from you, darling," Carlyle said, picking up before the second ring.

"Hey," she said. "It's me. Sorry I haven't been home yet. Things got a little out of hand."

"All's well, I hope?"

"Yeah. We're a little the worse for wear, but we gave better than we got."

"Did you have to shoot anyone?" he asked, suddenly concerned.

"Not me personally, but some guys did get shot," she said. "It'll be in today's *Times*, if the reporters got hold of it in time. Otherwise it'll be online. The main thing is, we got the bad guy... the worst guy of the bunch, I mean. And we recovered the computer, so everybody's data ought to be safe. I just need to run to Bellevue to pick up my car and talk to our perp. Once he gives up the password, we can verify the database is secure and figure out how to unplug that damn gadget."

"So I take it you'll be a little while yet?"

"I might be able to make a late lunch," she said. "Sorry again."

"All's forgiven, darling. I'm simply glad you're well."

"I hope you weren't worrying."

"You've proven you can take care of yourself," he said. "Absent evidence to the contrary, I'll assume you're still breathing. But there was something you wanted to talk to me about."

"It can wait a couple more hours. I'll tell you over lunch."

"Grand."

Erin went back to her paperwork. She was just wrapping it up when the elevator doors opened again and Vic and Piekarski emerged.

"How long does it take to drop off files?" Webb demanded.

"Sorry, sir," Piekarski said. "We got a little sidetracked."

Erin examined her fellow detectives. They looked surprisingly out of breath for having ridden an elevator. Both were slightly flushed and disheveled. Vic had a big, dopey grin on his face.

She turned back to her computer with a smile, saying nothing. It was none of her business.

# Chapter 21

Robbie Black smirked as much as the pain would let him. "You heard my lawyer," he said.

"Your client is a murderer," Erin growled at the lawyer

"*Allegedly*," the lawyer replied. He didn't smirk, which was just as well. Erin might have punched him, and that would definitely not have helped their case.

"He blackmailed a buddy into helping him plant a spy device on a computer server," she said. "He's the reason we've got a cop in the hospital in Brooklyn."

"You're accusing my client of attacking a police officer?" the lawyer asked.

"No," she grated out.

"Then I don't see how that's pertinent," the lawyer said. "And I don't see the reason for any unpleasantness. My client is prepared to fully cooperate with your investigation, in exchange for certain concessions from the District Attorney. In the meantime, absent a signed agreement, he has nothing further to say to you. Your previous interrogation was conducted while he was under the influence of narcotics, without the benefit of legal counsel."

"He didn't ask for a lawyer," Erin said. She recognized a sulky tone in her own voice but couldn't help it.

"But now, happily, he has availed himself of his constitutional rights," the lawyer said. "I have already informed the DA's office of my client's intentions. He will be joining us shortly. That meeting will not concern you, Detective."

The last words bounced off Erin's back. She was already on her way out of the hospital room. She was being unreasonable, she knew it, and she didn't care.

"Damn it, damn it, *damn it!*" she kept repeating. She could feel Robbie Black slipping through her fingers. But District Attorney Markham was a stand-up guy. He'd done a good job putting bad guys away. Maybe he'd be in their corner. He'd drive a hard bargain, at the very least. He didn't like murderers any more than Major Crimes did.

As if he'd been conjured up by her thoughts, the District Attorney emerged from the elevator just a few feet in front of her, flanked by a pair of aides. Markham's eyes met hers. He nodded politely.

"Detective," he said.

"District Attorney," she replied.

"I assume you've been talking to the man I'm on my way to see?" he asked.

"Yeah," she said. "Listen, sir, don't—"

He held up a hand. "You've done an excellent job bringing him in," he said. "I've familiarized myself with the charges against him. Now it's my job to see what we can get to stick. I'm glad I've run into you, Ms. O'Reilly. We need to talk."

"Anytime, sir," she said.

"If you check your e-mail, you'll find a request for a meeting," he said. "It will include your squad, your commanding officer, and your precinct captain. By odd coincidence, Captain Holliday is already in this very building."

"He is?" Erin said. "Why?"

"I understand he's visiting a wounded NYPD officer," Markham said, carefully avoiding using Phil's name in an open corridor. "If you could contact him and extend my invitation, and summon the rest of your unit, I think we can take over a room somewhere in the hospital and have our meeting shortly. Please make the arrangements and let me know. I expect my encounter with Mr. Black won't take more than an hour."

"Yes, sir," Erin said glumly.

In the half hour it took Vic, Webb, and Piekarski to arrive, Erin got hold of a hospital admin and arranged for the use of a lounge. She checked lines of sight and made sure the door could be secured from the inside. Captain Holliday joined her there.

"Good morning, Detective," he said, handing her a spare cup of coffee. The Captain was thoughtful that way.

"Thank you, sir," she said, taking a sip.

"Is that any good?" he asked. "I haven't dared try mine yet."

"It reminds me of a joke, sir," she said.

He raised his eyebrows. "Yes?"

"It's not exactly appropriate."

Holliday smiled. "Then I'm particularly interested in hearing it."

Erin didn't want to tell it to her commanding officer, but she'd trapped herself. This was the sort of thing that happened on too little sleep, with a head injury compounding poor judgment.

"This coffee is like making love in a canoe," she said.

"How so?" Holliday asked.

"It's fucking close to water," she said with a straight face. "Sorry, sir."

Holliday cracked a smile. "That's actually not bad," he said. "I'll remember that one."

"I don't think I've ever heard you swear, Captain."

"That doesn't mean I don't know how," he said. "It's good to keep all your linguistic tools handy. You never know when you'll need to drop a conversational hammer. I was a street cop once upon a time. They don't stamp captains out of a mold at One PP, you know."

"Thank God for that," she said. "Do you know what the DA wants to talk about?"

"We'll soon find out," he said. He tried his own coffee. "I see what you mean. Some parts of the city, the tap water's got more flavor. That was excellent work with the Russians, by the way."

"It was a near thing," she said. "Even with all our planning, they still caught us by surprise."

"I've been checking up on Yuri Vatutin," Holliday said. "He's a very dangerous man. Even if he'd been the only one we'd caught, it would be a good night's work."

"Yes, sir," Erin said, thinking of Webb and that shotgun blast. If the Lieutenant had taken it in the head instead of the vest, she didn't think she'd be getting congratulated. They'd be planning a departmental funeral instead.

"I think it might be good for you to stop in and see Lieutenant Stachowski on your way out," he added.

"Of course," she said.

Holliday shook his head sadly. "Poor man," he said. "I wish there was something we could do for him."

"There is," Erin said. "We can nail all the bastards. We can make it mean something."

"Of course," Holliday said. "I admire your dedication, O'Reilly."

"This isn't dedication, sir," she said. "It's anger."

"Whatever it is, hold onto it," he said. "I think you'll need it."

\*  \*  \*

"You're joking," Erin said flatly, half an hour later. She was doing a great job taking Holliday's advice. Her anger felt like a fundamental part of her.

Charles Markham, District Attorney, shook his head. "I'm dead serious," he said.

"No," Erin said. She looked around the table in the hospital lounge, hoping to see the same outrage on the faces of the others in the meeting. Vic's face mirrored her own. Piekarski was too stunned to speak. Webb just looked tired. Captain Holliday was inscrutable. Rolf was napping under the table and had no idea what was going on.

"It's not really up to you, Detective," Markham said gently.

"No!" she said again, louder. "Robbie Black murdered a man! He caved Floyd Shelton's skull in with a hammer!"

"True," Markham said.

"He's working with the Russian Mob!" she continued.

"Also true," Markham said with perfect calmness. "But he has valuable information about an ongoing criminal enterprise."

"That 'Fingernail' bastard?" Vic said. "So what? We'll get him on something else, sooner or later."

"He's also willing to provide the password to unlock the device that's compromised the St. John's database," Markham reminded them.

"Which means he's holding a college for ransom," Erin said angrily. "No deal!"

"O'Reilly, please," Webb said. "Let's look at the big picture."

"People are *dead*!" she snapped. "That's the big picture! For God's sake, Lieutenant, you got shot because of this guy!"

"If anyone has cause to resent that, it's me," Webb replied. "I'm not fond of the man, but he isn't the one who took a shotgun to my back. The shooter is dead, thanks to Lieutenant Lewis's marksmanship."

"Nobody is suggesting Vatutin and his gang of violent thugs get a deal," Markham added. "They tried to murder police officers."

"Black *succeeded* in murdering Shelton!" Erin insisted.

"Floyd Shelton, paroled convict?" Markham said.

"Floyd Shelton, harmless pizza deliveryman," she retorted.

"He was an accomplice in the university attack," Markham said.

"Only because Black threatened his sister," Erin said.

"We have no proof of that," Markham said. "Ms. Shelton did not hear the conversation. Vatutin's people assumed she had some knowledge of the heist. It's reasonable to presume Mr. Shelton was a willing co-conspirator who was betrayed, probably over money."

"That's not what happened," Erin said through gritted teeth.

"Regardless, the decision has been made," Markham said. "Robert Black pleads guilty to manslaughter."

"Manslaughter? It's Murder One," Vic said in a stage whisper.

Markham took no notice. "He will be kept under guard while he recovers from his gunshot wounds," he continued. "When he is released from the hospital, he will be placed in witness protection. In return, he will testify against the gang in which he was a member. He will also testify against Yuri Vatutin and provide the necessary information to disable the Odysseus device. We'll put a large number of violent gangsters behind bars, and protect an unknown number of victims from financial and identity theft. It's a win on all counts."

"Except for our murder victim," Vic muttered. "He loses."

"I'm informing your squad of this as a courtesy," Markham said with icy politeness. "I'm sorry you're not pleased with the outcome."

"It's the game," Webb said, shrugging. "We arrest the bad guys. The DA's office decides whether to charge them and what to charge them with. We know how it works."

"We need to keep our eyes on the larger prizes," Markham said. He looked around the table. "I understand all of you are read into the O'Malley investigation?"

"That's correct," Webb said.

"As you know, our timetable has been thrown into some confusion by the late unpleasantness involving Lieutenant Stachowski," Markham said. "There's no point waiting for him to recover. We have no idea how long his recovery will take, nor how complete it will be. In fact, I've been informed Captain Rydell at Precinct Ten has received Stachowski's letter of resignation."

"What?" Erin burst out.

"We knew it was coming," Webb said. "He'll have one hundred percent medical disability. Don't worry, O'Reilly. The NYPD looks after its own."

"Be that as it may," Markham went on, "Captain Holliday has officially taken over command of the operation. I've been in close communication with him. We're going on the Twenty-Sixth. That's five days from now."

"The day after Christmas?" Piekarski said. "Is that... I don't know, appropriate?"

"It's the best time to do it," Markham said. "The O'Malleys will be recovering from their holiday celebrations. They'll be vulnerable. The NYPD's surveillance teams are in place. At four in the morning, that's 0400 hours, we'll move on all the O'Malleys simultaneously. If all goes according to plan, it'll be a clean sweep. Every single associate of Evan O'Malley will be arrested. At the same time, officers will arrest Lucarelli don Valentino Vitelli."

"Wow," Piekarski murmured.

"I hope you didn't have plans to be out of town for Christmas," Markham said. "If so, I apologize for the inconvenience."

"No, this is a great Christmas present," Vic said, his voice dripping with sarcasm. "It's just what I asked Santa for."

"Come on," Piekarski said, nudging him. "It'll be fun."

"She's right," Erin said. "You get to arrest a bunch of guys you've had your eye on for months."

"That's true," Vic said, brightening slightly. "You did promise I could put the cuffs on that Finnegan punk."

"I'll leave the tactical decisions to the Department, of course," Markham said. He stood up. "Captain Holliday will have operational command. Good day ladies, gentlemen."

The door swung shut behind him, leaving the Major Crimes squad looking at one another.

"The guy's got a fancy job title," Vic said, "so sometimes I forget he's just another friggin' lawyer. We're letting murderers walk now? Is that what we're doing?"

"It's complicated," Webb said.

"It really isn't," Vic retorted.

"He's not walking," Webb said. "He still has to plead guilty."

"To manslaughter!" Vic snapped. "That's like giving a guy a speeding ticket after he runs over a little old lady."

Erin didn't say anything. She was thinking about Carlyle and a story he'd told about himself, another Irishman, and a bar stool. Even murder wasn't always as clear-cut as guys like Vic wanted it to be.

"I think we're done here," Holliday said. "I don't need to remind you to keep this information close. Don't tell anyone outside this room. Surprise is essential. When you see the finish line is no time to get careless. Five days, people. In the meantime, it's business as usual."

"For some of us," Vic said, grinning nastily at Webb. "Some of our more trigger-happy squad members are looking at modified assignment. Not Erin, of course. She exercised restraint and didn't fire her weapon."

Erin didn't take the bait. "If it's okay, sir, I think I'll drop in on Phil Stachowski," she said to Webb. "Then I'll be back at my desk after lunch."

"No, you won't," Webb said. "You've been up all night. I don't care whether you shot anybody or not. You're done for the day. Go home and get some rest. Piekarski and I can handle the rest of the paperwork."

"You've been up all night, too," she reminded him.

"Yes, but nobody's ordering me to go home," Webb said blandly.

"That's what you think, Lieutenant," Holliday said.

"Damnation," Webb said under his breath.

"I guess it's just me," Piekarski said. "Can I at least have the dog to keep me company?"

"No," Erin said.

Rolf opened his eyes, yawned, and stretched. Then he got up and followed Erin out of the room.

# Chapter 22

Phil Stachowski smiled at Erin as she and Rolf entered his room. His color looked almost normal and his eyes were focused on her.

"How're you feeling, Phil?" she asked, pulling a chair over. Phil's family had built the hospital room into a base of operations. Camilla Stachowski had brought a couple of comfy chairs from their house since the last time Erin had been in the room. There was even a little bookcase now.

"Not bad," he said, speaking slowly and carefully, enunciating each word. "Good day."

"That's great," Erin said as cheerfully as she could. "Have they told you when you're getting out of this place?"

"Not for a while," he said. "Weeks, maybe moons. No, not moons. Cycles? No, that's not right."

"Months?" Erin guessed.

"Yes," Phil said, nodding. His smile turned rueful. "It's hard. Can see in my head what I want to say, can't transfer... transcribe... damn."

"Don't worry about it," she said. "It'll come back, in time."

"Maybe," he said. "Screwed up my motorcycle functions, too. Can't stand up. Can feel legs, but they don't listen. Probably need to put in ramps at home."

"It's early days yet," Erin said, stubbornly optimistic.

"I know," Phil said. "It's okay. Really. Grace comes after school, reads to me. I see my daughters, see Cam, and that's what's important. Not legs."

Erin told herself she wasn't going to start crying. Not in front of this battered, wounded, indomitable man. What the hell did she have to cry about? She blinked a few times, rapidly, and cleared her throat.

"That's good," she said once she trusted her voice enough to risk saying something. "And don't worry, everything's in good hands at work. I just closed a big case."

Phil's eyes lit up. "Tell me about it."

"There's this tech company that developed a piece of spy equipment," she said. "If you plug it into a computer, it worms itself into the database and gives remote access to the hacker. You can't unplug it without the right code, or it fries the network."

"Sounds... illegal," Phil said.

"Depends on what you do with it," Erin said. "I bet the NSA and CIA would love to have it. Anyway, the problem was, one of the investors in the company was a front for the Russian Mob. Word got down to one of their little guys, an ex-con named Black. He'd learned computers in prison and figured he could use this thing to make a quick buck.

"He talked to a rival Russian organization and made a deal with them. He'd give them access to account information for this Russian billionaire. His way in was through the billionaire's son's college database. See, he was using the kid's trust account to pay his tuition and other expenses.

"Black knew how to steal the device. But he figured he couldn't just walk into the campus server room and plant the thing. Word would eventually get back to Vladimir Ludovic, and that guy's not just rich. He's powerful and he's dangerous. So Black needed someone to take the fall for him.

"He thought of an old accomplice, Floyd Shelton, who'd recently gotten out of prison. Shelton was working as a deliveryman for a pizzeria that's run by another ex-con who likes giving parolees a chance. Black approached Shelton, but Shelton didn't want any part of it.

"Gangsters don't like to take 'no' for an answer. Black threatened Shelton's sister, and Shelton went along with it. He wasn't really doing anything bad, after all; just delivering a pizza the way he was supposed to. What he didn't know was that Black was impersonating him while he committed a crime, wearing a Ninja Pizza jacket and a hat to make it hard for cameras to ID him. Black broke into the server room, planted the device, and got out.

"Maybe he always meant to kill Shelton. Maybe they had a fight. I don't know, and it doesn't matter. Either way, Black knew Shelton was a liability as long as he was alive, so he killed him and left him in his truck, hoping it would look like a garden-variety mugging. Then, when Ludovic's guys—or the NYPD, for that matter—came looking, they'd find a dead end.

"But Black's cronies double-crossed him, which was no more than he deserved. Instead of a briefcase full of cash, all he got was two bullets in the gut. They would've killed him if Vic, Rolf, and I hadn't intervened. Black's partner, Yuri the Squid, got away with Black's computer, but couldn't unlock the files.

"We knew that, so we laid a trap for Yuri and he fell into it. ESU nailed the Squid and his goons, we got the computer, and as soon as the DA finishes making his bullshit deal with Black, we're home free."

Phil nodded. "And the other thing?" he asked quietly.

"We're on the homestretch," Erin said, leaning forward. "I'm not supposed to say exactly when it's happening, but we're just days away. By New Year's, it'll all be over."

"You okay?" he asked.

"Of course I am," she said, her hand reflexively coming up to touch the scab on the side of her scalp.

"Not talking about injury," he said. "I mean you. Inside. Now it's almost over. It's... pipe wrench? Damn. Not what I meant. When you need to change something."

"An adjustment?"

"Yes." He nodded. "Big one. It'll be different."

"I know," she said. "But as long as Carlyle and I come through okay, we'll be fine. It'll be great to be able to breathe again. I'm getting tired of checking under my car for bombs."

"Might want to keep doing that," he said. "A little while, at least. We think we'll get all of them, but might miss a couple little guys."

"A cop's always got enemies." Erin said it lightly, but she felt something twist inside her.

"You'll tell me?" he said. "When it's over?"

"Absolutely," she promised. "We'll have a party right here in your room. I'm talking booze, cake, the works."

His smile was gentle but genuine. "You deserve it," he said.

"No, Phil," she said. "You do."

Those damned tears were back again, threatening to choke her. She squeezed his hand. "Take care of yourself," she said.

"Back at you, Erin," Phil said.

*       *       *

It was well past noon when Erin and Rolf finally got back to the Barley Corner. Erin had called Carlyle when she left the hospital, so he'd had a little warning. He was waiting for her upstairs with a big bowl of Irish stew, a basket of fresh oatbread rolls, and a pint of Guinness.

"Careful," she said. "I might think you're trying to seduce me. Sorry I'm so late."

He helped her into her chair. "What would our Ian say? It's not a problem, ma'am."

She made a face. "Please don't call me ma'am."

"Is everything sorted?" he asked, taking his own seat and passing the rolls.

"Yeah," she sighed. "But it got messy."

"So I understand. Your lads aren't too badly hurt, I hope?"

"They'll mend." Between mouthfuls, she explained what had happened. Carlyle listened attentively, asking only a few questions.

"And yourself?" he asked when she finished.

"I'll be okay."

His eyes narrowed slightly. "Meaning you aren't at this particular moment?"

"I'm just tired. And maybe a little scrambled."

"The bullet?" he asked, nodding toward her scalp wound.

"Yeah. I thought it was nothing, but I'm a little... off."

"You need to tell your physician," he said.

"I will," she said. "After."

"After what?"

"The arrests. I can't sit on the sidelines yet."

"How much longer?" he asked.

"Soon," she said.

"That's no answer at all. I'm worried about you, darling. How long?"

"The Captain said not to tell anyone," she said.

"And you're thinking I'll spill something to Evan?" Carlyle retorted. "I've been keeping your secrets a sight longer than Holliday has."

"Okay," Erin said. "But nobody else hears this, you get me? *Nobody*. Not Corky, not even Ian."

He nodded.

"And you can't be one bit different," she went on. "No matter what happens."

"Mum's the word," he said.

"Boxing Day," she said quietly. "The Twenty-Sixth. In the morning, early."

"Will they be taking me along with the others?" he asked.

"Yeah. To keep up appearances to the last minute, and to keep you safe."

Carlyle nodded again. "Very well. Five days. Then you go back for all manner of tests. I'll not be losing you, darling."

"You're not going to lose me," she said. "I'm okay, I swear. It's just headaches and a little blurriness."

"That's as may be," he said. "Have you given thought to what comes after?"

"Oh, God," she said. "Not you, too. I've already had this talk with Webb, and again with Captain Holliday. I don't want to be Commissioner, I don't want my own precinct, they don't even have to give me a damn medal. I just want to keep doing my job, with my dog and my squad."

"And what about that fine Irishman you've been keeping time with?"

She smiled. "I hope we'll stay together and see where it goes. Hopefully somewhere without quite so many bullets flying around."

"I'll drink to that," he said, taking a sip of Guinness. "But your dog won't be working forever. How long's he been running with you?"

"A little less than five years," Erin said.

"And how long is the typical career of a lad like Rolf?"

Erin didn't need to look up the number. They'd told her in handler training and she knew it by heart. "Seven to nine years," she said. "If everything goes well."

"Would you say Rolf's had a typical career thus far?"

"No," she admitted. "He's had a rougher ride than most. He's been shot a couple times, Tased, and beat up. Mickey Connor gave him a pretty good knock on the head and broke a few ribs. He's lucky to still be alive, let alone working. But I can't ask him to stop. He loves the Job, lives for it, just like me. It'd break his heart."

"Nonetheless, the day's coming when he won't be able to keep up with you," Carlyle said gently. "What happens then?"

"He retires," Erin said. "He becomes a couch potato and lives with me. I'll pay the Department a dollar, since he's technically a piece of NYPD equipment. It wouldn't be legal to just give him to me."

"And what will you do?"

"Spoil him rotten, of course." She reached down under the table and scratched Rolf's ears.

"I meant as regards your own career."

"Oh." She shrugged. "I don't know. I haven't given it much thought."

"It might be wise to put your mind to it, before it becomes pressing," he said. "You're happy as a detective, I know, but your circumstances may change."

"What do you mean?" she asked.

He smiled thinly. "What I said."

Erin scowled. "If you think you can yank me around just because you bought me lunch..."

Carlyle's phone rang. He held up a placating hand and answered. "Aye?"

There was a short pause. Carlyle listened.

"Thank you, lad," he said. "We'll be down directly. Nay, there's no cause for alarm. But you'd best keep an eye on them, just in case."

He put the phone away.

"What's that all about?" Erin asked.

"Ian, downstairs," Carlyle said. "A pair of rather suspicious lads have shown up asking for you. Russians, he thinks."

"Russians?" she echoed, springing to her feet and dropping a hand to her Glock. "Shit, I need to get this thing fixed. Why don't you have guns?"

"It's illegal, darling," he said. "And surely you're worrying needlessly. They'll not try anything here, and if they do, Ian will handle it. He's armed, you'll recall."

"Yeah, I remember," she said grimly, kneeling and pulling her snub-nosed .38 from its ankle clip. She put the gun in the right-hand pocket of her leather jacket, within easy reach. "But I'd prefer to be prepared. If these are some of the Squid's guys, you don't know what they might do."

"If you'd prefer not to talk to them...?" Carlyle prompted.

"No way," Erin said. "This is my home, and your pub. I'm going down to see what these assholes want, and they'd better be goddamned polite or they're going out through the window."

"Please don't go throwing lads out my windows," Carlyle said with a pained expression. "Plate glass is expensive."

"That'll be up to them," she growled.

# Chapter 23

Erin was thinking like Ian as she went down the stairs. She pictured the layout of the Barley Corner, envisioning fields of fire, good cover, and possible exits. She'd have Ian and at least one of his guys for backup, plus whatever O'Malley goons might happen to be having a late lunch. Some of them would be armed. It was weird to think of them as allies, when in less than a week they'd all be in jail cells because of her, but that was undercover work for you.

Ian had said there were only two Russians. That wasn't so bad, even if they'd brought automatic weapons. And she couldn't see Ian being so calm about it if they were carrying AK-47s. She wondered who they were working for. The NYPD had taken care of Vatutin's best shooters. Nogti, Black's boss at Far Horizon? But what would he want with Erin? If he was smart, he was either hiding or running for his life. She didn't think he'd be crazy enough to make a suicide run at an NYPD detective.

She slipped a hand into her pocket and took hold of the .38. Rolf was at her side, ready for action. Carlyle was two steps behind her, calm but alert. She took a deep breath and opened the door.

The pub was sparsely populated. Three guys sat at the bar, drinking beer and eating sandwiches. Two more were sitting in a booth, one of whom appeared to be asleep. Ian Thompson had chosen a position along the far wall. His backup man, another former Marine named Ken Mason, had picked a spot near the front door. Between them, they had their guests in a perfect crossfire position, though neither man had drawn a weapon.

The Russians weren't what Erin had expected. They were clad in expensive-looking suits and topcoats. The one on the right looked like some sort of businessman, maybe a CPA, and was probably in his mid-forties. The one on the left, younger and more muscular, sported a military-style buzz cut and held a briefcase in his left hand. The briefcase was handcuffed to his wrist. Both men had Bluetooth earpieces.

The older man stepped forward. "Ms. O'Reilly?" he said.

"That's me," Erin said cautiously. She was watching their hands. Hands were the thing that would hurt you.

"It is my great pleasure to meet you," he said with a thick accent but excellent diction, extending an empty hand. "Pyotr Ozerov."

"How's it going?" Erin replied, risking taking her hand out of her pocket to shake his. Ian and Mason were watching, she reminded herself. They wouldn't let these guys try anything.

"My business is proceeding well," Ozerov said. "I apologize for disturbing you, but I have urgent business. I have come directly from the airport."

"Airport?" Erin repeated, confused.

"John Fitzgerald Kennedy International Airport, to be precise," Ozerov said. "My colleague and I flew from Moscow by the first available aircraft. We arrived only a short while ago. And you would be, sir?"

"Morton Carlyle," Carlyle said. "I'm the proprietor of this establishment, and I welcome you to it. You must be thirsty after so long a journey. Would you care for a fine beverage? I've several grand varieties of vodka."

"Once we have concluded our business, it would be my honor to drink with you," Ozerov said.

"And just what is your business, Mr. Ozerov?" Erin asked.

"Maxim?" Ozerov said, gesturing to his comrade. The other Russian stepped forward. He laid the briefcase on the bar. Ozerov reached into a pocket and took out a pair of keys. One key unfastened the bracelet on Maxim's handcuff, the other unlocked the case itself.

Erin stood back. She remembered another case, on this very bar, that had contained an explosive device. Rolf hadn't alerted to the presence of a bomb this time, but that didn't mean it was safe.

Ozerov raised the lid. Nothing exploded. Erin took a careful step closer and peered inside.

A dozen copies of Benjamin Franklin's face stared back at her from twelve stacks of hundred-dollar bills, green and crisp, three wide by four deep. Bank straps were wrapped around each stack, as if they'd come straight from the Federal Reserve vaults.

"What the hell is this?" she blurted, surprise getting the better of etiquette.

"A small gesture of my employer's appreciation," Ozerov said. "I am to deliver it, with his personal thanks."

"And who, exactly, is your employer?" Carlyle asked. Erin had temporarily lost the power of speech.

"Mr. Ludovic," Ozerov said, seeming surprised by the question. "He requested I deliver this into your personal possession, Ms. O'Reilly. I have now done so, and my orders are fulfilled."

"What am I supposed to do with this?" Erin demanded, recovering slightly.

Ozerov smiled politely. "Whatever you wish, Ms. O'Reilly," he said. "I believe spending it is customary. Now, I would very much enjoy sampling one of your excellent vodkas, Mr. Carlyle. Which would you recommend?"

"The Grey Goose is popular," Carlyle said. "But I'd personally recommend the Chopin Family Reserve. Matt, if you'd get a bottle of the Chopin and four glasses, please?"

"On the way, boss." The Corner's daytime bartender laid out four shot glasses and a pricy bottle of clear liquor.

"On the house, gentlemen," Carlyle said as Matt opened the bottle and filled the glasses.

Erin tossed back her drink. The vodka slid down smooth. It was too bad Vic wasn't here, she thought. He'd appreciate good vodka more than she did. Ozerov and Maxim drained their glasses just as fast. Carlyle sipped his more slowly.

"Perhaps one more," Ozerov said. He raised his glass. "I toast the New York Police Department and its excellent detectives, who have worked so hard to safeguard my employer's interests and his son's future."

Numbly, Erin hoisted her own glass and clinked it. She kept looking at the briefcase, as if it would sprout legs and scuttle away.

The Russians finished their drinks and left. Maxim favored Ian with a professional nod on the way out, which Ian returned. Erin wondered which man would win in a fight. She decided she'd put her money on Ian, but not by much.

"Let's take this upstairs," Carlyle suggested. "Once we've counted it, we'll decide what's to be done with it."

\*     \*     \*

"Twenty-four stacks of a hundred bills each," Erin said, a short while later. They were in Carlyle's office. The briefcase lay on his desk. The money was piled beside it.

"At one hundred dollars per bill, that's two hundred forty thousand dollars," Carlyle said.

"Jesus Christ," Erin said. "And I let them leave that on the bar and walk out? I can't accept this."

"I rather think you already did."

"No, I can't! There's rules about this sort of thing!"

"You didn't do anything for your own benefit, darling," he said.

"That doesn't matter," Erin said. "It's the appearance of it. How many times have you told me it doesn't matter what really happened? What matters is what it *looks* like, and if I keep this, it looks like I was a hired gun for a Russian billionaire! Why'd he have to do this?"

"It's my opinion he believes you did him a great service," Carlyle said.

"Then he can send me a thank-you note at Christmas," she said. She ran a hand through her hair and stared at the pile of cash. "Seriously, what can I do with this?"

"Make a down payment on a house in the Hamptons?" he suggested, a twinkle in his eye.

"You've already got one," she said.

"Hardly," he said. "That house belongs to Evan O'Malley, and I expect it'll be seized when he's arrested. The same with that place in the Bahamas, if they can finagle it with the local authorities. It's a pity. I did enjoy the place."

"Quit screwing around," Erin said. "I'm serious. I'll have to turn it in."

"Of course you will," he said. "I'd expect no less from you. You're incorruptible."

"I'm crazy is what I am," she muttered. "Three years' pay, tax-free, and I'm throwing it away. I ought to have my head examined."

"And you will," he said, taking her by the shoulders. "I'm worried about you, darling. Not for the money. For your health. I don't want you keeling over on me."

"All right, all right," Erin said. "This really isn't a big deal."

"Erin, my first wife died," Carlyle said quietly. "Don't put me through that again, I'm begging you."

"I'll do my best," she said. "I'm pretty hard to kill. It'll take more than a bullet to the skull to put me down, especially while Evan and his boys are still running around. Five more days, that's all."

"Five days," he agreed. "That's not so long."

Erin nodded, but a thought crawled out of some dark corner of her mind. She didn't say it, and hoped Carlyle couldn't read it in her eyes.

An awful lot could happen in five days.

# Here's a sneak peek from Book 25: Celtic Twilight

# Coming 9/23/2024

"The Captain wants everyone in position by two-thirty at the absolute latest," Webb said when Erin and Rolf came back downstairs.

"That means we'd better be streetside by two," Vic said. "Just in case."

"I still think I ought to come," Piekarski said.

"And I'll remind you once again, Officer Piekarski, that your temporary assignment to Major Crimes is for medical reasons," Webb said.

"Not just medical," Piekarski said. "I'm getting experience for when I get my gold shield. Besides, I'm not due until March."

"This isn't up for discussion," Webb said. "And this isn't a democracy, so while I'll listen to your opinions, they carry exactly as much weight as I want them to and no more."

"We need someone in the office manning the phones," Erin said, trying to soften the order. "If anything unexpected happens, you may need to coordinate a response."

"Yeah," Vic said. "The Captain's gonna be on the street, same as the rest of us."

"So you're saying an old fogey like Holliday can run around busting bad guys, but because I got knocked up I have to sit here and play house," Piekarski said, pouting. "What about Vic? He's as responsible for this as I am."

"I'd leave Neshenko, but he hasn't been housebroken," Webb said, deadpan.

Vic had his Sig-Sauer automatic field-stripped on his desk. He was cleaning the pistol and pretended not to hear Webb. "Hey, Erin?" he said.

"Yeah?"

"You ever get your Glock fixed? Remember how it misfired last time you needed it?"

"I'm not likely to forget," she said. "I got a new one from the armory."

"Did you test-fire it?" Vic asked. "You know, even with the same make of pistol, there's little differences that can screw with you if you're not used to the new piece."

"I took it on the range," she said. "Relax."

"When's the last time you cleaned and oiled it?"

"Vic!"

"What?"

"Stop it."

"Stop what?"

"Fretting. You sound like my mom on my first day of grade school."

Vic blinked. "Your mom double-checked your guns before putting you on the bus? Jesus, where'd you go to school?"

"Don't worry about him," Piekarski said to Erin. "He gets like this when he's nervous."

"Who says I'm nervous?" Vic snapped. "I used to kick down doors with ESU every damn day. I just don't want anything to go wrong."

"Nothing's going to go wrong," Webb said.

The others all stared at their commanding officer in horrified disbelief.

"Please tell me he did not just say that," Vic muttered.

"I'll handle the O'Malley arrest in person," Webb said, ignoring their superstitious reaction. "O'Reilly, you'll be with me. Neshenko will be in charge of taking Finnegan. Lieutenant Lewis and his team will tackle Pritchard. He's probably the most dangerous individual, so we want our top ESU guys on him. But watch out for Finnegan, Neshenko. He's unpredictable."

"By which you mean he's bat-shit crazy," Vic said. "I know. I saw him eat a guy's face."

"Those are the three absolutely essential targets," Webb went on. "With luck, we'll catch all the others, too. With the exception of a very few people, nobody knows the full extent of the operation. The other Patrol and ESU elements all think they're serving specific, individual warrants. That should eliminate any chance of O'Malley thinking he's under a coordinated attack until it's too late. We've got a good plan and good people carrying it out. Everything's going to be fine. In the morning we can read all about it in the *Times*."

"I don't read the *Times*," Vic said.

"Having seen your reports, I can believe it," Webb said. "I'm sometimes surprised you can read anything."

"I've got a college degree!" Vic protested. "Just because I went to community college instead of some fancy Ivy League bullshit school doesn't mean you gotta shit all over my education."

"I'd love to hear where you think I went to school," Webb said. "Do I look like a Harvard man?"

"Where *did* you go, sir?" Erin asked.

"UCLA," Webb said. "I majored in psych. If I'd known where I was going to end up, I would've done a concentration in abnormal psychology. It would've served me well."

"Yeah, that would've been helpful cracking perps in interrogation," Erin said.

"Perps?" Webb echoed. "I'm talking about this squad."

Vic had picked the wrong moment to take a sip of Mountain Dew. He sprayed it clear across his desk. He spluttered a curse and started wiping down his monitor.

\*     \*     \*

It ought to snow on Christmas; white, soft, magical flakes. But New Yorkers had experienced one of the worst blizzards in its history earlier that month and they'd expended their allotment of enchantment. What they were getting now was what the weather guys called "wintry mix," a nasty slurry of cold rain and sleet that left puddles of slush and sheets of black ice everywhere.

Erin drove Webb toward O'Malley's Tribeca apartment, going carefully. They were early; it was about one in the morning. Her Charger had good tires, but it would be far too easy to spin out into another late-night driver. She squinted into the glare from the streetlights on her rain-spattered windshield. The wipers were going, but the little droplets kept freezing on contact with the glass and couldn't be wiped away.

"Is all this shit going to cause problems with our timetable?" she asked.

"It shouldn't," Webb said. "If anything, it'll make it harder for the bad guys if they try to make a run for it."

"I guess so," Erin said. "They'd probably get about fifty yards and wrap themselves around a lamppost."

"You think O'Malley's going to run?" Webb asked.

She'd been thinking about that. "No," she said. "He's an old gangster. The young ones try to run or fight. He'll try to beat us in court."

"He doesn't have a chance," Webb said. "The case is airtight. DA Markham is practically drooling over it."

"Evan doesn't know that," she pointed out. "He doesn't know we've got everything."

She was referring not only to Corky and Carlyle having switched sides, but also to Evan's ledger. The meticulous accounting of his criminal empire had been well hidden. It had taken months for her to discover he'd been using the brain of his ward Maggie Callahan as a data repository. Maggie's mind didn't work like a normal human's; she was the only person Erin had ever met who possessed a truly photographic memory. Corky had been the one to convince Maggie to write down an emergency backup of her mental files—a backup that was now in the possession of the New York District Attorney's office.

"He also thinks he has leverage on you," Webb said.

"Yeah," she said, smiling grimly. "I'm kind of looking forward to it when he tries to drag me down with him. It's like when a guy tries to shoot you and the gun clicks empty."

"I had a man shoot at me with blanks once," Webb said. "It wasn't much of a relief when I found out afterward."

"Who've we got for backup?" she asked.

"Half a dozen ESU," Webb said. "We'll have Patrol units on perimeter duty. We're ready to come heavy, but the plan is to just knock politely and show him our warrant. If you're right, he'll come quietly. No muss, no fuss."

"And we can't tip our hand," she said.

"We're setting up down the block," Webb said. "We've got a cover story of a high-risk warrant nearby, in case O'Malley has people monitoring the airwaves and ESU assignments."

"I guess the planners thought of everything," she said.

"That's why this took so long to set up," Webb said dryly. "It's been hard on you. I honestly don't know how you manage without cigarettes."

"There's always whiskey," she said. "What's your brand, sir?"

"Jim Beam. Johnnie Walker for special occasions."

Erin made a face. "Really? Tell me you at least get the Blue Label."

"Red," Webb said. "I've got alimony and child support on a Lieutenant's salary, remember? I can't afford the good stuff."

"My brother Mike said I was crazy to become a cop," she said. "He told me the private sector's where the money is. He was right, dammit. Crime may not pay, but neither does law enforcement."

"Not if you're doing it right," Webb agreed. "Tell you what, after this is all over, you can have your boyfriend get me a drink on the house. Top-shelf whiskey."

"What makes you think he'd do that?" Erin asked, grinning.

"It's the least he can do," Webb replied. "We're keeping him out of jail, aren't we? Not to mention protecting him from a large number of unpleasant people who'll want to hurt him. And speaking of unpleasant, violent people, take the next left and pull into that parking garage. The rest of the team should be showing up soon, if they're not already here."

Erin unloaded Rolf and walked him around the garage for a couple of minutes. The K-9, unlike Vic, was thoroughly housebroken, and parking garages were an odd sort of no-man's-land, halfway between indoors and outdoors. But Erin said it was okay, so he cocked a leg on a support column. Then he trotted up to the next level with her, where they found a group of ESU officers standing around a black SUV. Their commander was talking with Webb.

"Hey, O'Reilly," one of the officers said, raising a gloved hand in greeting.

"Five Cent!" she said, recognizing Nichols, one of Vic's old ESU buddies. "Merry Christmas."

"Now I have a machine-gun," Nichols quoted, hefting his assault rifle. "Ho, ho, ho. Campbell says hi, and he's sorry he can't be here."

"How's he doing?" she asked. Officer Campbell had been badly injured in a botched assassination attempt on a judge earlier that autumn.

"Getting there," Nichols said. "He had to get a bunch of skin grafts on account of the burns, but the docs say he's doing well. He might even get cleared for duty sometime next year."

"That's great news!" she said.

"Yeah," Nichols said. "He says to tell you if you want to set one or two of these bastards on fire for him, it wouldn't be the worst idea."

"Yes, it would," Webb said. "There'll be no lighting perps on fire. That's an order."

"Goddamn lieutenants, always spoiling our fun," Nichols said, pretending to scowl.

"Let's move this inside," the ESU Lieutenant said. "We've got a place lined up next door with good visual lines on the target building."

Erin found herself in an empty corporate office, apparently part of an architectural firm. The Lieutenant laid out a set of blueprints on a drafting table.

"O'Reilly, I understand you've been inside," he said. "Are these plans accurate?"

Erin spent the next fifteen minutes going over the floor plan of Evan's penthouse, describing the layout from memory. She noted the positions where guards had been on her prior visits, and what sorts of weapons they'd been carrying. The ESU guys listened attentively, asking a few questions but mostly just absorbing the information.

"Shouldn't be too bad," the Lieutenant said. "The elevator's the only really dicey spot."

"Ready-made kill-box," Erin said, giving Ian's favorite description of an elevator car.

"But assuming this guy's not ready to go to war with the NYPD, he won't hit us in the elevator," the Lieutenant said. "All the same, we'll stop two floors down from the penthouse. We'll hold the elevators there and take the stairs the rest of the way. Full tactical gear. Nobody take any chances. I'm damned if I'll be delivering death notices on Christmas."

"Too late for that, boss," one of the ESU guys said. "Midnight was an hour and a half ago."

"You know what I mean, Booth," the Lieutenant growled. "I don't want any surprises, I don't want any accidents, and I don't want any friendly casualties. You get me?"

"Yes, sir," came the chorus of replies.

"Lieutenant Webb and Detective O'Reilly will be coming in with us," he went on. "Because this is some sort of big, fancy Major Crimes case. And we'll have O'Reilly's K-9, which might be useful. Any questions?"

"Can I say 'yippee-ki-yay' when we bust the bad guys?" Nichols asked, still in a *Die Hard* frame of mind.

"Only if you make the bust barefoot," the Lieutenant replied. "Okay, we've got the green light to go in at 0400. We'll move into the lobby at 0355, which means I want boots on the street at 0350. You've got till then to nap or jerk off or whatever the hell you do when you're not earning your paychecks."

The tinny, recorded strains of "Jingle Bells" sounded from Webb's direction. He patted his trench coat and fished out his phone. "Sorry," he said, bringing it to his ear. "Webb. Talk to me."

There was a short pause while he listened to the voice on the other end.

"I don't see why you're calling me, sir," he said. "That doesn't sound like a Major Crimes situation. And besides, you know what we're doing right now."

There was another pause. Erin watched her commanding officer and waited, fighting an irrational, crawling dread seeping up from her stomach. Rolf, at her side, nosed her hand. She absentmindedly rubbed his ears.

"I see," Webb said. "Yes, I'll send O'Reilly right away. I'd better stay here. Yes, Neshenko should be available, too. Yes, sir, I'm aware of the time constraints. I'll keep you posted."

He hung up and turned to Erin. "We've got a problem," he said.

"I was afraid of that," she said. Her throat was suddenly very dry. "What's up?"

"That was Captain Holliday," he said. "We have a possible home invasion. Patrol units responded to a report of shots fired in an apartment. One casualty, multiple GSW. I don't know if he's alive or not."

"I'm with you, sir," Erin said, mystified. "That sounds like a job for our Homicide boys. Or Robbery, if the victim's not dead. And we really don't have time to screw around. Not tonight. Why is this our problem?"

Webb sighed. "It's James Corcoran," he said. "Somebody broke into his place and shot him."

# Author's Note

In October of 2008, while driving to an out-of-state wedding, my wife and I were in a serious car accident. A badly-secured piece of scrap metal apparently came loose from the flatbed truck that was hauling it and fell into the highway, where we struck it. We blew out a tire and spun into another car. My wife and the other driver, thankfully, were not badly injured, though very shaken. I suffered a broken collarbone and a concussion of moderate severity.

One of the things I learned over the course of that experience was that traumatic brain injuries are rarely depicted accurately in fiction. In the movies, a hero or heroine can be knocked unconscious, often repeatedly, and bounce right back up. Our hero will be none the worse for the encounter and will not suffer any lasting symptoms from such an injury.

My own experience was quite different, or so I've been told. The only things I know about the accident are based on the accounts of others. Though I was only unconscious for a few minutes, I have a six-hour gap in my memory of that day, including two hours before the crash and four hours after. In my memory, I jump from a motel parking lot to a hospital bed, where I found myself with my arm in a sling, a splitting headache, and bits of automobile glass embedded in my arm and head.

I was temporarily afflicted with anterograde amnesia; the inability to create new short-term memories. If you've seen the movie "Memento," you may have some idea what that is like from the outside. From the inside, I don't remember a bit of it, but I apparently asked my wife dozens of times what had happened, whether she was all right, and where we were. She patiently answered every time, forcing down her own fear and trauma to try to comfort and reassure me as well as she could.

I was exceptionally lucky in that my symptoms were temporary. By the end of that weekend in a small hospital in Oklahoma, I had largely recovered from my TBI. But many who are afflicted with these injuries continue to wrestle with symptoms for weeks, months, or even indefinitely. Their lives are significantly affected. Often they cannot continue with their jobs. I personally know one case of a man who, after a very bad car accident, underwent a personality change which destroyed his marriage.

Concussions are no joke. Erin O'Reilly has had more than her share of hard knocks, including being far too close to several explosions, getting punched in the head by a very large, strong man, and most recently taking a bullet to the skull, along with any number of more moderate bumps and thumps. In a real-world context her career, like that of her mentor Phil Stachowski, would almost certainly be over. This is a work of fiction, so I have bent reality somewhat, but it would be dishonest of me, as well as unreasonable, to expect Erin to walk off so much cumulative damage with no ill effects.

If you are ever unfortunate enough to suffer a significant head injury, by which I mean a knock on the head hard enough to render you unconscious or even dizzy and disoriented, *go to a hospital as soon as possible.* A hit that can knock you out may have caused a brain bleed, which can be debilitating or fatal if untreated. These things can kill in a matter of hours, often with no further warning.

Also, wear your seatbelt. Always. If my wife and I had not been wearing our belts, it is almost certain we both would have been killed. Erin O'Reilly would never have existed, and I would not be writing these words.

# Ready for more?

Join the Clickworks Press email list
for the latest on new releases, upcoming books and
series, behind-the-scenes details, events, and more.

Be the first to know about new releases in the Erin
O'Reilly Mysteries by signing up at
clickworkspress.com/join/erin

# About the Author

Steven Henry learned how to read almost before he learned how to walk. Ever since he began reading stories, he wanted to put his own on the page. He lives a very quiet and ordinary life in Minnesota with his wife and dog.

# Also by Steven Henry

## Fathers
### *A Modern Christmas Story*

**When you strip away everything else, what's left is the truth**

Life taught Joe Davidson not to believe in miracles. A blue-collar wood-worker, Joe is trying to build a future. His father drank himself to death and his mother succumbed to cancer, leaving a broken, struggling family. He and his brother and sisters are faced with failed marriages, growing pains, and lingering trauma.

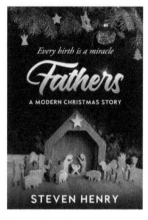

Then a chance meeting at his local diner brings Mary Elizabeth Reynolds into his life. Suddenly, Joe finds himself reaching for something more, a dream of happiness. The wood-worker and the poor girl from a trailer park connect and fall in love, and for a little while, everything is right with their world.

But suddenly Joe is confronted with a situation he never imagined. What do you do if your fiancée is expecting a child you know isn't yours? Torn between betrayal and love, trying to do the right thing when nothing seems right anymore, Joe has to strip life down to its truth and learn that, in spite of the pain, love can be the greatest miracle of all.

Learn more at clickworkspress.com/fathers.